• • • • • •

He told her, "I love it when you wear jeans. But your skirts make me hard."

The disclosure made Korah's eyes widen. A tingle between her legs settled on her clitoris and drummed pleasantly.

"I can give you ten million dollars," he said. He took another step, until his body pressed against hers. His hands moved slowly towards her ass. He gripped both cheeks tightly and drew her even closer.

The pleasant sensation between Korah's legs suddenly burst into flames, causing her nipples and pubic hairs to stand erect. Brick kissed her again. This time he slipped his tongue past her lips. He tasted her, until her blood flowed like lava.

"Brick, I gotta go," she panted between succulent kisses.

"What about your ten million?"

Korah cried out when he hiked her skirt up and fondled her ass through her panties. She felt her body immediately become moist for him. Her juices were hot and sweet. She wanted him to taste her. She wanted to climb on top of him – right then and there – but this was a little too kinky, even for them.

She reached and pulled her skirt down. Brick reluctantly allowed her to do so.

"We, we'll have to finish this later," she told him as she backed away.

Her legs felt as weak as blades of grass, but she had to get away from him. At that moment she didn't know why she'd want to escape such a fine specimen of a man, but she knew the reasons would come to her once she was no longer within range of his mind control.

Brick turned to watch her, but he didn't follow. His right hand moved to adjust his erection – or so Korah thought. As she watched, he began to rub the bulge in his pants. His eyes remained glued to hers.

"You're a freak," she told him.

"Only for you," he said.

Korah was surprised by how happy that declaration made her feel.

• • • • • •

1

KEITH THOMAS WALKER

I0589320

BRICK HOUSE 2

KEITH THOMAS WALKER

KEITHWALKERBOOKS, INC
This is a UMS production

3

BRICK HOUSE 2

KEITHWALKERBOOKS

Publishing Company
KeithWalkerBooks, Inc.
P.O. Box 331585
Fort Worth, TX 76163

For information write
KeithWalkerBooks, Inc.
P.O. Box 331585
Fort Worth, TX 76163

All characters in this book have no existence outside the
imagination of the author and have no relation whatsoever to
anyone bearing the same name or names. They are not even
distantly inspired by any individual known or unknown to the
author and all incidents are pure invention.

ISBN-13 DIGIT: 978-0-9882180-6-2
ISBN-10 DIGIT: 0988218062
Library of Congress Control Number: 2014918578
Manufactured in the United States of America

Second Edition

Visit us at www.keithwalkerbooks.com

This book is for Deloris Harper

MORE BOOKS BY KEITH THOMAS WALKER

Fixin' Tyrone
How to Kill Your Husband
A Good Dude
Riding the Corporate Ladder
The Finley Sisters' Oath of Romance
Blow by Blow
Jewell and the Dapper Dan
Harlot
Plan C (And More KWB Shorts)
Dripping Chocolate
The Realest Ever
Jackson Memorial
Sleeping With the Strangler
Life After
Blood for Isaiah
Brick House

NOVELLAS

Might be Bi (Part One)
Harder

POETRY COLLECTION

Poor Righteous Poet

Visit keithwalkerbooks.com for information about these and upcoming titles from KeithWalkerBooks

ACKNOWLEGMENTS

Of course I would like to thank God, first and foremost, for giving me the creativity and drive to pursue my dreams and the understanding that I am nothing without Him. I would like to thank my wife for being my first and most important critic, and I would like to thank my mother for always pushing me to be the best I can be. I would like to thank Janae Hampton for being the best advisor, supporter and little sister a brother could ever have. I would also like to thank (in no particular order) Denise Bolds, Sabrina Scott, Beulah Neveu, Jason Owens, Sharon Blount, BRAB Book Club, and Uncle Steven Thomas, one love. I'd like to thank everyone who purchased and enjoyed one of my books. Everything I do has always been to please you. I know there are folks who mean the world to me that I'm failing to mention. I apologize ahead of time. Rest assured I'm grateful for everything you've done for me!

CHAPTER ONE
THE AVERY RANCH

The forest painted. The autumn leaves
Crinkle beneath your steps. I breathe
But slightly, though my heartbeats peak
I'm smitten by your loveliness

Perchance to hold your hand in mine
I'm weakened by your pulse. Each time
You smile a tremor sweeps my spine
I praise God for your loveliness

The weather on Saturday, October 4th was perfect. The few clouds in the sky above the majestic Avery Ranch were bright and beautiful and not numerous enough to block out the warm sun, which provided a perfect temperature of 76 degrees.

Korah held on tightly to a pair of worn, leather reins that were fastened to a bridle that didn't feel strong enough to fully control a half-ton beast that seemed friendly enough when Brick introduced them ten minutes ago. But now that she felt the horse's powerful muscles flexing between her legs and she watched the hair on the animal's mane flowing like silk as they picked up speed, Korah felt like she'd bitten off more than she could chew. But that feeling was far too common when it came to Brick and many of his delightful endeavors.

Rosie was a beautiful paint horse who had an easy-going temperament – according to Brick. Brick also told her Rosie was gracious when accepting new riders. Korah agreed with that description initially, but when Brick pulled ahead of her on a golden Palomino and instructed her to "*Hold on!*" as he brought his horse to a gallop, Korah had to accept that she had no control over her situation, their route, or even the speed in which Brick propelled them towards their destination.

The trail they followed was easy to trace in the beginning, but as they entered a wooded area nearly a mile away from the ranch, Korah could not predict their path at all. Thankfully Brick never gave her more than she could handle, and Rosie was completely at ease as she followed the Palomino. Gradually Korah's heart rate decreased to a beat that was slower than the sound of horse hooves clapping on the hard earth, and she was able to relax a little and enjoy the ride.

Autumn was upon them, and the scenery was picturesque. Many of the trees were decked out in beautiful oranges and browns that mingled charmingly with the evergreens. Korah had been at the Avery Ranch for less than a day, but she already felt fully immersed in the splendor Mother Nature had always offered, regardless of humans' repeated attempts to remove themselves from it.

Not surprisingly, Korah decided that the most splendid sight was the one right in front of her. Brick sat so comfortably atop the Palomino, she wondered why he ever bothered to do anything else. He and the horse seemed to move as one. His perfect ass didn't bounce around on the saddle, like Korah's did, and he showed no hesitance at all as they galloped past trees that wouldn't yield one inch if there was a collision.

Brick's shoulders rose and fell at the same rate of his gallant steed's, and by the time they burst through a clearance that revealed a massive, yet cozy lake, Korah was a little dismayed that their ride had ended so soon. But then again, her legs felt like noodles when Brick brought his horse to a stop and ambled over to help Korah off hers. She couldn't remember the last time she felt so happy to have both feet firmly planted on the ground.

Brick wore faded blue jeans with a white collar shirt that was tucked in. The top three buttons of his shirt were unfastened. As she admired him, Korah hated that he wore a shirt at all. She could see the deep crease between his pectorals, which were wonderfully hard and smooth. His grip on her hand was both strong and gentle. She didn't want him to let her go, even after she regained control of her equilibrium. She smiled as she stared into his hazelnut colored eyes.

His smile deepened as he returned the gaze.

"Why are you looking at me like that?" he asked, with a slight southern drawl. "Did you enjoy the ride? Did I go too fast for you?"

Korah shook her head but said, "You know you went too fast. But it was nice. Your horse is awesome."

Brick rubbed the animal's mane affectionately. "You treat her good, Rosie?"

The horse turned slightly, so that Brick could caress her head as well. The contact was brief, but it was enough to show Korah how close Brick and his equine was; how Rosie lived to please him. Apparently Brick's effect on females transcended species.

"So you're glad you came?" he asked as he turned back to Korah.

"Yes. Of course I am."

She stepped closer and sighed pleasantly when he wrapped his strong arms around her. Brick didn't wear a ton of cologne on a regular day, and this afternoon he wore even less. Korah inhaled the scent of his unfaltering manliness as she buried her face in the crook of his neck. Never in a million years did she think she'd be so happy and falling so hard for a man who beat her out of her dream job less than one week ago.

"You ready to catch some fish?" he asked when their embrace ended. He grinned as he took a step back to admire her outfit.

Korah wore jeans as well, with a new pair of boots and a Brick House tee-shirt that stretched nicely over her swollen bosoms. She still had no plans to work for Brick's company or merge their businesses to create the *ultimate* contracting corporation. But Korah knew what her man liked, and she liked to please him.

Her hair was shoulder-length and loosely curled. She was a foot shorter than her man and more curvaceous than slender. Her skin was dark, her lips full. She knew that her hips and ass looked awesome in her jeans. Brick's eyes had been enslaved since he picked her up from home.

"You sho' look good with my logo on you," he said.

"Stop staring at my breasts," she teased.

11

"Nope. Can't do that," Brick said, and he made no attempt to avert his attention. "If this lake didn't have so many fish in it, I'd ask you to go skinny dipping."

"I don't know how to fish," Korah told him, not for the first time.

"It's okay," Brick replied. "The odds are highly stacked in your favor. There's so many fish in here," he said as he scanned the vast area of water, "I had to introduce a school of largemouth bass to keep the population in check. If you can't catch a fish in this lake, I dare say you need another spanking."

His eyes twinkled as Korah blushed and an embarrassed smile spread across her face. Last week Brick made good on his promise to spank her, for a much more serious infraction, the memory of which made Korah's ass burn and tingle unexpectedly.

"This whole lake is yours?" she asked, her gaze returning to the water.

The lake was manmade and the grounds along the bank were well-kept.

Brick nodded. "This ranch is nearly one-tenth the size of the whole county. At least once a month Carl and his boy have to run a few of our neighbors off the property. This lake is a hot commodity."

Korah knew that Carl was the ranch hand who maintained the estate when Brick was away, which was virtually all the time. In addition to feeding and caring for the six horses Brick had in his stable, Carl took care of all of the landscaping, maintenance and apparently the security needs at the ranch.

"Maybe you should share," Korah said, "then people wouldn't have to sneak onto your property."

"How many squatters you got living at your mansion?" Brick countered.

"That's different," Korah said with a giggle. "I don't have a whole, freaking lake."

"My family worked hard for this land," Brick said. "Blood, sweat and tears."

Korah's breath caught as she watched his mood darken slightly. She grew up in Chicago, but she knew full well how much harder it was for black people in the south. She knew that Brick's family had a working class background, which made their achievements that much more impressive. Plus there was sure to be some antagonism as the Avery clan amassed their fortune and enough property to own such a large portion of the county.

"I'm sorry," she said. "You don't have to let anyone fish in your lake, if you don't want to."

"Carl never runs the children off," Brick said, his mood still reflective.

"I knew you had a soft spot for kids," Korah said with a smirk, hoping to lighten the mood.

"I do," Brick said, his smile back in place. "But I don't know about *your* kids. I get the feeling they don't like me."

"Stephanie likes you just fine," Korah said.

Brick raised an eyebrow but didn't ask why she left Devin out of that comment.

"Come on," he said, walking towards the lake. "Let's catch us some dinner."

"*Dinner?*" Korah couldn't hide her surprise. "I thought this was going to be a friendly catch-and-release activity."

"We'll release most of them. But *two* of those lucky bastards will have the pleasure of going on our plates this evening."

Korah laughed. "Really Brick? I don't think they would consider themselves lucky."

He stopped and turned to stare at her. "Yeah, you're right, little lady. I'm the one who's lucky. I'm at my favorite place with my favorite girl. It doesn't get any better."

"You are such a charmer," Korah said sarcastically, though her heart fluttered every time he looked at her like that.

"Yeah, I know," Brick said. "Now get over here and grab one of these here frogs."

He laughed when her smile slipped. Korah hesitantly followed him to the dock to check out his supplies.

• • • • • •

Before Brick gave Carl the weekend off, he asked him to drop their fishing supplies off at the lake. In addition to the rods and reels, Carl left a couple of beach chairs on the dock along with a cooler filled with ice and Dos Equis. And, much to Korah's relief, the frogs Brick intended to use as bait were artificial. Korah didn't know much about fishing, but she thought the lures were extremely lifelike, right down to their wiggly, rubbery legs.

Rather than toss their lines simultaneously, Brick wisely chose to help Korah get a bite first.

"I'm pretty sure you'll lose my rod in the lake, if you and me get to fighting a big one at the same time."

Korah didn't think she was that much of a wuss, but once again Brick's prediction was accurate. The fish in his lake were so voracious, she got a tug on her line less than ten minutes after Brick casted it nearly halfway across the shimmering body of water.

Korah shot to her feet and secured the pole with both hands as her float submerged and the line jerked roughly to the left.

"I got one!" she exclaimed excitedly.

"Yeah, you do," Brick said casually as he approached and stood beside her. "You know what to do?"

"Hell no!" Korah's smile was wide, her eyes anxious. "I reel it in, right?" She searched for the correct lever without taking her eyes off the water. "Oh my God, Brick! He's so strong!"

Brick moved behind her, and the hairs stood on the back of Korah's neck, even before he placed his hands on her hips and instructed her to, "Spread your legs. Move this foot back a little. Make sure your stance is secure. Don't want you falling in."

"I'm not gonna fall off the dock," Korah assured him, but she did as he asked her to.

"Keep the line tense," Brick told her. "Don't let it slack up at all."

"No problem there!" Korah said. Her catch was trying its best to get away. "I think it's gonna break the rod!" she shrieked. The top half of her pole was bent at what looked like an unsafe level.

"You need help?" Brick asked calmly. He reached around her to help secure the pole, but Korah pushed him back with her shoulder.

"No. *I* wanna catch it!"

"Oh, alright then," Brick said and gave her some space. "You sounded like you needed help."

"I just want *instruction*," Korah said and then she gasped when her line jerked hard in the opposite direction. "I think I got a *shark*!" she screeched.

"Maybe," Brick said. "No telling what's in that water. Could be the creature from the black lagoon."

Korah looked over at him and rolled her eyes at his cocky grin. "Shut up and tell me what to do!"

Brick coached her on how to reel in her catch, and he watched carefully as Korah delighted in the task. Her jeans weren't skin-tight, but they fit her nicely. The sexy swell of her hips and ass was a constant turn-on. The way she took control of her catch and skillfully used his rod was just as enticing.

At forty-six years of age, Korah was remarkably strong and fit and limber. Brick loved her smooth, brown skin. Her curves made him want to caress her body each time he laid eyes on her. He no longer wondered why, out of all the women he had access to, Korah was the one who had him thinking about things like COMMITMENT and PERMANENCE.

He didn't know if those words were part of his essential being, but sometimes Korah made him feel like they were.

Sometimes she did.

He asked again if she wanted help as she reeled the fish closer to the dock and they could both see it writhing near the surface of the water.

"*Yes!*" she exclaimed. "What do I do now? Your pole is gonna break, Brick! I know it is. *This fish is huge!*"

Her cowboy beau was casual as he hefted a large net from the dock and knelt to scoop her fish from the water. Korah stepped back in revulsion as he brought the dripping net towards her. The fish continued to fight for freedom with everything it had in him.

"*Eww!*" She dropped her pole and backpedaled. "*Get that away from me!*"

Brick laughed. "You don't wanna see your fish?"

"I don't wanna get that nasty water on me," Korah replied.

Brick cracked up even more, which made a few crow's feet appear in the corners of his eyes. Korah loved to see him smile. Brick was one year younger than her, but his body and his features didn't reflect that. His close-cropped hair had no grays at all. He never wore a beard or moustache. His jawline was hard and commanding. The muscles in his shoulders and arms were always detectable, even with the button-down he wore today.

"Alright," he said. "Well, can you at least hold the net, while I get some water in that bucket?"

Korah gave him a look before reluctantly taking the net. She had to secure it with both hands to keep from dropping it.

"*Brick, this is a big fish!*" she squealed.

"Way to go," he said as he hefted a six gallon pail and took it to the edge of the dock. He knelt and scooped up enough water to nearly fill it. He placed the bucket on the dock and returned to his uncharacteristically squeamish girlfriend.

"Alright. Let me see that."

Korah thought he was reaching for the net, but he reached inside and secured the fish instead. She was both amazed and spooked when he stuck his thumb in the fish's mouth without hesitation and lifted it from the net. And then the stupid fish whipped his tail, flicking a few drops of stinky water right at Korah's face.

"*Eww, Brick! That's disgusting!*" she screamed. She dropped the net and wiped her mug furiously.

"Aw, baby. I'm sorry," Brick said, but he was grinning.

"*No you're not!*"

"I am. Come here. I didn't mean to."

He wrapped his free arm around her waist, still holding the fish at arm's length.

"You still look beautiful to me," he said.

Korah's frown melted away as he leaned in and kissed her softly. When he backed away, she was cheerful again. She checked out her catch and was startled to see that it was only ten inches long. She would've sworn she was reeling in something more spectacular, like a dolphin.

"You wanna keep it?" Brick asked as he removed the hook from its mouth.

"Yeah, what's wrong with it?" Korah asked.

"Nothing. Didn't know if you wanted something bigger."

"You got bigger fish in there?"

"Carl says he caught a sixteen-incher once. But he didn't take a picture, so you know I don't believe that. Personally, I catch fourteen-inchers all the time."

"Alright, well I want a *bigger* one," Korah decided.

"I figured you might."

Brick returned to the end of the dock to release her catch.

"Good luck!" Korah said as the fish disappeared beneath the surface of the water with its predatory instincts still intact.

"I wouldn't be surprised if we catch him again today," Brick said.

"If we do, that means he's meant to be our supper," Korah declared. She returned to her man's side with a childlike smile lighting her features. "Okay, so where's the hand sanitizer?" she asked.

Brick shook his head as he reached for a box of sanitizing wipes Carl left with the other equipment.

"This can hardly be considered *roughing it*," he said as he passed the container to her.

"You know you like me soft and clean and sweet-smelling," she replied.

"Yeah, I do," Brick agreed. "And I like you dirty, too. You can do no wrong, Ms. Stewart."

The intensity of his gaze heated Korah's whole body by a few degrees. Sometimes she loved how dreamy he made her feel. Other times she recognized the danger of such fierce emotions. She hefted her pole and returned her attention to the task at hand.

"I'm ready to go again," she said with a smile. "Set me up, boss."

"Yes'm," Brick said as he approached and helped with her line.

● ● ● ● ● ●

The bass weren't the only fish in the lake, but Brick said they were the only ones big enough to go after with the frog lures he brought. It only took an hour for them to catch six more fish, two of which were big enough for the meal he planned to prepare that evening. He left them in the water bucket and led Korah to a canoe he had tied to a post further down the bank. There were already two lifejackets waiting inside.

Brick adamantly refused to wear his jacket initially, but Korah was just as strong-minded. She said she wouldn't wear one if he didn't, so Brick finally relented. They climbed aboard the canoe with the ice-cold Dos Equis. Korah felt like the luckiest girl

17

in the world as Brick paddled them towards the center of the lake. The moment he got there, he removed his lifejacket and set it aside. Korah rolled her eyes and quickly did the same.

"You are so stubborn," Brick murmured.

"I must've picked that up from you."

Brick popped the top on two of the beers and handed her one. Korah relaxed in the small boat and took a drink. The beer was delightful. She didn't realize how thirsty she was. Brick downed half his bottle and then set it aside. He lifted her feet into his lap and carefully removed her boots. She was surprised but didn't object as he pulled her socks off as well.

She closed her eyes and sighed pleasantly as he began to massage her bare feet. It no longer struck her as odd that he would do such a thing without request or even drawing much attention to it. He wanted Korah to think it was no big deal, but she refused to downplay his romantic gestures. The things he did for her and the way he made her feel was a very big deal.

It was the best thing that had happened to her in a very long time.

After nearly an hour of lounging and floating and sipping her imported beer, Korah felt fully relaxed and pampered. All she needed was a parasol to dangle over her shoulder, to make her feel like an official southern belle.

In the short time they'd been together, she knew that Brick was very dedicated to his business. But she was surprised that even now he had work in the back of his mind.

"Did you decide if you would accept my offer?"

At that moment, Korah didn't care what he asked of her. She'd fly all the way to the moon with him. If he wanted to elope, she thought she'd be down for that as well.

"The school," Brick said. "Did you talk to your son about my offer?"

Korah shook her head. On Monday the Overbrook Meadows school board broke her heart by granting the deal of a lifetime to Brick's contracting and construction company rather than her own. While it was true that Brick House was a little bigger and they had actually built a school before, Korah had hoped the project would propel her company, Texas Builders, to the forefront of the construction scene.

But it wasn't meant to be.

Korah believed she'd lost the contract because of a bad construction deal that came back to haunt her nearly a decade later. But she would never be completely sure. Maybe the school board picked Brick because of his rugged cowboy swagger. Or maybe Brick House really was the best company for the job.

But every dark cloud has a silver lining. Within an hour of losing the bid, Brick called and offered Korah an opportunity to work together on the fifteen million dollar project. He told Korah that she was his woman, and she should share the spoils of his success. The only hang-up was her son Devin, who ran her construction company and didn't care too much for Mr. Brock "Brick" Avery.

Korah shook her head as she watched the shimmering water reflect off her boyfriend's pretty brown eyes.

"Why not?" he asked, still cradling her feet in his lap. He ran a finger down the sole of her left foot, which made her leg shudder.

"That tickles," she said.

"Why haven't you talked to your son?" Brick pressed. "You don't want to work with me?"

"Of course I do."

She closed her eyes, enjoying the sound of the water, the birds, the sweet, calming effect of Brick's voice.

"When do you plan to make a decision?" he asked her.

"I already have," she said and opened her eyes. "I would love to be a part of your project."

The smile that spread across Brick's face made Korah's heart flutter. She loved to make him happy, mainly because he was so good and so relentless when it came to doing the same for her.

"That's great, baby. But what about your son?"

"Devin wants what's good for the company," she assured him.

"Are you sure about that?"

Korah wished that question wasn't warranted, but unfortunately it was. Before the school board awarded Brick House the new contract, Korah's company was a serious contender. To give Texas Builders a fighting chance, Korah instructed her son to renovate a badly constructed shopping center that was falling apart from the roof down. Devin eventually

19

completed the repairs, but he disagreed with his mom's line of thinking and fought her tooth and nail.

"Devin and I did have some disagreements in the past few weeks," Korah acknowledged, "but we're better now. We're on the same page."

She didn't know if that was completely true or not, but she wasn't speaking to her boyfriend now. If Brick wanted to discuss the school contract, then this lazy canoe ride had just become a business meeting.

"What about me?" he asked knowingly. "He's gonna be okay working with me?"

"That's not a—"

"Work *for* me, that is," Brick corrected. "I don't wanna bring anyone on my site who's gonna roll their eyes every time I show up."

"Business is business," Korah said. "Devin doesn't *love* every property owner we work for. But he knows how to put his personal feelings aside and provide the excellence all of our customers expect from Texas Builders."

Brick chuckled at her sales pitch. "But I am correct in assuming he doesn't like me..."

"He likes you a lot more, since you helped find that guy who broke into our office."

"Is that right?" Brick asked, his sexy, southern swag in full effect.

He had his sleeves rolled up to the elbows, his shirt still mostly unbuttoned. The sun set gradually behind him. Korah thought he looked like a freaking postcard!

Absolutely yummy.

"Regardless of what that knucklehead thinks about you," she said, "I like you a whole bunch. And it's my company. So that's that."

Brick smirked and then repeated his comment. "Is that right?"

"Yes, that's right," Korah said. "And you'd better stop looking at me like that."

"Like what?"

"Like you plan on spanking me again," she said with a grin.

Brick chuckled. "You know you liked it. You wouldn't keep bringing it up – unless you wanted it to happen again."

Jeez, Korah thought. Was she that transparent? Before he did it, she would've cringed at the thought of a man trying to spank her. But things were certainly different with Brick. And now Korah was in the awkward position of pretending she didn't like it, though she kinda, sorta wanted him to do it again.

Or did she?

Surely not.

Thankfully, her boyfriend let her off the hook.

"You ready to head back to the ranch?" he asked as he took hold of the canoe paddles.

"Yeah, I suppose so."

"We can come back here tomorrow," he said. "Maybe you'll let me talk you into skinny dipping."

"I'm not swimming with all of those *nasty fish*," Korah assured him.

"I like it when you tell me what you not gon' do," Brick told her. "Makes me feel like I accomplished something, when you end up doing it."

Korah's clit swelled unexpectedly. She shuddered and then giggled to herself.

Of course Brick could get her to go skinny-dipping. All he had to do was tell her *Take off your clothes, and get in the water*, and she'd be butt-naked and fully submerged in less than a minute.

She had a good feeling he knew that as well.

CHAPTER TWO
GIDDYUP!

There was still a little fire left in the sky when Brick paddled the canoe to the bank and secured it to a post that was planted deep in the ground. Korah followed him to the dock and saw that the two fish they caught were still swimming in the bucket of water they left them in. Brick retrieved them and wrapped them in butcher paper – another supply he had the foresight to request from his ranch hand.

He placed the wrapped fish in separate freezer bags and took them to the painted horse named Rosie, who hadn't left the area despite not being tethered to anything. Her companion, the golden Palomino, was still grazing near the shoreline as well.

Once Brick got the fish stashed safely in the saddlebag, he surprised Korah by instructing Rosie to "*Go home!*" accompanied by a swift smack on the hindquarters. The horse took off in the direction of the ranch, and Korah quickly lost sight of her in the woods.

"What'd you do that for?" she asked.

"Don't you want to ride back with me?" Brick asked.

His grin made Korah smile in return. "You want me to ride on your horse?"

"I think it'll be fun," he said. "We couldn't go very fast on the way out here. But if I don't have to worry about you keeping up, we can have a little fun with Roscoe."

The palomino perked up and began to step in their direction.

Surprised, Korah asked, "He knows his name?"

"Course he does," Brick said.

He ran a large hand down the bridge of the beast's nose when it approached them. He then planted a foot in Roscoe's stirrup and grabbed the saddle horn to help pull himself atop the horse.

Korah thought he mounted the animal like a true cowboy. She didn't think she'd ever stop being impressed by this man. He reached down, and she slipped her dainty hand into his. Brick's grip was very strong. He removed his foot from the stirrup and told Korah, "Put your foot in there."

She followed his instruction and was surprised by how little pulling she had to do to get up on the saddle. She was not a tiny woman, but Brick hefted her with no trouble at all. When she was firmly planted on the seat, Korah was immediately grateful that Brick had suggested this. The saddle was built for one, so she had to get *very* close to him. Almost every part of their body touched from the chest down.

"I like this," she cooed.

"I thought you might," Brick replied. "You know you gotta hold on tight, right? If you fall off without a helmet on, it won't be good."

A wave of dread rolled through her and made the hairs stand on Korah's arms. She reached and held Brick around the midsection.

"*Tighter*," he muttered.

Her arms weren't long enough to clasp her hands together, and Brick didn't have any official handles. She wasn't sure what to hold onto.

Brick released the reins and took hold of her hands. He placed her palms on his stomach. Through the shirt, Korah felt his six-pack, which was as hard as ever. She smiled and hummed pleasantly as she ran her hands up and down his stomach. Brick was the first man she ever dated who had real-live *washboard abs*.

Her greedy hands moved up to his chest, which was equally delightful. Korah smiled and closed her eyes as she rested the side of her face against his back. She thought she was in cowboy heaven when he took her to the stockyards and showed off a sexy, country swing dance. But that was nothing compared to this day, this ranch, this horse-riding hunk.

"You figured out what you wanna hold onto?" he asked after a few seconds.

"No," Korah replied. "I reckon I'll figure it out once we get moving."

"You *reckon*, huh?"

She giggled. "Yeah."

"Alright, little lady," he said and took hold of the reins again.

"Wait," Korah said. "I wanted to ask you: How do you keep your butt from bouncing around in the saddle? On the way down here, I was all over the place, but you weren't."

"You have to relax your hips," Brick explained. "It's kinda like dancing. You don't go left when your partner is going right. And you don't go up when the saddle is going down. Pay attention to the movements of the horse, and let your hips roll with him. In this case, you can let your hips roll with mine. I'll show you how it's done."

"I'd like that."

"I thought you might." He snapped the reins slightly and told Roscoe to, "Come on," and they all got moving.

Korah was able to keep up with him at first, but as they increased speed, her body felt less secure. Brick remained firmly planted in the seat. She held onto his midsection as she tried to relax her muscles and flow with the horse.

"If you can't feel what Roscoe's doing, then feel me," Brick urged her. "Feel how my hips are going back and forth a little, kinda like I'm making slow, sweet love to this saddle."

Korah grinned. She loved that description, and she loved being this close to him. She took a deep breath and managed to calm her nerves. She knew that Brick wouldn't let her fall. She always felt safe with him. She concentrated on their movements, and she did feel Brick's hips moving back and forth, slowly and, well, *sensually*. Korah wasn't the best dancer, but after a little while she was able to match his movements.

She didn't realize that her butt wasn't bouncing around anymore until Brick said, "There you go. You're getting it."

"I am," Korah said. "This is fun!"

"You ready to go faster?"

"Yes!"

She tightened her grip, and Brick clicked his heels on the horse's flank.

"*Giddyup, boy! Come on, Roscoe. Let's get it!*"

He snapped the reins, and the palomino responded with an explosion of speed that nearly toppled Korah. She reached and found that her arms were in fact long enough to wrap around her boyfriend completely. She clasped her hands together over his stomach and held on for dear life as the horse transitioned into a full gallop.

Brick leaned forward in the saddle, and Korah did the same. The sound of Roscoe's hooves clapping the hard soil filled her ears as the world flew by them in a blur. The smell of the lake and the trees was all around them.

"*You alright*?" Brick yelled.

"*Yes!*" Korah shouted back.

Her body was completely flat against his now. She had her head turned to the side, her face pressed between his shoulder blades. The friction between her breasts and the powerful muscles in Brick's back was surprisingly erotic, but that was nothing compared to the rubbing between her legs. She wasn't sure if it was the way they moved on the saddle or their high rate of speed or the life-threatening thrill of it all, but Korah felt herself becoming more and more aroused as she rocked her hips with Brick, leaving nary a sliver of space between them.

The smile on her face grew steadily, even as her heart rate increased. She felt the palomino's strong muscles extending and contracting beneath her. She felt equally impressive muscles in Brick's back and stomach tightening as he strengthened his grip on the reins and led Roscoe towards the trees.

Korah knew there was a trail beneath them, but once again she couldn't see it. Fright got the best of her, and she squeezed her eyes closed as they zipped past shrubbery that was close enough to reach out and touch.

Surely this was the most dangerous thing she'd ever done. But as death-defying as this ride was, she knew that Brick wouldn't let any harm come to her. She trusted him as much as she trusted the safety bar on an amusement park roller coaster. She even had enough faith in him to open her eyes after a while, so she could fully admire the beauty of his land and the majesty of his steed.

Brick was surprised that Korah had gone along with his plan, and he was impressed that she wasn't screaming like a banshee along the way. When they emerged on the other side of the tree line and the ranch was once again in view, Korah surprised him yet again by releasing the grip on her own hands and grabbing hold of him instead. Her hands were soft, but her grip was strong. Her nails dug into his chest and stomach, which caused an unexpected plume of heat to stir deep inside him.

Brick's eyes narrowed in confusion.

No matter how many times he tried to put Korah in a box and prove that her femininity made her weaker, less knowledgeable of construction or even less willing to ride a horse, she always found a way to destroy his preconceptions. Brick was still not ready to acknowledge that he'd met his match, but he had to admit that the woman clinging to him was a fireball. She was smart and sexy and possibly just as much of a daredevil as him.

Was it possible that Korah was *The One*?

Brick didn't know how to answer that, because as far as he was concerned there was no such thing. He was forty-five years old, and he had yet to encounter a woman he couldn't bear to be without. He didn't purposely avoid lengthy relationships, but *forever* was not a concept he could affix to one girl. At least that had been the case with him.

But Korah was different. She was not the type of woman he could compare to the rest. Was that why thoughts like *forever* kept popping into his mind nowadays? They had only been dating for a month. Was he tripping?

He had to be.

"*Why are you slowing down*?" she screamed very close to his ear.

Brick felt the fire consuming his soul once again. He knew that it was ignited by her energy, her touch and her words. He knew that she had the power to burn him down completely, and he realized there was somewhere he wanted to get to very quickly.

Why was he slowing down?

No longer racing for fun, he snapped the reins again and beckoned Roscoe to hurry to their destination.

"*Come on, now! Giddyup, boy! Get!*"

Korah confounded him further when she began to shriek with laughter, totally oblivious to the inner turmoil her defiance was producing.

● ● ● ● ● ●

When they got to the stable, Rosie was dutifully waiting for them. Brick had four more horses that were all strong and robust, healthy and well fed. Each one of them stopped grazing for a moment and took notice as the palomino roared through the gate with his two passengers. The horse's nostrils flared as big as a fist as it sucked down enough oxygen to fuel his massive muscles.

"Whoa."

Brick pulled up on the reins and led the animal to the water trough. Roscoe immediately began to quench his thirst, taking no notice as Brick helped Korah off first and then hopped off of the saddle himself.

The stable was new, made mostly of wood that was fashioned like a traditional log cabin. But inside it was state of the art, with all of the amenities one would expect from a professional breeder.

The ranch house never gave the pretense of being old-fashioned. It was a two story mansion with 16,000 square feet of living space, a guest house, a cabana, a wine cellar and one of the most impressive home theaters Korah had ever seen. She only had a little time to admire the home before they went fishing. Korah was eager to explore more of the property over the next two days she planned to stay at the ranch.

Brick was unusually quiet as he retrieved their dinner from Rosie's saddle bag. Korah was on cloud nine. The exhilaration from their furious ride had her blood racing hot and fast.

She didn't realize Brick's pulse was racing as well until they entered the ranch through the back and he reached out and stopped her in the foyer. Korah was surprised to feel his strong hand on the waistline of her jeans, hooking her at the small of her back, bringing her to an immediate halt.

She turned and her eyes narrowed when she gazed into his hazel orbs. His expression was deep and serious. For a moment, Korah feared that she had done something wrong. Brick tossed the fish haphazardly onto a wooden end table and reached again, this time gripping the front of her jeans. Her heart froze as he pulled her to him roughly, nearly hard enough to pop the buckle. When they were chest to chest, her lips parted as she gasped and then sighed weakly.

Brick kissed her hard and passionately. His hands moved from her sides down to her hips and finally settled on her ass as he deepened the kiss, slipping his tongue inside her mouth, sucking and tasting until Korah's chest heaved against his. She felt feeble in his arms. She closed her eyes, and her mind spun in a sea of erotic bliss.

Suddenly he began walking towards her, forcing her backwards.

Korah's lovesick eyes flashed open as she stepped back blindly. Brick continued to march forward, his mouth never leaving hers. After a few steps, Korah's back encountered a wall, and a startled "*Uhn,*" escaped her mouth.

Brick grunted as he sucked her tongue and lips. His hands squeezed her ass. *Hard.* He didn't look angry, but he didn't look happy, either. He reached and pulled her shirt up her stomach and over her chest. Korah had no choice but to raise her arms to facilitate the garment's removal.

Her bra unfastened from the back, but Brick maintained eye contact as he grabbed it with two hands from the front. He yanked hard, and the fabric tore easily. Her breasts spilled forward like a cornucopia. Her skin was cocoa brown. Her nipples a shade darker.

"*Brick,*" she breathed. "*What are you doing?*"

The question was mostly rhetorical. As he palmed both of her breasts with his large hands and dipped his head to tug at her sensitive nipples with his lips and teeth, *what* he was doing was very apparent. It was the *why* Korah was curious about. Why here, why now? Why like this?

But as these questions swirled through her mind, Brick's hot tongue swirled around her areola, and Korah realized she wasn't opposed to this treatment *at all.* In the past it was their shared love for construction that put him in this type of frenzy. Korah didn't think she had done anything recently to bring out this side of him. If so, she desperately wanted to know what it was, so she could do it again in the future!

Brick's mouth left her chest, and he pushed her squarely against the wall. He restrained her with two strong hands on her shoulders. Korah stared up at him with large, nearly frightful eyes. He stared down at her with much stronger intensity.

"I don't know what it is about you," he finally said, though it was more like a growl. His jaws clenched. He inhaled deeply, causing his nostrils to flare.

Korah was at a loss for words. Her chest continued to heave between them. She wasn't afraid, but her body was trembling, mostly between her legs. She squirmed. The movement caused her to feel how wet her panties were.

Jeez, I'm a mess, she thought.

"*You, broke my bra*," she whispered.

She realized how trivial her comment was at the same moment as Brick. He sneered slightly and made a *humph* sound.

"That's all you got to say?" he asked.

Korah's heart fluttered. "I – I don't know what to say."

"Then don't say anything."

Korah agreed that was probably for the best, but she couldn't stop a slight scream from slipping past her lips when Brick reached down suddenly and grabbed her pants again. He yanked at the buckle forcibly but managed to get it open without tearing the fabric. He unzipped them as he dropped to his knees. He lifted her legs, one foot at a time.

He tugged her boots and socks off in one smooth motion. He then pulled her jeans down to her ankles with the panties still entwined. He stood and ordered her to "*Get 'em off*," as he removed his own shirt.

The mansion had enough bedrooms to create a bed and breakfast, but Brick wanted her in the foyer, and Korah knew that she was powerless to stop it. Or was she a willing participant? She stepped out of her jeans stiffly, each movement creating a ripple of ecstasy between her legs that caused her body to produce more lubrication for him. Her clitoris swelled and began to throb rhythmically.

She watched as Brick unbuttoned his own jeans and pushed them down to his knees. She was curious about how he'd get them off with his boots still on, but her boyfriend had a sense of urgency that wouldn't allow such minor details to delay him. Another thing he didn't have to slow down for was a condom.

Last week Brick proposed that they get checked out by their physicians, so that they could eliminate the use of condoms from their love life. This was also Brick's way of ensuring they were in a monogamous relationship. Korah was pleased that the incurable playboy picked her to be his only girl. And she was surprised that he managed to make such a clinical request sound romantic.

29

He pushed his boxers down and stepped to her with his hard dick in hand. The sight of it made Korah's legs grow weak. Her mouth watered, but her throat clicked dryly when she swallowed.

Brick closed the distance between them and planted hot kisses on her mouth and neck. Korah threw her head back and placed her hands on his broad shoulders. Brick's hands returned to her soft backside. His hands and fingers gently explored every inch of her ass, and then he squeezed her cheeks hard enough to make her cry out with pleasure.

"*Brick*," she panted. "*Baby, let's go to the bedroom.*"

"I want to," he said.

He rested his forehead against hers and squeezed his eyes closed. Korah closed her eyes as well. She ran her hands from his shoulders up to his trapezius muscles. The feel of the raw power coiled beneath his burning flesh made her clit swell even more.

"But I can't make it," Brick continued. "... not unless you wanna see me duck walk."

Korah grinned at the image of him shuffling through the mansion with his pants around his ankles. And then she cried out when he tightened his grip on her ass and began to lift her from the floor.

"*Whoa! Baby–*"

He did not respond. When her bare feet were completely off the floor, he leaned her against the wall again. Korah's grip on his neck and shoulders tightened. He lifted her higher. He stepped closer until she felt his dick pressing against her wet opening.

Korah's clit got the first taste of his meat, and it quivered in anticipation. She didn't think he could manage insertion without reaching down to guide himself, but it was high time she stopped doubting this man. He pushed his hips forward slowly, and the head found the warm, wetness it desired.

"*Damn*," Brick said softly as he slid inside her, inch by inch.

He backed away slightly and stared down at her nude physique. Korah's spine rested against the wall. She watched his eyes as Brick watched himself slide in deeper, until their skin met. The look on his face made Korah's heart thump slow and sweet. The feel of him entering her from this angle was highly sensual.

30

"*Damn*," Brick groaned again. "*You feel so good, baby. I knew you'd feel this good.*"

Korah knew he was referring to his first plunge without protection. He pushed in even more, and a heavenly shudder rolled down her entire body. When it reached her labia, her walls clenched around him. Brick's eyes widened for a second and then narrowed. That was the first time Korah had ever watched his reaction to her body's involuntary response to him.

"*I like it when you do that,*" he said as he began to stroke slowly, in an upward motion.

From this position, every inch of his shaft provided titillation to her clit as he slid in and out. Korah began to moan softly. Her eyelids fluttered, but she would not allow them to close. She didn't want to miss any of this – this man – this bronze god who had brains and brawn and a relentless hankering for Korah that baffled them equally.

Her eyes followed the swell of his pecs, down to his six pack and the sexy lines under his love handles. She was never one to stare, but the sight of his dick plunging in and out of her was hypnotizing. She was crazy to want to take this to the bedroom. Brick could do no wrong.

And that was why she didn't object when he pulled her away from the wall, drawing her to him until they were chest to chest. His hands moved under her thighs until he supported her fully. And Korah found that she could contribute now. She wrapped her legs around his waist and was able to move her body up and down on his pole. Brick kept his feet planted and let her take over completely.

Korah stared into his eyes as she rode him. He was rock hard. Without a condom, she felt every vein on his dick. The sound of their lovemaking was moist and raucous. She felt wetter than she had ever been, but her body was still tight for him. Her clit drummed with urgency as her orgasm began to consume her, originating in her heart and mind.

He kissed her softly. He tugged at her bottom lip with his teeth.

He told her, "*I been waiting to feel all of you, like this.*"

Korah knew that was the case, but it excited her to hear him say it.

"*I, I have too,*" she said.

31

He grinned. *"Not as much as me."*

Up and down she went.

She felt him throbbing, growing harder.

"Why are you looking at me like that?" he grunted. His smile was impish.

"I want... Uhn. I want to watch you," she moaned.

Up.

And down.

"Watch..." He swallowed. His Adam's apple was stiff and bulbous. *"Watch me what?"*

Korah's eyes darkened. She surprised herself by being bold enough to articulate her naughty desires. *"Cum."*

He grunted again. He turned suddenly and deposited her on an ottoman. It was only big enough for her upper body. Everything below her backside hung over the side. Brick dropped to his knees and lifted her legs in the same motion. He spread her thighs wide and stared at the extraordinary sight between them. Feeling self-conscious, Korah closed her eyes. Her head rolled back on the cushion.

"I wanna watch too," Brick said, and he entered her again, slowly.

He continued to hold her legs open. The sight of his caramel colored dick pushing inside her darker skin made a fierce shudder roll down his body, tightening his chest and abdominal muscles along the way. He pulled out completely and submerged again. He did it a third time and muttered, *"Shit,"* this time staying buried inside her, pushing hard until his hips pressed her ass.

A deep quiver in Korah's belly snowballed down her womb. It raced down her legs and left them tingling when it headed back up. The quiver felt like a cannonball when it collided with her clitoris. Her mouth fell open and she moaned mightily. Her hands gripped the cushion on the ottoman. Brick began to pump hard and fast, causing her orgasm to split in two, the second one more dynamic than the first.

Korah screamed, her voice laced with pain and pleasure. Brick didn't let up.

He told her, *"You're creaming, baby,"* and Korah knew that she was.

He continued to hold her trembling legs, and somewhere faraway Korah heard him say, "*I thought you wanted to watch.*"

She didn't know what that meant – didn't think she ever said such a thing, but then she remembered.

"*Uhn.*" Brick blew a plume of hot air from his nostrils. Korah felt his grip on her legs tighten. She looked up in time to see a look of pure bliss overtake him. The light shining behind her man's face made him look ethereal. He was the god of passion. His bottom lip was half-tucked between his teeth. His eyes were concentrated between her legs. His purpose and his desire made him look like he had never made love before in his life.

"*Uh-uhn.*"

He looked up at her as his seed spilled from him. His dick pulsated, and her walls caressed him. Thanking him for the offering.

This was Korah's first night at the Avery Ranch. She still had Saturday and Sunday to look forward to.

She absolutely loved her life.

CHAPTER THREE
LIVING THE LIFE

Brick marinated their bass with olive oil, lemon juice, parsley and pepper while Korah lounged in an oval shaped bathtub that had silver metal work and was held a foot off the floor by four elegant dragon legs. Brick served the fish alongside rice and sautéed vegetables. Later the couple retired to the den and talked and snuggled long into the night while sipping Laroche Chablis.

On Saturday Brick showed her more of the property, including a run-down shack near the lake that was out of sync with the extravagance of the ranch house. Brick told her the two-room shanty was once the home of his great-grandparents. Korah was immediately enthralled. She saw that the land around the small house was well kept, so it hadn't been totally abandoned.

She asked, "Is it safe if I have a look?"

He nodded and Korah slowly made her way up the creaky steps.

Once inside she had a strong sense that the shack might fall down on her at any moment, but Brick's assurance stayed her, as did her fascination. The home was dusty but not too stuffy. It was furnished relatively well with a row of courier shelves against one wall and two desks that hugged the central support column.

In one corner there was a bed that was low to the floor and without a mattress. The smell of old wood was rich and pleasant. Korah gasped and rushed over to a classic Glenwood stove in the kitchenette that was manufactured in the early 1900's.

"Oh my God, Brick! This place needs to be in a museum!"

He stood in the doorway watching her. "Yeah. One day, maybe."

Korah was transported back in time as she inspected the rest of the house. The shack was from a simple era; a time before televisions or even indoor plumbing.

"When was this place built?" she exclaimed.

"1895," Brick said without the need to think about it.

Korah turned back to look at him. Brick wore faded jeans with a tee-shirt and a brown Stetson. He fit right into the old-timey backdrop. It was clear that he took a lot of pride in the little house.

"My great-grandfather Abe built this place by hand," he said. "That's always been in our blood; building things and owning property. He was a carpenter, first black man to own a shop downtown. He specialized in desks, but he could make anything, if he had enough wood.

"They burnt his shop down," Brick continued. His eyes were soft and reflective. "*Twice.* He rebuilt it. And then he saved up enough money to buy more land in Lewisville. He built another house there. I can take you to see it today, if you want."

Korah nodded. She stepped closer, hanging on each one of his words. "I'd love to see it."

"When I became the renowned construction and contracting *god* you know and love," Brick said, pausing long enough for Korah to roll her eyes and grin at him, "I started taking steps to restore this old cabin." He looked around the front room with a gleam in his eyes. "I didn't want to change anything, just reinforce all of the supports, to make sure it wouldn't fall down any time soon.

"I also added fifty more acres to the ranch, which included the other half of the lake. I started building the ranch house and the new stable. Bought some more horses."

"And now you're living high on the hog," Korah joked. "A chocolate J. R. Ewing. The richest man in Lewisville."

He grinned. Korah smiled as well. Even in jeans Brick exuded power and confidence.

"Well, the city's not that big," he said modestly. "But yeah, I am."

And he's all mine, Korah thought as she stepped closer and kissed him softly on the lips. She didn't even allow the ugly little words *for now* to spoil the mood.

● ● ● ● ● ●

Brick followed through with his promise to take her to the big city that day. Lewisville had a population of just under 100,000. It was one of those rare places where American commerce had taken hold, but there were still a lot of areas with barely paved roads and farms sitting on vast swaths of land.

Among the highlights was a downtown relic called "Abe's Carpentry Store." Korah was as giddy as a school girl when Brick pulled to a stop in front of the building and told her, "This is it; my great-grandfather's store."

"You're kidding me," Korah said, her eyes wide and disbelieving. "It's still open?"

"Sure," Brick said.

"Since the late 1800's?"

"1905," Brick said. He nodded at a placard next to the front door that announced this information elegantly.

"This is amazing," Korah said. She was truly awed. "What do they build? Who runs it?"

"Everything's still made in the shop out back," Brick said, "which is probably why we haven't opened any national chains yet. But they do alright. My uncle's a master carpenter. He runs the store with his wife and kids. They'll make anything on request, but they specialize in desks and tables, bedroom furniture. This little shop put me and a lot more of us through college."

"We're going in, right?" Korah asked. "They're open now?"

"Yes'm," Brick said as he opened his door and hopped out of his truck. "They'd better be open on a Saturday afternoon," he said when he opened Korah's door and helped her out of her seat. "Might not have anyone in the workshop, but someone's manning the register."

The store seemed to double in size once they entered. A doorbell rang quaintly to announce their arrival. The layout of the store was typical of a furniture shop, with some collections fully assembled. The floor was hardwood. The dressers and headboards on display ranged from cherry wood to maple, all polished to an impeccable shine. Most of the designs were intricate and engaging.

Korah left Brick's side and was caught up in the beauty of the woodwork when a fair-skinned woman approached and threw her hands around him.

"*Brick*! Oh my goodness! Baby, why didn't you tell us you were coming down?"

He grinned as he wrapped his arms around the older woman and squeezed tightly.

"I'm just hanging out at the ranch for the weekend," he replied when they separated. The woman held him at arms' length, looking him up and down.

Korah could see the gleam of love in her eyes and Brick's as well.

"Are you going down to the house to see Clarence and them?" the woman asked.

Brick shook his head but said, "I might. I came down with a friend."

He left the woman and went to Korah, who was headed their way. Brick took hold of her hand as he introduced her.

"Aunt Ruth, this is Korah. She owns a contracting company in Overbrook Meadows. Korah, this is my Aunt Ruth. She runs this here shop with my Uncle Clarence."

"Pleased to meet you," Korah said. She pulled away from Brick, so she could shake her hand.

Aunt Ruth was a tall woman with wide hips and huge boobs. She looked like she could hold her own against the hardworking men she was around every day, but the smile she fixed on Korah was as sweet as honey.

"Nice to meet you, young lady! You sure are pretty! I love your dress."

Korah's sundress was knee-length with floral patterns. "Thank you!" she replied. "I've heard a lot about this place."

Aunt Ruth continued to smile at her, and then she grinned at Brick. "You're lucky to have a woman this beautiful on your arm," she announced.

Korah blushed.

Brick nodded. "I agree."

"And you're a contractor, huh?" Aunt Ruth said to Korah.

"We're not as big as Brick House," Korah conceded. "But we're getting there."

"Hogwash," Brick interjected. "Texas Builders is just as big as us," he assured his aunt. "Korah almost beat me out of a school contract last week. I don't think we would've made this trip, if that was the case."

Korah's mouth fell open. "Wow. The truth comes out."

Aunt Ruth laughed. "I'm sure y'all have a lot in common, both working in construction and all..."

Korah nodded. "We do." And then her face heated as she thought about their mutual love of tools – the bigger the better – and the aphrodisiac they had become. "I love your furniture," she said, changing the subject.

Aunt Ruth's eyes became even brighter. "Why thank you! You know we build every piece by hand."

"Brick told me. And I find that completely incredible," Korah said as she returned her attention to a nearby desk. "I really like the style of this one. Is it oak?"

"Mmm hmm," Aunt Ruth said. She followed her, in full salesman mode now. "That desk is as sturdy as you'll ever see. And it comes with a lifetime warranty."

Brick frowned slightly as he followed them. "Come on, Auntie. Everyone I bring into this store is not a customer."

"Why can't I be a customer?" Korah asked without looking back. "I need a new desk for my office."

"Well, the one you have *is* ugly," Brick agreed.

Korah turned and slapped him playfully on the arm. "Well thanks a lot!"

"I'm just saying you shouldn't feel obligated to purchase anything – just because I brought you here."

"I don't have to buy a desk to impress you," Korah quipped.

"Mmm," Aunt Ruth said, raising an eyebrow. "Brick, I think this one can give you a run for your money. I was wondering how you'd been putting up with his cockiness," she said to Korah. "But I can see that you're no pushover."

"Not at all," Brick agreed.

Korah looked into his eyes and smiled warmly.

"So tell me," Aunt Ruth said, interrupting their tender moment. "How big is your office, sugar...?

• • • • • •

Korah purchased a beautiful oak desk and made arrangements to have it shipped to her office. Afterwards, Brick showed her more of his not-so-little hometown, and he took her to a real-live butcher shop, where he purchased two fresh rib eyes for dinner.

Korah was thoroughly impressed with Brick already. Seeing the humble environment he grew up in furthered her admiration. But it was the places he did *not* show her that were most notable.

Brick did not take her to his uncle's house, as his aunt suggested. And he did not take Korah to meet his parents, who were both still very much alive. She wasn't sure how she should interpret that, or whether she should read anything into it at all.

She and Brick had only been dating for a month, so it was probably premature to think he was ready to take her home to meet the folks. But since he did bring her to his hometown and show her locales that were only a few miles away from his childhood home, why wouldn't he stop to visit with his family? It didn't seem like a mere oversight. Did he avoid this natural progression of their relationship because Korah wasn't *the one*?

She decided it would be best not to mention it. If the shoe was on the other foot, she would certainly have introduced him to her family. But Brick was a different creature, and she knew that going in. He constantly did things to show Korah that she was his only girl. Pointing out things he didn't do would make her seem clingy and unsure of herself.

● ● ● ● ● ●

When they got back to the ranch, Brick showed her some of the upkeep that was involved with the property, which included caring for the horses and cleaning their stable.

With so many employees at his disposal, Korah was surprised to see him work so hard. He could've easily left the task for his ranch hand, who would return on Monday. But Brick seemed to delight in the labor. Korah delighted in watching him break a sweat that made his tee-shirt cling to his muscular chest and back.

When he finished, he pulled his work gloves off and planted his pitchfork in the soft dirt near the stable. He leaned on it as he wiped his brow. His brown, sun-beaten skin glistened with sweat.

"Did you learn anything?" he asked her.

"I learned that I like seeing you work," Korah said. She hadn't done anything in the past hour but play with Rosie, who was her favorite of his equines.

"You like watching me work, huh?" Brick said. He placed his Stetson atop his head as he approached her with a southern swagger that came natural to him.

"I do," Korah said. She backed away as he drew nearer.

"What's wrong?" Brick asked. "You don't wanna give me a hug?"

"No! Get away from me, stinky!" Korah laughed as she turned tail and sprinted towards the house.

Brick gave chase, but he also gave her a reprieve and headed for the shower once inside.

While he bathed, Korah checked her phone and responded to a few emails. Her daughter Stephanie was respectful enough not to call during Korah's weekend retreat, but she did send her mom a text message that morning:

How's it going?

Korah reclined on a plush easy chair in the sitting room as she dialed her number.

"Hey sweetie."

"Hi, Mama!" Her baby girl sounded very excited.

"How's everything going?"

"Great! How are things going with *you*? Whatcha doing over there?"

"Nothing. Relaxing," Korah said.

"Had a hard day?" The question was filled with innuendos.

"No. It's been nice," Korah said. "Saw some beautiful things. I bought a new desk. It should be delivered next week."

"You bought a desk? For the office?"

"Um hmm."

"Why would you buy a desk? He took you furniture shopping?"

"No," Korah said with a chuckle. "Brick comes from a long line of carpenters. He took me to a shop his great-grandfather built in 1905. They still do great woodwork. I saw a desk I liked, and I bought it."

"You did that to help with the contract right?" Stephanie guessed. At twenty years of age, she was heir to the Texas Builders' throne one day – she and her big brother Devin. Stephanie could be a little cutthroat at times, but she knew that her mother had never resorted to underhanded tactics to win a bid.

"No. I bought it because I fell in love with it," Korah informed her. "It had nothing to do with Brick."

"Did he bring up the sub-contracting?" Stephanie pressed.

"Yes," Korah said. "I told him I accepted the offer."

"*Sweet!*" her daughter exclaimed. "Did he give you a contract?"

"No, not yet," Korah said. "But you know this weekend isn't about business."

"Yes, I wanna talk about that too. How y'all getting along over there? Did he let you ride his horses?"

Korah eyed Brick through a large picture window. He casually attended to their steaks on a humongous stainless steel grill outside. He wore a new pair of jeans and a different tee-shirt. Korah smiled as she stared at his strong back and perfectly squeezable butt.

"I did ride a horse," she said. "And I drifted in a canoe. And I caught some fish. I'll send you a picture. It's been great. Very relaxing."

"Mama, you're gonna fall in love," Stephanie warned. She was both happy and anxious. "Are you worried about that?"

Korah gave it some thought. She sighed. "I know who Brick is. I knew who he was before I even met him."

"You keep saying that, but it doesn't mean you won't get hurt."

Korah appreciated the insight, but she didn't know how to resolve her current situation. Should she keep her heart from Brick, so it wouldn't hurt so badly when he decided it was time to move on? If so, she might as well stop seeing him right now. Or should she give in to love, hoping that he *wouldn't* decide to move on? That didn't seem wise at all.

"Mama?"

"Baby girl, you're looking way too far into the future," Korah said. "And now you got me doing it. Brick's making us dinner right now. And later he promised to take me on a carriage ride. I can't say what our future holds past that."

"Okay," Stephanie said. "Well, you go right ahead and *live that life*, Mama! Forget I said anything!"

Korah chuckled. "I love you, sweet pea. Tell your brother I said I love him, too."

• • • • • •

After supper Brick led two of his horses, Sally and Jezebel, to the barn, where he had an old-fashioned carriage stored away. He hitched the animals like he'd been working on a farm his whole life, and then he helped Korah aboard with the casual chivalry that came so natural for him.

They set off as the sun retreated in the western skies, casting a beautiful auburn glow about the land. The ride was slow and breathtaking. The dirt roads that circled and ran through the property were surprisingly smooth. They were both dressed casually, but Korah felt like she was headed for a ball as Brick manned the reins, sitting tall on the bench seat. Even the horses seemed much more majestic in their shiny, leather harnesses.

Korah reached and placed a hand on her man's thigh. Brick looked over at her and smiled affectionately. As far as weekend getaways went, Korah knew this trip would always rank among her favorites. The accommodations and dining alone would've been enough to keep her coming back. The fact that she was spending so much time with a man she was falling in love with made the ranch even more enchanting.

"I'm going to build the best school they've ever seen," Brick said twenty minutes into the ride.

Korah wasn't surprised to hear him boasting again, though he hadn't spoken much about the school all weekend.

"Are you?" she asked, her smile soft and wistful.

"It'll be the best thing you've ever seen," he continued. He stared straight ahead as he spoke. His hat and shoulders rocked gently with the easy swaying of the carriage.

"I know you strive for perfection," he said. "And I do too. So I don't envision us bumping heads on your subcontracting. In addition to the football field, I'm going to give you guys the training center. It's a state of the art weight room. They want it to rival the one at TCU. I haven't seen the plans yet, but I know what they're expecting."

Korah's pulse quickened, but she tried not to show how excited she was.

"But the school," Brick went on. He shook his head. "It'll be my crowning achievement. And it only gets better from here. In three years, Brick House signs will be at all the major construction sites. I'm gonna be so big, baby. Getting this school is the validation I've been looking for since I started the company. It's everything I've ever wanted."

Korah couldn't have been happier for him. There was a tinge of envy, because she had been in the running for the school contract as well. If things had gone her way, she'd be feeling the same euphoria Brick was basking in. But the cards didn't fall that way.

But that didn't mean she wouldn't take part in the success. The school district allotted 15 million dollars for the project. The work Brick was offering would amount to a third of that, if not more. Korah's company was poised to grow by leaps and bounds as well, simply because Brick felt like his woman should share the bounty.

That was something he did not have to do. Korah was thankful on a business level and even more so on a personal level. She knew that she didn't owe him anything more than a job well done, but that didn't seem like enough to show the full depth of her gratitude.

● ● ● ● ● ●

Later that evening, Korah returned to the bathroom with the oval-shaped tub while Brick bathed in a room Korah had never seen five doors down. They reunited in one of the two dens downstairs. Brick waited for her wearing only a pair of black boxers. He toted a bucket of ice with a bottled of chilled wine, two elegant wine glasses. He also had a bottle of heated lotion, mango scented. Korah was surprised that he remembered.

The room was beautifully furnished, designed to showcase a huge bearskin rug that drew your attention as quickly as a living bear would. When she first saw it, Korah was not a fan. But as she approached wearing nothing but a bra and panties under her robe,

43

Brick looked befitting enough to deserve such a savage monument. They sat on the thick, black fur and enjoyed a glass of wine as well as a few delicious kisses.

Korah rejected Brick's offer to give her a massage.

"No. You lay down. I want to massage you," she offered.

Brick didn't protest. He lay on his stomach. Korah was giddy as she straddled his thighs. Her hands were magical that night. His bulging muscles melted beneath her kneading fingers and thumbs. But when she rolled him over, she saw that at least one of his muscles hadn't melted. It was as hard as a brick.

Korah took her robe off and scooted down between his legs. She peeled his boxers down and wasted no time taking him into her mouth. Brick's stomach tensed. He sat up on his elbows and watched as her lips slid slowly down his shaft. Korah's mouth was hot, but his dick was hotter.

She looked up at him as she began to slowly bob her head up and down. Her tongue slithered around his meat like a serpent. Brick's eyes darkened. Korah wondered if he could read her mind; if he knew that she loved the taste and feel of him in her mouth. He probably wouldn't believe that she enjoyed pleasing him in this manner more than he enjoyed the pleasure she provided.

Earlier that week she told him she was curious about what his cum tasted like. Did he remember? The look in his eyes made her feel like he did. The throbbing against her tongue and cheeks assured her that she would know soon enough.

She smiled around his dick and then did something with her jaws that made Brick's nostrils flare. He reached and placed a hand on the side of her face. His fingers slipped into her hair, softly at first, but gradually his grip on her head tightened. It didn't feel like he would let her go when he came. Korah felt naughty for hoping that was the case.

She closed her eyes and continued to suck him down greedily.

CHAPTER FOUR
THE BIG ONE

On Sunday, Korah surprised herself by sleeping till 10:00. She couldn't remember the last time that happened, even while on vacation. She rolled over and saw that Brick had the curtains in the bedroom pulled closed. The curtains were dark and thick, which prevented the sunlight from peeking through. The only light source came from the open doorway.

Brick rolled onto his back when he noticed she was awake. He reached and pulled her close to his body. Korah smiled and kissed his bare chest.

"Been up long?" she asked.

"About ten minutes," he replied. "Been laying here thinking."

"About what?"

"About how much fun I've had with you over the past two days. I don't wanna go back to my regular life. But at the same time, I kinda do. I'm eager to get back to work."

"I feel the same way," Korah said. "I'm glad we have one more day left."

"That's not all I've been thinking about…"

"Oh?" Korah looked up at him. She expected something profound, but Brick had more primitive things in mind.

"Not sure what to do about my morning wood," he murmured.

Korah giggled as she looked down and saw the tent he was pitching under the sheets.

She rolled away from him. "Sounds like a personal problem to me."

"Yeah," Brick grunted. "That's what I figured. But then again, I have a naked angel in my bed. So it might not be a problem at all."

He placed a hand on her hip and rubbed seductively.

Korah rolled again until she was on her stomach. She yawned, feigning disinterest.

Brick pulled the sheets back unexpectedly, fully exposing her.

"How rude," she muttered.

He reached and caressed her ass. He used his free hand to pull her legs apart slightly. His other hand inched lower. When his fingers struck gold, he titillated the outer lips before slipping his longest finger inside her.

"Do you wake up like this?" he asked, noticing how wet she was.

"No, I don't think so."

"Why am I so lucky?"

"I saw you were hard," she explained. "And then you started touching me."

"That's it?" he asked. "That's all it took?"

Korah didn't know how to respond. Surely he knew by now how much control he had over her body. Voicing it seemed like total surrender.

Brick rose to his knees and hiked her hips up as he positioned himself behind her. Korah kept her face down on the pillow.

He rubbed the head of his meat around her moist opening and said, "I told you, baby. No problem at all."

Korah sucked air between her teeth as he slid in all the way to the hilt. She gripped the pillow tightly and delighted in the colors dancing behind her closed eyelids.

● ● ● ● ● ●

After another lazy day at the ranch, the lovebirds climbed into Brick's Navigator and put the stables in their rearview mirror at sunset. Korah was not eager to leave the place or Brick's presence, but the real world beckoned, and there was much work to be done in their hometowns.

Brick brought up the contract again when they entered Overbrook Meadows' city limits. Korah shook off the last of her vacation mind state and put her thinking cap back on.

"Have you ever built anything similar to a football field?" Brick asked. "I didn't see anything like that on your website."

"I think the closest we've done is a soccer field," Korah said. "The one at the school, do you think it will have stadium seating or collapsible bleachers?"

"Collapsible," Brick said. "But everything has to be perfect. They'll have their track meets there in addition to the football and soccer games. I think they want a professional concession stand. And locker rooms, of course."

"That doesn't sound too taxing," Korah said.

"The community center you built in Forest Hill, it has a weight room inside?"

"Yes, and basketball courts in the gym. You checked out my community center?"

"Only the outside," Brick stated. "They weren't open when I stopped by. I'll go again sometime next week."

Korah was surprised to hear that. "Are you still checking up on me?"

"Of course."

"Don't you think you should've done all of that before you offered me the subcontracting?"

"You haven't signed a contract yet," he said. "Until then, nothing's official."

Korah bristled visibly, but she kept her mouth closed.

He laughed. "Babe, I'm just kidding. I said I was going to bring you in on this project, and I meant it. I'm not going back on my word."

Korah didn't share his humor. And now she had other concerns.

"Brick, what if we break up? What happens to our agreement then?"

He frowned and then said, "We won't break ground on the school until January. That gives us three months to decide if we really like each other."

That comment only made her feel more unsure of herself. "What does that mean? I don't want to walk on eggshells for the next three months; thinking I can't do anything to piss you off, or

47

you'll snatch this job away from us. That's not fair. You might as well tell me we're not doing business together right now and get it over with."

"Whoa. Where's this aggression coming from?"

"This is business, Brick. If you wanna string my heart along, and I choose to accept it, that's fine. But I'm not going to allow you to do that to Texas Builders."

His eyes widened. He turned to stare at her.

"Keep your eyes on the road," she instructed.

He grinned but did as he was told.

"I don't think I said anything funny," she snapped.

"Baby, you are feisty as hell. First off, I'm not stringing you or your heart along. And, frankly, I'm offended you would say such a thing."

Korah rolled her eyes and kept her next thought to herself.

Brick surprised her by saying, "Second, you're right. What I said a moment ago is not fair to you. The day I got the contract, I offered you subcontracting work. You don't have to walk on eggshells until I give you a formal contract. The conversations we've already had constitute a verbal agreement, so you could sue me for breach of contract if I back out."

Korah didn't look comforted by that, so he said, "Do you want me to call your phone and leave the offer on your voicemail, so you'll have phonographic proof?"

That made her laugh. Brick smiled as well.

"What's funny?"

"I think you used the wrong word," she said. "Also phonographic sounds a lot like *pornographic*."

"I could leave some pornographic proof as well," he said.

That cracked her up even more.

"The school board is allowing three years for the new project," Brick said, back to business. "I know you think I'm only bringing you aboard because you give me good loving. But the truth is if it wasn't you, I'd hire some other construction company, because I want to finish at least six months ahead of schedule, if not a full year.

"The more construction I have going on at the same time, the sooner we'll get finished. And the sooner I complete my masterpiece, the sooner I can take on bigger and better jobs. If you wait until after you sign the contract to tell me you hate me, and the job is all you were after the whole time, I wouldn't try to kick you off my site. As long as you build the football field perfectly, we'll have no problem. Business is business, and I never lose."

His statement was a bit crass, but it did a lot to settle Korah's nerves. She should've known Brick was too smart to let his emotions be the driving factor in such a big decision.

"So we're good?" he asked. "You still like me?"

I love you, Korah thought, and then she kicked herself for allowing such a thing to happen. But at least she was being honest with herself, even if she couldn't be honest with him just yet.

"Yes," she told him. "I still like you, Brick."

"Do you want to come home with me tonight?"

She laughed. "No. I think I need a little time to recoup. Rain check?"

"Sure, babe. Just don't forget about me, while you're recouping."

Lord! Was this man serious? Did he think he was in any way forgettable? Even if Korah was a caterpillar in her next life, she'd try to make it back to the Avery Ranch the moment she sprouted wings.

"Okay," she told him. "I'll try not to."

● ● ● ● ● ●

Over the next few months Brick met with a lot of important people, shook a lot of hands and basked in the glory of his biggest achievement. On average it takes anywhere from 26 to 36 months to build a new high school. Brick wouldn't rush the work, but finishing ahead of schedule would be beneficial for everyone involved.

In addition to the actual construction, he had to deal with a lot of legalities, such as acquiring building permits, approving the architectural design, surveying the land and land acquisition. The permit process alone wouldn't be completed until early December.

In the meantime, Brick and Korah's relationship continued to thrive, growing deeper by the day. For Korah, the hardest part was accepting that her man truly was as fantastic as he appeared. She found that Brick really did enjoy touching her and massaging her and wining and dining her to the fullest. He showered her with gifts, sometimes rather expensive ones, without the prerequisite of a special occasion. She never opened a door when they were together. Brick made her feel secure and protected and always appreciated.

Korah continued to worry that someone who had lived most of their life as a playboy would have trouble settling down, even for a little while, but she never found evidence of infidelity. And over time she stopped looking. She didn't want to drive herself or Brick crazy with wild, unfounded accusations. Plus it felt good to trust him and sit back and enjoy the new lifestyle that came with being his woman. Sometimes it felt so good, she wanted to pinch herself, to make sure he wouldn't disappear when she batted her eyes.

On Monday, December 8th, Brick stopped by Texas Builders' main office at the end of the work day to drop off the official contract. Korah was so excited, she couldn't stop herself from throwing her arms around him and planting hot kisses on his mouth and cheeks.

Brick grinned and took a seat across from her desk. He wore a dark suit with a white shirt and blue tie. He looked as handsome as ever. His cocky, cowboy swag was in full stride.

"Nice desk you got here," he said as he leaned back and took in the ambiance of her office.

In addition to the new desk, Korah had made a few more changes that gave the room a more welcoming feel.

"Thank you," she said, returning to her seat. "I have a connection in Lewisville. I could give you their number, if you're looking to upgrade."

He laughed briskly. Overall, Brick had a smug air of superiority that offended Korah when they first met. Now she thought his arrogance was well warranted. Mr. Avery was definitely the man.

She flipped through the contract casually before placing it on her desk. She clasped her hands together and continued to smile at him.

"I'm giving you the football field and the training center," Brick said. "I can get you the designs as early as tomorrow. You will need your lawyer to go through the contract, to make sure everything's on the up and up."

"Of course," Korah agreed.

"Just because you're my woman," Brick went on, "doesn't mean I won't sue the shit out of you, if you screw up my job. Hopefully we can leave the courtroom and make sweet love in the parking lot, after I take you to the cleaners. I'd hate for anything like that to ruin our relationship."

"Yeah right," Korah replied. "Don't worry about me, sir. We take care of business over here. You won't have any problems."

"What else does your little company have going on?" Brick inquired. "Working on more convenience stores these days?"

"Kiss my ass," Korah said, but she was still smiling. "My *big* company is building the new AMC theater downtown. We have so much work lined-up, your little project may get pushed to the back burner."

"You'd better not put my school on the back burner."

"*Ooh*," Korah teased. "He can dish it, but he can't take it."

Brick chuckled. He told her, "I've doubled the size of my construction team in the past couple of months. Have you hired more people? I'd hate for you to have to leave the rest of your sites deserted, while you're working on my school."

"Gee, I didn't know we had a new-hire in human resources," Korah quipped. "When did you start? I don't believe anyone showed me your resume."

Brick rolled his eyes.

"Oh, you don't work here?" Korah said. "Well, I guess you'd better let me make the decisions about our employees then. We will have enough workers for your job and all of our other important projects, Mr. Avery. Don't you worry your pretty, little head about us."

"I'm gonna accept that from you – only because I've been thinking about your titties all day."

Korah's eyes and mouth flew open at the same pace. "*Mr. Avery! How dare you!*"

He laughed as he gingerly rose from his seat. "I apologize, Ms. Stewart. Sometimes I do get carried away."

Korah had to purse her lips to keep from smiling. She stood as well.

"Congratulations," Brick said. He reached across the desk to shake her hand.

"Thank you," Korah replied as she slipped her small hand into his. "Where are you off to?" she asked when he backed away.

"Meeting some important people," Brick said. "That's all I do nowadays; meet people, shake hands, make promises and cash checks. I wanna take you and those titties out to celebrate."

Korah tried to maintain a professional demeanor, but it was hard when his eyes swam over her body, heating her like a July sunbeam.

"I think I can make arrangements for that," she said. Her boldness made her nipples harden beneath her blouse.

Brick nodded and then winked at her before turning to leave. "Great. Have your people call my people."

"*You're such a jerk*," Korah mumbled, but she stared after him longingly until he rounded the corner and was out of sight.

• • • • • •

The next morning Korah dressed sharply in a blue skirt suit with a teal blouse and two-inch pumps. She generally scheduled morning meetings for the company on Monday, but this was a special occasion. She had to make a few moves that couldn't wait another week.

Korah's core group of employees was relatively small, but that was one of the things she planned to change. As vice-president and accountant, Priscilla Levin was one of her most valuable assets. Priscilla had been with Texas Builders since Korah's late husband founded the company in 1990. After Devin Sr.'s untimely passing, she kept the company afloat while Korah grieved and subsequently returned to school to complete her degree in contracting and construction management.

Next to Priscilla was Yolanda, who, over the years, had become much more than Korah's administrative assistant. Not only was Yolanda strikingly beautiful, but she was smart, career-minded and fiercely loyal. Her only flaw was an ill-advised relationship she was having with her boss' son, but Korah had yet to confront her about that.

Stephanie and Devin were Korah's only children, and they were heirs to the Texas Builders' empire she was constantly expanding. Stephanie was currently studying construction at Texas Christian University. If Korah let her have her way, her daughter would've dropped out by now and devoted all of her time to the family business. But Korah refused to let her take on more responsibilities until she completed her higher education.

Stephanie's ultimate goal was to take on the CEO position, once her mother decided to retire. In the meantime she was an office assistant, eager to learn as much as she could about the business from Priscilla and Yolanda as well as her professors.

Devin Jr. was so much like his father, sometimes it tugged at Korah's heart when she stared at him. He graduated from Texas Lutheran, like his dad. And he preferred to work with his hands, rather than push papers. When Korah added a 30-man construction crew to the business in 2010, Devin took over as head foreman, and he thrived in that role.

Aside from sleeping with Yolanda, Korah's only gripe with her son was that he had a bad temper and was developing a reputation of being a "hard ass." But Devin's constructions were always stellar, so Korah backed off and let him do things his way.

The biggest debate in her family at the moment was whether Devin would seek the CEO position when Korah vacated it, or if he would relinquish the role to his little sister. Korah doubted if Devin would ever be willing to take instruction from Stephanie, so the transition was not something she looked forward to.

In the meantime, the four people who sat at the table with her had increased the net worth of Texas Builders twentyfold over the past ten years. Korah smiled at each of them individually before she got down to business.

"Well, as you all know I've been in negotiations with Brick House about the new school they won the contract for in September."

All of her employees had a reaction to that, but Stephanie's snicker said it all. Before Brick won the school bid, Texas Builders was a front-runner. Their competitive rivalry somehow led to a love-connection that some members of Korah's team didn't understand or appreciate.

"Yes, I'm still dating Brick," she said. "And I'm sure all of you know this opportunity probably wouldn't have been presented to us if not for that fact – but business is business. And as far as business goes, the subcontracting we've been hired to do is one of the most important projects we've ever had."

All of the women in the room nodded at that. Yolanda and Priscilla thought Brick was too conceited, but they couldn't help but admire the work he'd done. Stephanie only wanted her mother to be happy. If her relationship caused Brick to throw a lucrative project their way, that was even better. Only Devin continued to have a problem with Brick as his mother's boyfriend or business partner. Korah knew she couldn't send him to lead the work at the school unless he got over it.

"We've been hired to build the football field as well as a state-of-the-art training center," she went on. "Brick is allotting us five million for the project. It's official. He brought the contract by yesterday."

The announcement brought boisterous cheers and applause from the ladies, but Devin remained reserved. Korah decided not to confront him about his personal hang-ups until after the meeting.

"Some of that money will be sent to our account next week," Korah said. "We won't break ground on the new school for another month, but we have a lot of work to do in preparation.

"Obviously we'll have to hire more construction workers," she said. "We may need to double the size of our current crew. And we'll need to delegate our responsibilities differently. We'll need a new foreman to oversee our other projects, while Devin devotes his time and expertise to the school.

"Even though Brick and I are in a relationship, this contract is very important to him, and it is now our most important project as well. Not only will this school bring in a lot of revenue, but the experience and contacts we establish will lead to more lucrative contracts in the years to come. I hope you guys are as excited as I am, because Texas Builders is about to blow up – bigger than our wildest dreams. You are all very fortunate to be a part of it."

The room once again erupted in exaltations, but it was the one silent voice that stood out the most.

"Alright, y'all, let's get to work," Korah said, officially ending their meeting. Before her son could take off, she said, "Devin, Yolanda can you two meet with me in my office for a second."

The busted lovebirds shot each other glances laced with uncertainty before they followed their boss down the hallway.

CHAPTER FIVE
THE CHRISTMAS PARTY

"So, how long have you two been dating?"

Korah sat behind her desk wearing a stern look of disapproval. Yolanda looked like she might hop out of her seat and make a run for it. Devin knew his position in the company was secure, so he maintained an air of muted defiance.

Korah cleared her throat and frowned at both of them. "That's not a rhetorical question."

"We, um..." Yolanda was generally straightforward and confident, but she couldn't find the courage to tell her boss that she'd been sneaking around behind her back – with her only son, no less.

Today Korah's assistant wore a pencil skirt with a pink top that was both sexy and professional. Her micro braids were tied back in a ponytail. Yolanda had fair skin and full lips and more curves than a mountain road. It was no wonder Devin chose to pursue her, despite Korah's warning that he should never do such a thing.

"It's been almost a year," Devin said, glad to finally come clean. "We started talking at the Christmas party. I think you caught us that night. You asked me if I liked Yolanda, and I told you I didn't. I'm sorry, Mama. That was a lie."

Devin was tall and dark-skinned like his father. He was a strong young man who spent his days turning a folder full of designs into architectural marvels. Devin wasn't as athletic as he was in school, but he still had a chiseled physique that constantly drew attention from the opposite sex. He kept his hair trimmed short and rarely wore a beard or moustache.

Korah shook her head in disappointment.

"Mama, it's not a bad thing, like you said it would be," Devin offered.

"How do you figure that?" Korah wanted to know.

"Because the whole time we've been together, it hasn't had any negative effects on the company," Devin explained. He looked over at Yolanda and smiled.

She was still far from at ease.

"We've had our fights," Devin went on. "We're not always happy-go-lucky. But when it's time to go to work, we know how to take care of business."

He reached with his left hand and tried to take hold of Yolanda's trembling mitt. She pulled her arm away from him and swallowed roughly.

"It's okay," Devin told her. "She knows about it now. Isn't this what you always wanted?"

"I don't really feel good about this," Yolanda said, her face red and heated. "I'm sorry, Ms. Stewart. I hope you're not upset with me."

"I was disappointed when I figured it out," Korah said. "I feel like you two went behind my back and did something I specifically asked you not to do. But feelings can't always be controlled, and I know that love will find a way."

Yolanda sighed with relief, but it was short-lived.

"What bothers me the most," Korah went on, "is both of you have been lying to my face for a long time. Yolanda, we talk about *everything*. I don't know why you felt like you couldn't tell me about this."

"Ms. Stewart, I am truly sorry," the girl said. "I can't tell you how many times I wanted to tell you. But it just never felt like the right time."

"And Devin," Korah said, returning her angst to her son, "what about all the times I asked who you were dating? I told you to bring her by the house, invite her to dinner. For a whole year you swore up and down there wasn't anyone special. I was starting to think you were going out with some nasty skank."

Devin chuckled, but Korah was clearly offended. He wiped the smile off his face.

"But, Mama," he said, "doesn't it matter that you were wrong about us?"

"How was I wrong?"

"You said it would hurt the business if we started dating. But it hasn't."

"No, I said it would hurt the business if you started dating and then you *broke up*," Korah corrected him. "That's what I was worried about. And I'm still worried about that, Devin. How do you think our meeting this morning would've gone, if you two hated each other? Our company is too small to have you rolling your eyes at someone you have to see every day."

"What about you?" Devin asked.

Korah narrowed one eye and raised the eyebrow on the other. It was an interesting expression that warned him to tread lightly.

"I'm not trying to disrespect you," he said. "But you got into a business deal with Brick *after* y'all started dating. Basically you're worried about us doing something that you don't seem to mind doing yourself."

Yolanda sighed loudly, hoping her boyfriend would shut the hell up.

But Korah didn't mind pointing out the flaws in his thinking. "The difference is Brick and I do not work for the same company," she stated. "And I won't be doing any direct work on his site. I never even have to see that school, if I don't want to. He hired us to do construction. That's *your* job. I'm a contractor. Once the school is finished, Brick and I never have to speak again, and I'll still get paid. So tell me how that's the same as what you and Yolanda are doing?"

Her son didn't have a response for that.

"Furthermore," Korah continued, "Brick and I discussed how our working relationship would continue in the event that we did grow to hate each other. I seriously doubt you and Yolanda did the same..."

Their silence confirmed they had not.

Korah sighed. "It's really a moot point. You two have made a decision, and we have to live with it." Her features softened. "So how is your relationship going anyway? Yolanda looks like she wants to break up with you right now."

Devin made eye contact with his woman, and he feared his mother was correct.

"She's just upset because of the way you're confronting us," he guessed. "Yolanda and I are fine. I love her, and I want to marry her one day."

As apprehensive as she felt, Yolanda's heart couldn't help but respond to that. Devin had never expressed his love for her in such a public setting. In that regard, it did feel good to get it all out in the open.

She smiled. Her face reddened again as she looked up at her boss.

"I do love him, Ms. Stewart. He can be a jerk at times, but he makes me happy."

"I know *exactly* how you feel," Korah said and she returned the smile. "Yolanda, could you leave me and Devin alone for a moment?"

"Yes, ma'am, Ms. Stewart." The girl couldn't get out of the office quickly enough.

"It appears to me you still have issues with Brick," Korah told her son when they were alone.

Devin frowned and looked down at his hands.

"I thought you got over it, after he helped us catch those people who were vandalizing our sites," Korah said.

"Man, I... I'm glad he helped us," Devin conceded. "But I remember how he lied to me when I first met him."

Korah understood that. Back in September, when Brick learned that Texas Builders was his biggest competition for the school bid, he decided that he had to meet the woman in charge. Rather than simply request a face-to-face, he created a ruse: He told Devin that he needed some construction work done, and he would only discuss the project with Korah.

She smiled now, thinking about how determined he was. Brick always found a way to get what he wanted. Korah considered herself fortunate that it was her he set his sights on that day.

"He already apologized to you for that misunderstanding."

"It wasn't a misunderstanding, Mama. He flat-out lied."

"And you've been lying to me for a year," Korah countered. "People sometimes lie about who they like and who they're dating. If I can get over what you and Yolanda did, then you can get over what Brick did."

Devin met her eyes but didn't respond.

"I guess the main thing I need to know is whether you're going to be in charge of the work at the school," Korah said.

Devin's eyes widened. He thought that was a forgone conclusion.

"I love you with all my heart," his mother said. "But this job is way too important for me to let you jack it up because you're all in your feelings. You can come up with whatever excuse you want to not like Brick, but I know you don't like him simply because I'm dating him."

He didn't respond to that, which confirmed her thinking.

"If this is too much for you to handle right now," Korah went on, "that's fine. I won't have any hard feelings. Just tell me who you want to put in charge of the project, so I can meet with him tomorrow."

Devin couldn't believe she would suggest such a thing. While he did have a few excellent workers who were born leaders and would jump at this opportunity, Devin couldn't imagine anyone working on the new school but himself. He was stunned that his mother was so nonchalant about assigning the lead role to someone else.

"Okay, Mama. You're right about me not liking him. But I don't want to put anyone else in charge of that school. I promise you I will be respectful. Brick and me won't have any problems. I know how to put business first. I won't let you down."

Korah was glad to hear that, but it would've been better if Devin let go of his grievances altogether. But then again, maybe that was asking too much. Devin didn't like the idea of his mother dating *anyone*, and Brick didn't help matters much by being such a prick.

She decided to take what she could get, for now. Hopefully Brick would grow on Devin the same way he did with her.

"Okay, son. Remember, a positive attitude goes a long way. Regardless of how you feel about Brick, I need you to be genuinely excited about this job."

"I am," Devin assured her. "I'm sorry I didn't sound like it in the meeting."

Korah nodded. "Okay. I should get the designs sometime today. Make sure you stop by at the end of the day to check them out."

"Alright," Devin said as he stood to leave.

"I love you, boy."

"I love you too," he said and left Korah to her work.

• • • • • •

In an effort to bridge the gap between their two companies and show appreciation for the mega subcontracting deal, Korah invited Brick and his employees to the Texas Builders' annual Christmas party on Saturday, December 20th. She rented the ballroom at the downtown Hilton for the affair, which was professionally catered, including an open bar.

Korah even went as far as purchasing a huge banner that hung near the main entrance with the words "WELCOME BRICK HOUSE!" printed in bold, glittery letters. Her daughter Stephanie wondered if the banner was a little over the top, but Korah didn't think so. She reminded her that Brick gave them a five million dollar contract *just because*, and it was never wrong to show a little gratitude.

That night Korah dressed in a midnight blue evening gown with four inch heels and pearls on her neck and wrist. Brick told her she looked *ravishing* when he showed up wearing a black suit with gator loafers that were polished to perfection.

Nearly a hundred people attended the party, including Korah's core office crew and their guests as well as all of Devin's construction workers and their wives or girlfriends. On Brick's side, his partner Isaac came with his lovely wife Lisa and their son Myron. Brick's top foreman, Hector attended with his wife, in addition to a dozen more of Brick's construction workers and their significant others.

By ten p.m. the party was in full swing. The DJ was excellent, making sure to include a lot of oldies with the newer tunes. The drinks and the buffet kept everyone's belly full and their hearts happy. Korah was delighted to see her and Brick's employees mingling and getting to know one another. Of course Brick was the main attraction, but the people on his side were just as eager to meet the woman behind the Texas Builders' empire.

Isaac approached with his wife and reached to shake her hand.

"Ms. Stewart?"

She turned and smiled brightly. "Hi! Please, call me Korah."

"It's very nice to meet you," he said. Isaac was a dark-skinned gentleman, short in stature and stout. He wore a cropped beard with wire-rimmed glasses. He kept his head shaved completely bald. "This is my wife, Lisa," he said, introducing the woman on his arm.

"It's great to meet you!" Korah said as she shook their hands. "I've heard so much about you," she told Isaac.

"Same here," Brick's business partner said. "I've been very eager to meet the woman who has Brick's head in the clouds these days. He's told me a lot about you."

Korah was flattered to hear that. Brick expressed affection whenever they were together, but she didn't think he was the type to discuss his fondness of her with his friends.

"I can see that he wasn't exaggerating about your beauty," Isaac went on.

"Why thank you," Korah gushed. "Isn't he a sweetie," she told his wife.

Lisa nodded. Her smile was bright and filled with holiday cheer. "He is. Your party is wonderful," she said.

"Thank you," Korah replied. "I'm glad you're enjoying yourselves. I understand you're the true brains behind Brick House," she told Isaac.

He chuckled. "Where'd you hear that from?"

"From Brick, of course. He says you've saved his butt many times over the years. He credits you for all of your company's growth over the past decade."

"Hmph. He never told me that," Isaac said with a grin. "Maybe I should ask for a raise."

"You should!" Korah said with a laugh.

On the other side of the room, Brick had a glass of brandy over ice in one hand and two beautiful women standing before him. Korah's assistant Yolanda and her daughter Stephanie held off for as long as they could. But after a few drinks, they grew courageous enough to confront the man who stole their boss' heart and gave them a whopper of a subcontracting deal.

Both ladies looked gorgeous for the occasion. Their hair and makeup was without a flaw. Yolanda was tall and curvy, with fair skin the color of a croissant. Stephanie's complexion was dark and rich like her mother's. She was shorter and a little chubby but just as appealing.

"So, *Mr. Brock Avery*," Stephanie said, staring up into his cool, brown eyes.

"Good evening," Brick said. "Please, call me Brick." He reached and took her hand in his. "And who might you be?"

His voice was deep and drenched with southern charm. His touch gave Stephanie a belly full of butterflies.

"I'm Stephanie, Korah's daughter."

"Oh." Brick's eyes brightened. "It's very nice to meet you." He brought her hand to his mouth and kissed it as he spoke.

Stephanie giggled like a school girl.

"I think I met you before," Brick said, "when I stopped by your office one day."

She nodded. "Yes, you did."

"I met you, too," Brick told Yolanda. He took her hand and kissed the back of it in the same manner. "It's very nice to see you again."

Yolanda wasn't accustomed to such a greeting, and she immediately took a liking to it. It was much better than the, "*Yo, girl! What's your name?*" greeting she was accustomed to hearing from men in her generation.

"I'm Korah's assistant," she told him.

"Then your name must be Yolanda," Brick guessed.

She nodded. "Yes."

"Korah talks about you all the time," he said. "She says she'd be lost without you."

"I don't think that's true," she replied. "But it's nice of her to say that."

"Don't be modest," Brick said. "Between the two of you, Texas Builders has become more and more successful each year."

"Well, aren't you a charmer?" Yolanda noticed.

"Yes," Stephanie agreed. "But what we came to talk about is what's going on with you and my mama."

Yolanda's mouth fell open. "I, I didn't come to ask about that."

"I did," Stephanie said. "Why'd you offer us the subcontracting on the school?"

Brick continued to smile confidently. "Why wouldn't I? Texas Builders does great work."

"We almost won that contract," Stephanie told him.

"I'm aware of that."

"Do you consider us your competition?"

Stephanie was smiling, but Yolanda was taken aback by her approach. This was not the conversation they discussed a moment ago, when they were deciding what they could get away with saying to the Brick House CEO.

"Mr. Avery," Yolanda said, "I'm sorry for this. We're not trying to come down on you."

"Oh, it's no problem," he said. "And please, call me Brick."

"Well," Yolanda said, "if you don't mind talking about it, I would like to know why you offered us the subcontracting. We do appreciate it – don't get me wrong. But you could've had the whole pie for yourself."

"I'm not a greedy man," Brick said. "I don't mind sharing, with people I care about."

"Do you love my mama?" Stephanie asked.

Yolanda's eyes widened. She nudged Stephanie with her elbow. "Um, that is not our business."

"I'm sorry," Stephanie said with a smirk. "I'm just kidding."

Brick chuckled. "I like you," he said.

Stephanie blushed. Yolanda rolled her eyes.

"So, you have a ranch?" Yolanda asked.

"Yes, he does," Stephanie answered for him. "It's a big one. They have horses and everything. He took Mama on a canoe ride and a carriage ride."

Brick raised an eyebrow. Yolanda shook her head in embarrassment.

"Girl, how much did you drink?" she mumbled under her breath.

"Not a lot," Stephanie said. "Three or four."

Brick laughed heartily. He looked over her shoulder and spotted Korah across the ballroom. She looked radiant. Breathtaking. She was busy entertaining other guests, so there was no hope in her rescuing him.

"I'm curious about something," Stephanie said. "Why haven't you ever been married?"

Yolanda forced a smile and apologized with her eyes while Brick considered how he would respond to that one.

• • • • • •

Two hours later the clock struck midnight, and the party started to wind down. Everyone had a great time, but the meet and greet had one glaring exception. Brick had waited all night for the head of construction at Texas Builders to make his acquaintance, but Devin had not stepped or even looked in his direction.

Brick didn't know what to make of that. He didn't expect the boy to welcome him with open arms, but total avoidance was not acceptable – not if they were going to work together on a Brick House project.

Brick understood he was probably the one at fault. He disrespected Devin the first time they met by lying about who he was and what his intentions were. He remembered the way Devin glared at him when Korah revealed his true identity. Now he was dating Korah, and Devin probably took offense to that as well.

Brick found it easy to win women over, but apologizing to another man was not something he was comfortable with. For Korah, he would do his best. He ambled over to the bar when he spotted Devin standing there alone. Korah's son wore a dark-colored suit with a collar shirt and no tie. He was nearly as tall as Brick and almost as brawny, but not quite.

Devin's eyes narrowed when he turned and saw Brick headed his way. He managed to keep his expression neutral, despite the inner turmoil his mother's boyfriend created.

"Good evening," Brick said.

Devin faced him and leaned with his back against the bar. "Mr. Avery."

Brick did not like the fact that he didn't initiate a handshake. Unlike everyone else he met that night, he did not ask Korah's son to call him *Brick*.

"Listen," he said, "I think we got off on the wrong foot."

Devin nodded slightly. He maintained eye contact, which was something Brick could respect. He also didn't wilt under Brick's powerful aura. Brick didn't like that, but it was also something he could respect.

"When we first met, I lied about who I was," he said. "I lied about my intentions. I know you're protective of your mother,

64

because I'm the same way with my mother. So I understand that I may have upset you."

Devin nodded again.

Brick sighed quietly. He wasn't used to eating humble pie. It made him nauseous.

"Now Korah and I are dating," he said. "And I assume that bothers you. You're probably not sure who I am, what my intentions are or what interest I have in your mother. I suspect you may not be totally comfortable about us working together, which would make you even more suspicious. Is that about right?"

Devin hesitated. He didn't expect him to know exactly what he was feeling. He nodded.

Brick smiled good-naturedly. "I, uh, I would appreciate it if this conversation wasn't so one-sided."

Devin surprised himself by chuckling. "Sorry, Mr. Avery. I was just listening to you. Not really sure what to say."

"Well, saying anything is a start," Brick stated. "Tell me, do you think we're gonna be able to get along well enough to work together for the next couple of years?"

That question was loaded. Devin felt like he was being lured into a casual conversation that was anything but.

"Of course we can, sir. I don't know you well enough to have any negative feelings about you."

"Are you sure?" Brick asked. "You seemed kinda uptight when I approached you. You didn't even shake my hand."

Devin's eyes widened. His mother would kill him if he did something to jeopardize this deal.

"I'm, I'm sorry, sir." He stuck his hand out. "Let's, can we take it from the top?"

Brick didn't consider himself sadistic, but he did enjoy watching the boy squirm. Whether Devin liked him or not was irrelevant. The only thing that mattered in this world was money and power. Brick had more of both. He and Devin would have a better relationship when the boy recognized that.

After a few beats, his smile returned as he reached to shake Devin's hand.

"Good evening," Brick said. "It's nice to meet you again..."

• • • • • •

The party was mostly over by the time Brick and Korah got a chance to spend a moment of quality time together. They embraced on the deserted dance floor while the DJ played a sultry Luther Vandross tune and the caterers collected the last of their dishes.

Korah felt lightheaded when Brick wrapped his arms around her and they rocked slowly to the beat. He made her feel warm and safe and successful. She didn't think anything could go wrong, as long as they were together.

"How you holding up?" he asked.

"Exhausted. My feet hurt."

"You wanna come home with me, let me massage your feet?"

The mere prospect made Korah's heart sigh.

"Yes. I would like that very much."

Brick's hand moved to the small of her back. His touch made her clit perk up. His cologne was still enticing, despite the fact that he put it on more than three hours ago.

"I think your party was a huge success," he said, speaking softly, right next to her ear.

Korah closed her eyes and smiled. She rested her head on his chest. It felt good to have their relationship out in the open, for everyone to see.

"Thank you for bringing so many of your people," she said. "It seemed like everyone got along well."

"They did," Brick agreed. "Isaac had been dying to meet you."

"He's a great guy," Korah said. "His wife is beautiful."

"I think Priscilla is a genius," Brick told her. "You're lucky to have her."

"You talked to Priscilla?"

"For a little bit. She's very soft spoken, but when she's talking business, her eyes light up. It's not hard to see how smart she is. If you ever want to get rid of her, please send her my way."

"Not on your life," Korah replied with a grin. She sighed with contentment. "I saw that Stephanie and Yolanda had you hemmed up for a little while."

Brick chuckled. "Your daughter is something else."

"I hope she didn't bother you too much."

"Nah. She's curious. A little concerned. It's to be expected."

"Thank you so much for talking to Devin," Korah said. She backed away a little, so she could look him in the eyes. "How did it go between you two?"

"It went fine," Brick said. "He's a little more concerned about us than Stephanie is, but that's to be expected, too."

"So everything is alright?"

"Of course." He pulled her closer. "We're gonna make a lot of money together. All of us."

Money wasn't Korah's primary goal, but she did want her company to flourish, for the sake of her children and her employees. She rested her head on Brick's chest again, and they continued to rock slowly in the middle of the dance floor.

They didn't realize so many eyes were watching them, but the two richest people in the building drew a lot of attention. The DJ stifled a yawn as he transitioned to another track, content to let the party continue as long as Korah wanted it to.

With the help of half a dozen chicken wings, Stephanie had sobered up quite a bit. She watched her mother and Brick with a delightful lump in her throat. Yolanda was happy for her boss, too. But when she turned and smiled at her boyfriend, she saw that Devin looked downright gloomy.

She took hold of his hand, and his attention gradually rolled towards her.

"What's wrong?" she asked him, though she was pretty sure she already knew.

"Dude got everybody fooled," Devin said. "He tried to check me a little while ago. Now he's hugged up with my mama, like it didn't even happen."

His comment made Yolanda's expression change and her heart sink. She watched from a distance when Brick and Devin had their little talk. From her vantage point, the two men seemed to have gotten over their differences. They even smiled and shook hands, like proper gentlemen. Brick did seem happier afterwards, but Devin was behaving like a spoiled brat. Yolanda wondered why she couldn't have a more mature man in her life.

She stepped closer to Devin and placed his hand on her waist. She began to rock her hips seductively. Devin looked down

and seemed to notice her cleavage for the first time. He smiled.
Yolanda winked at him.

"You wanna dance?" she cooed.

"Not really," he said, but he placed his other hand on her
hip.

"You ready to go home?"

He nodded.

"Good," Yolanda said. She turned and led the way to the
exit.

Devin meant to tell his mother goodbye, but he didn't want
to interrupt her special moment with Prick Avery. Plus the swell
of Yolanda's ass in her dress nearly had him drooling. It was hard
to focus on anything else.

CHAPTER SIX
CHRISTMAS

Salivating tongues bless the meal
The young ones also say grace
And lick their lips
Here come the plates!
So packed
So overwhelmed with food
That touches and blends
The smell fills the room
The smiles do, too
And eager spoons
Dig into sweet potatoes and mashed potatoes
And Ooh
Have you tasted the gravy?
No, I'm dieting. Well, maybe
Just a little
A little more
Oh, just turn it up and pour!

Korah loved Christmas. It was the one holiday she didn't mind the hustle and bustle and excessive commercialism. This year she was even more excited because several of her relatives from Chicago were coming to Overbrook Meadows to make the season even brighter.

When she was a child, Korah's home was the destination for family gatherings. Her father Franklin had thirteen brothers and sisters, which made for a packed house full of love and holiday cheer. That all changed when Korah's parents divorced when she was in middle school. Franklin had an affair with one of his co-workers, which would have been bad enough, but he also got his mistress pregnant and decided he wanted to leave his wife to be with her.

Korah was mostly confused at the time. Her mother Debbie was completely devastated. But despite the turmoil, the divorce was surprisingly smooth. Debbie was granted custody of the couple's only child, and Franklin didn't object too much when she decided to move to Texas to get a fresh start at life.

Initially Korah didn't want to go. She had always been a daddy's girl. The thought of leaving all of her family and friends behind was frightening. She didn't know one single person in Texas, and neither did her mother.

Later, she came to look up to her mom for the brave decision she made. Debbie had always been strong-minded and fiercely independent. She taught Korah that life is what you make of it, and depending on a husband or anyone else for your personal happiness was a fool's venture.

Debbie was a nurse in Chicago. She had her master's degree and was able to obtain a manager position in an ICU unit at Jackson Memorial Hospital in Overbrook Meadows. She and Korah packed up most of their belongings and boarded a plane one bitterly cold morning in 1980. Debbie wasn't hostile about the divorce, but once their plane landed in Dallas, she vowed to never look back. Korah still loved her father, despite his faults, so she knew that she could never do the same.

Growing up in Texas presented a few dilemmas in the early years, most notably being the scorching summer heat and lack of friends and family. But eventually Korah and her mother grew to love the state. Debbie enjoyed a great career at Jackson Memorial for the next two and a half decades, and Korah met her late husband while attending school at Finley High. By the time Debbie passed away in 2010, Korah considered herself a true Texan. There was no other place she'd rather be.

Over the years she was also pleased to mend the relationship with her father. Franklin went on to marry his mistress Gayle, and the child she bore him grew into a handsome and successful young man. Korah met her half-brother Reggie many times. While they weren't as close as she'd like, they did share a familial bond that could never be severed. Korah referred to Reggie as her "little bro," and Reggie was constantly awed by his "amazing big sister."

● ● ● ● ● ●

Korah invited her father, Gayle and Reggie to her home for Christmas that year, and she was thrilled when they all agreed to come. Reggie even brought his wife and infant son. Korah also got a call from her two favorite cousins Tina and Patricia. They wanted to celebrate the holiday in Overbrook Meadows, if Korah didn't mind springing for their airfare. Texas Builders had been doing exceptionally well over the past few years, so she didn't hesitate.

And so it was that on Thursday, December 25th Korah's home was filled with warmth and laughter and the family love she'd been yearning for since her childhood years. In addition to her relatives from Chicago, Devin and Yolanda came as well as Stephanie and her new boyfriend from college. Priscilla and her husband Hiram arrived for dinner, too.

Korah served all of the traditional goodies, most of which she and Stephanie spent the past 24 hours making themselves. Her dining table was a virtual cornucopia; with a huge turkey, an even bigger duck, dressings and gravy and wine and vegetables and more sweets than you could shake a stick at. But as beautiful as her spread was, the most wonderful sight for Korah was the people seated around it.

The main topic of discussion that afternoon was the hostess herself. Korah's relatives from Chicago could not get over how successful she'd become.

"I thought you'd be a nurse, like your mom," her father said. "You were always so much like her. When you were little, nursing was in your blood. Do you remember when you'd bring those sick kittens home and try to get them better?"

Korah's father was a large man, tall and stout. Korah took after her mom, for the most part, but she could see a lot of herself in her father's features, mostly the eyes.

"I remember I brought *one kitten* home," she said. "Her name was Gracie, and she turned out just fine."

"There was a lot more than one," Franklin said to Gayle. "You should've seen her giving those cats flea-baths in the bathroom sink. They didn't like it one bit, but Korah would take those scratches for them. Afterwards she'd get them bundled up in a towel and carry them around, like they were babies."

Korah smiled at the story, even though her memory was a little vague.

Gayle smiled warmly, too. Korah never lived with her, but her dad's wife had a sweetness to her that made her easy to like.

"I thought she'd be a pro-athlete's wife," Korah's cousin Patricia chipped in.

"*A pro-athlete's wife?*" Korah laughed, but she wasn't flattered by the lackluster prediction. "Why on earth did you think that?"

"You were always the pretty one," Patricia explained. "The boys were always chasing you around."

Korah chuckled. "Now, I don't remember that at all."

"You know it's true," her other cousin Tina agreed. "You dated *both* of the Hodge twins."

"*Dated?*" Korah's eyes widened. "I was only in the sixth grade! We never even went to the movies."

"Wow," Devin said before shoving a spoonful of mashed potatoes into his mouth. "Didn't know about that, Mama."

"*Player-player*," Stephanie said with a laugh.

Tina and Patricia were Korah's closest running buddies when she was a child, so their assessment couldn't be taken lightly. They actually had a lot more embarrassing stories Korah hoped they wouldn't bring up during dinner.

"I liked *Jason*," she said. "But we never kissed, or anything like that. Kevin gave me that cheap perfume he stole from Mott's, but I never said I liked him back. Plus he was the one who didn't believe in deodorant. Remember everybody called him *Stinky Twin*?"

That cracked everyone up.

"I was just kidding about you being some rich guy's wife," Patricia said. "But you did have a lot of *admirers* back then. And that was at a time when a dark-skinned girl couldn't catch a break."

"Yeah," Tina said, with a hint of childhood rivalry. "They would push me out the way to get to *Korah*."

"But she was too smart for them," Patricia recalled. "I knew you'd get rich one day – all by yourself."

"Well thank you ladies very much," Korah said, her face growing warm with embarrassment. "But I didn't accomplish all of this by myself. Devin Sr. started the company," she said, taking a moment to lock eyes with her children.

"But you've expanded it by leaps and bounds since you took over," Priscilla interjected.

Korah grinned at her vice-president and said, "Don't you sit there and act like you're not running the show. Trust me," she told everyone at the table, "Texas Builders would be *nothing* without Priscilla."

"That's great, but I wish she'd retire soon," her husband Hiram muttered.

Everyone laughed at that, but Korah knew he was quite serious.

"Let's have a toast," her father said, rising from his seat. He lifted his wine glass and said, "To Korah's success..."

"Here, here," Reggie said, and everyone drank to that.

Korah quickly rose to her feet and said, "I'd also like to toast to my father and Gayle for celebrating 33 years of marriage this year..." She paused to give everyone time to applaud. "... To my little brother Reggie and his wife Dana, for the new life they just brought into the world..." she continued. "... And to my babies Devin and Stephanie for everything they've accomplished with the company and in their personal lives. I'm very proud of all of you!"

Everyone clapped and drank up.

Before the commotion died down, Patricia said, "What about me and Tina? We don't get a toast?"

"I'm sorry," Korah said. "Of course you do. What have you two been up to?"

"Not a goddamned thing," Tina said, which brought a chorus of laughter.

● ● ● ● ● ●

After dinner everyone went to the den to exchange gifts before some of the guests left to visit other relatives. Devin and Yolanda had to stop by her mother's house, and Stephanie was invited to her boyfriend's mother's home. Hiram started yawning towards the end of dinner, so Korah was not surprised when he and Priscilla were the first to bid them adieu.

She was not happy to see her guests leave, but she still had a house full of people to entertain. Her father and Gayle weren't going anywhere until New Year's Eve, and neither were her cousins or her brother and his family. Over the next six days, Korah planned to show them some of the awesome sights of Texas, before they headed back to the Windy City.

She followed Yolanda and Devin to his truck, when they had to take off at four p.m.

"Thanks for coming," she said, giving them big hugs. "Yolanda, you know you're family. I'm really glad you could make it."

"Of course, Ms. Stewart," her assistant said. "I wouldn't miss it for the world. Your dinner was excellent. I've never seen so much food."

"You're gonna have to stop calling me, 'Ms. Stewart,' when we're not at the office," Korah told her.

Yolanda continued to smile, but she said, "Sorry. I don't think I can do that. It wouldn't feel right."

"Sure it will," Korah said, but she didn't push the issue. One of the things that made Yolanda such a great asset to the company was her tenacious professionalism. "Are you two headed to your mother's house?"

"Yes," Yolanda said. "She knows we already ate, but everyone will be there for a while, watching the games."

"Tell her I said hello."

"I will, Ms. Stewart."

"Don't forget, you need to come back tomorrow to pack away some of this food," Korah told her son. "And your uncle wants to hang out with you for a little bit."

"I'll be here around noon," Devin promised her.

"Make sure he gets me some more of that duck and pecan pie," Yolanda said.

"I will," Korah said. "I'll pack it up for you tonight."

"Okay. Thanks, Ms. Stewart."

Korah gave her son another kiss before they climbed into his truck and rolled out of her driveway. Devin and Yolanda's love was such a blessing, it made her heart thump slow and sweet. Initially the thought of two of her employees dating filled her with dread. But now that Korah saw how beautiful it could be, she had nothing but love and praise for their union.

Maybe they'd give her a grandbaby one of these days. That thought made Korah's smile grow even bigger.

• • • • • •

Yolanda's family loved Devin. Her clan was a lot more close-knit, compared to Korah's family, and they were also a lot lower-class. Yolanda came from a long line of factory workers, broom pushers, welfare-mamas and prison inmates. She didn't think her job as Korah's assistant was anything spectacular, but compared to her cousins, Yolanda was one of the most successful members of her family.

Her mother was a strong woman who raised six kids (who had three different fathers) the best she could on the south side of Overbrook Meadows. Yolanda's grandmother was also a hard worker, but without a high school education, she never made it out of the service industry in the 55 years she was employed. Yolanda was happy that her Grammy was able to finally retire last year, and she was grateful for the work ethics the matriarch passed down to her.

Entering her childhood home made Yolanda feel like she was going from *riches to rags*, after enjoying the lavish accommodations at Ms. Stewart's mansion. But Yolanda also felt joyous and comfortable around her gang of misfits. Even her tattooed nephews and loud-mouth nieces reinforced the notion that home is where the heart is.

Surprisingly, Devin fit right in as well. He loved football, which automatically gave him something in common with the menfolk who crowded the living room and cheered for the Cowboys like they had money on the line – which was actually the case for most of them.

Plus Devin's construction job and his rough, hard-working hands garnished respect from Yolanda's brothers and uncles. Just because they couldn't get up every morning and step into a pair of work boots didn't mean they didn't admire a young brother who could.

Thirty minutes after the couple arrived, Devin and Yolanda split up and didn't spend much time together for the duration of their visit. Devin bounced from his spot in front of the TV in the living room to a lively dominoes game in the garage, while Yolanda visited with her relatives, changed and burped babies and helped her mother keep the house clean – which was no easy task. Soiled paper plates and empty liquor bottles and beer cans kept popping up as quickly as they could dispose of them.

Towards nightfall, Yolanda was exhausted. She lounged at the kitchen table with her three sisters and wasn't able to stifle a huge yawn that seemed to take forever to get out.

"*Ooh*. Excuse me," she said, wiping her eyes.

"Girl, you about to pass out," Crystal noticed. "What are y'all doing when you leave here?"

"Nothing," Yolanda said. "Going home. I'm going straight to sleep."

"Y'all not stopping by Devin's mama's house?" her older sister Verna asked.

Yolanda shook her head. "We already went earlier today. That's why it took so long for us to get here."

"That must've been nice," Crystal imagined. "What's it like kicking it with a bunch of rich people?"

"It was alright," Yolanda said casually.

"Stop lying," Verna said.

"Yeah," their youngest sibling Tasha piped in. "Bet y'all had *roasted duck*. Leg of lamb dipped in *caviar*."

"*Eww*. That sounds disgusting," Yolanda said. "But we did have roasted duck."

"I knew it!" Tasha said and they all laughed.

"So, when are you gonna hurry up and get pregnant?" Verna wanted to know.

"That's what I been asking her," Crystal said. "You already know Devin is paid. I would've been done popped out four or five babies by now. I wouldn't never let that nigga leave the bedroom!"

They all found that amusing, Yolanda included. When it came to love, most of the women in her family put finances first. Oddly these same women would have a child with a rich drug dealer, without considering the fact that their baby's father might be dead or in prison before the child finished potty-training.

"I don't know about all that," Yolanda said. "Y'all know I'm not having a baby unless I know his daddy is gonna stick around."

"Or *her* daddy," Tasha said with a grin.

"Or her daddy," Yolanda agreed.

"Why do you think Devin's not gon' be around?" Crystal wanted to know.

"Don't tell me you still tripping on that old shit," Verna said.

Yolanda frowned. She didn't think her problems with Devin were so insignificant.

"What old shit?" Crystal asked.

"She said Devin threw her under the bus a few months ago," Verna told them.

Crystal's eyes widened. "Really? What he do?"

"He was mad about his mama dating some dude," Verna said. "And then Yolanda—"

"Uh, I'm sitting right here," Yolanda said, with a smack of her lips. "I can tell the story myself."

"Well tell it then," Verna said.

Yolanda rolled her eyes at her. Verna was the oldest, and she'd always been very bossy.

"Devin was mad about his mom – who you know is my boss – dating one of our competitors. But he was also tripping about work we had to do on a shopping center. That's what started it all. I thought he was being real immature about the shopping center. If it was up to him, our company probably would've went bankrupt by now."

"Just get to the part about Brick," Verna urged.

"That's what you don't understand," Yolanda said with a hint of exasperation. "I was trying to tell you when it happened that it's not only about Brick. It's about Devin's whole attitude. He's very immature at times. I was already wondering if we were gonna make it before Brick came along."

"So what happened with the dude?" Crystal asked.

"Well, Ms. Stewart started dating a guy named Brick, and Devin hated him right off the bat – which was him being childish again. I tried to calm him down one day by telling him we had a big deal coming soon because of Brick, and he flipped out. I begged him not to tell Ms. Stewart that I was the one who told him about it, but he did anyway. He just threw me under the bus, like it wasn't nothing."

"So his mama got mad at you?" Tasha asked.

Yolanda shook her head. "No. Not really."

"Then what's the problem?" Crystal said.

"The problem is Devin is supposed to have my back, but he didn't. I trusted him with some confidential information, and he confronted his mom the same day. He didn't care if I got fired or what."

"What difference does it make if you get fired?" Crystal asked. "If you're still with Devin, then you're good."

"That's what I told her," Verna chipped in.

"Y'all don't understand," Yolanda said, shaking her head. "I don't want to depend on him – or anyone else – for my job or my future. And if I can't count on my man to do the one thing I asked him to, which was to not say *shit*, then how do I know I can trust him? When Devin gets mad, he just sees *red*. Straight black- out. Nothing anybody says matters anymore. I've never been with anyone who has a temper like him."

The table went quiet as everyone let that sink in.

"Has he ever hit you?" Tasha asked.

"Oh, hell no," Yolanda said, her eyebrows bunched. "I would've got Mike to kick his ass a long time ago, if he ever did that."

The girls all nodded in agreement. Their cousin was given the nickname *Psycho* Mike for a reason.

"So, are you going to break up with him?" Tasha asked.

Yolanda shook her head, but then she shrugged.

After another few beats of silence, Verna said, "You know Tyson called over here, looking for you."

"I know," Yolanda said, which caused everyone's eyebrows to rise. "Mama told me," she explained. "She gave me his number, and I called him back. I talked to him a couple of times."

That comment made her sisters even more curious.

Back when she was in high school, Tyson was all Yolanda could think about. Tall, dark and skinny, he had the air of a very important somebody, even when he was seventeen. Tyson led the debate team to the state finals, with his quick wit and skilled tongue. He was Yolanda's date to the prom their senior year.

"What'd you and Tyson talk about?" Verna asked.

The silence at the table, as they waited for her to respond, was poignant. And then it was interrupted. Devin stepped into the kitchen with a big, dopey grin on his face. He toted a cup of unknown intoxicants. His eyes were low and glistening with inebriation.

"Hey, baby," he said, when his eyes rolled to his woman. "You ready to go?"

"Uh, yeah," Yolanda said, rising to her feet. "What you been drinking?"

When she reached him, she took his cup away and sniffed it. The strong alcohol made her nose cringe.

"Your brothers are a trip," Devin said, still grinning. "How you ladies doing?" he asked her sisters.

"*We're fine,*" they all said, each of them sporting a crocodile smile.

"I'm driving," Yolanda told him.

"That's cool," Devin said, handing over his keys.

Yolanda put her arm around his waist, hoping he wouldn't send both of them falling to the floor before they made it outside. Her family consisted of caring people, for the most part. But some of them would laugh before they rushed to help them up.

Yolanda didn't like her man drunk, but she did like him happy, and Devin was generally a happy drunk. This Devin was acceptable.

She looked back at her sisters before they exited the kitchen.

"Talk to y'all later."

Verna looked very upset about the juicy gossip she'd just missed out on.

● ● ● ● ● ●

At twelve minutes after midnight, Korah was surprised to hear her doorbell ring. She and her cousins were having a cozy movie night in the den with her brother Reggie and his wife. Her father and Gayle had already turned in for the night.

Korah handed a bowl of popcorn to Patricia as she rose from the sofa.

"I'll be right back," she said with a puzzled look on her face.

"Who's that?" her cousin asked.

"I don't know," Korah said. "I'm not expecting anyone."

"It's after midnight," Tina said. "Want us to come with you?"

"No," Korah said with a smile. "I think I'll be alright."

When she got to the living room, her eyes lit up when she spied Brick through the peephole. She opened the door, and he immediately stepped inside and wrapped his strong arms around her. Korah stood on her tippy toes and nuzzled her face against his neck. His skin was warm, and he smelled delightful.

"You feel so good," she told him. His closeness heated her whole body.

"Merry Christmas!" Brick announced when they separated.

He wore a white button-down with faded jeans and a new pair of boots. His shirt wasn't tucked in, and he had the sleeves rolled midway up his forearms. He looked strong and super sexy.

Korah checked her grandfather clock and grinned. "You're late," she said. "It's not Christmas anymore."

"It's still Christmas in California," he said.

"You said you'd be here at ten," she told him. "I didn't think you'd still come."

"It was hard to get away."

Brick's voice was deep. His jawline was hard and rigid, but his eyes were soft. Korah was not upset about his tardiness. She knew that he spent the holiday with his family in Lewisville. The fact that he drove all the way to her home tonight, rather than retreat to his own mansion to recuperate from the long day, meant a lot to her.

"You look nice," Brick said.

His southern drawl made goose bumps sprout on Korah's arms. She wasn't wearing anything special, just a pair of shorts and a camisole. She knew that it was her exposed flesh that perked his attention. Her exposed cleavage made Brick's mouth water.

He reached and drew her in for another hug. The moment his hands slipped towards her ass, Korah heard a sound behind them, and she pulled away. She looked back and saw both of her cousins creeping in the hallway.

"Hi!" Patricia said, smiling brightly.

"Hey," Tina said. "Korah, who's your friend?"

Korah shook her head good-naturedly before introducing them. "Brick, these are my cousins from Chicago. Patricia and Tina."

The ladies rushed forward to get a better look.

80

"Hi," Patricia said again. She continued to smirk like a groupie as Brick shook her hand.

"Good evening," he said. "Nice to meet you."

"I'm Tina," the other woman said, offering her hand.

Brick shook it as well. "Very nice to meet you. Merry Christmas!"

"Merry Christmas to you, too!"

"Are you ladies enjoying Texas?"

"Yes, we are," Patricia said as she devoured Brick with her eyes.

Korah wasn't the jealous type, but these hoochies were out of control.

"I'll be back in there in a minute..." she said, giving them their cue to get lost.

"Okay. Goodbye, Brick," Tina said as she backed out of the room.

"See you later," Patricia added as she reluctantly did the same.

Korah rolled her eyes at them before she turned back to her boyfriend. She was surprised to see that Brick had removed a long jewelry box from his back pocket. He grinned as he offered it to her.

"Merry Christmas."

Korah's smile deepened. She opened the box, and her eyes widened.

"Oh, wow..."

Inside the jewelry box was a beautiful gold necklace with a panther head pendant affixed to it. The pendant was diamond encrusted with dark, emerald eyes. Korah's mouth hung open as she took in the details of the intricate design.

"This is beautiful," she said when her eyes returned to Brick's.

"And symbolic," he said. "Because you are a beautiful, black panther. Powerful and majestic, smooth and calculating. Fierce, but still nurturing."

Korah thought his description of her was just as wonderful as the necklace. She stepped to him and kissed him softly. Her heart rate increased when he wrapped both arms around her and slipped his tongue inside her mouth. Korah got lost in the kiss for a moment, but she backed away when she felt his hand inching towards her ass again.

"Baby, my dad's here. And I'm pretty sure my cousins are still standing in the hallway."

She closed the jewelry box. Her eyes were gleaming as bright as the diamonds on the pendant. "Come on, your gift is in the garage."

He wore a confused expression as she took his hand and led him through her home. They entered the garage through the kitchen. Korah flipped a light switch, and Brick paused when he saw a brand new saddle perched atop an equally new saddle rack. The saddle was black and shiny, with silver metal work and designer conchos that had "BRICK" etched into them.

He stepped past her and slowly approached his gift. He inspected it carefully, making a complete circle around it before he reached and felt the skirt, stirrups and fender. He looked back at Korah, who was watching his every move.

"I had to get in touch with Carl to find out Roscoe's size," she explained.

Brick cocked his head, and she said, "I got Carl's number from Isaac. Neither one of them told you?"

He shook his head.

"Great," she said. "Then it really is a surprise."

"It is," Brick murmured. He smiled warmly. She didn't get him a run-of-the-mill saddle. This one was luxury all the way. "I love it. I think it might be the best saddle I've ever seen."

"Really?" Korah beamed. She didn't realize how hard it was to shop for a millionaire until she began to contemplate his Christmas gift. She was happy to get him something he considered special.

"Can I take it home?" he asked. "I got my truck parked out front."

"Of course you can take it home," she said with a giggle. "I can get my brother out here to help you load it up, if you want."

"Nah, I can manage," Brick said, admiring the saddle again.

He looked back at Korah when he heard the garage door retracting. It was a beautiful night, a crisp 59 degrees. The weather forecasts predicted sunny days all the way through New Year's.

Brick approached her and hugged her tightly. When he kissed her, she felt the passion building in his chest and his touch. She was grateful when he backed away, but not really. Her breaths were heated. Brick noticed that her nipples were now erect. He reached and caressed one of them softly with his thumb.

"Maybe next year we can spend Christmas together," he suggested.

The comment could have been flippant, but maybe it wasn't. They had been dating for four months. Did he plan to still be with her a year from now? Brick was clearly not the playboy he used to be, but Korah was reluctant to hope for a commitment of that magnitude.

"I would like that," she whispered.

Brick kissed her again, tenderly, before he turned and exited through the open garage door. A few moments later Korah saw the taillights of his truck as he backed into her garage. She stepped forward, so that she could guide him in safely.

CHAPTER SEVEN
GROUNDBREAKING

Brick returned to Korah's home the following day to have lunch with her family. The menu consisted of leftovers from Christmas dinner, but no one complained. Brick was as charming as ever, and thankfully Korah's cousins didn't make a fool of themselves by flirting with him. After the incident last night, Korah had to put them in check when Brick left with his saddle.

"I'll cut one of you heifers, if you keep gushing over my man," she said in a tone that might have been serious, maybe not. Neither Patricia nor Tina was willing to risk it.

The most flirtatious thing they said to him when he came for lunch was, "Do you have any brothers, Brick? A twin, maybe?"

Brick chuckled and told them he had several brothers, but they were all married with children.

Korah's father thought Brick was a great suitor. After lunch the two of them went for a walk in the backyard, talking about God knew what. Korah joked with Gayle as she watched them from the kitchen window.

"I think it's too late for Daddy to screen my boyfriends."

"It's never too late for that," Gayle said with a chuckle. "You'll always be his baby girl."

Korah had grown to love her dad's wife over the years. She always appreciated the tender moments they shared.

"What if Daddy comes back in here and tells me Brick isn't the one for me?" she wondered.

"Then you'll have to elope," Gayle said with a straight face. "'Cause that man is *super* fine."

Korah laughed. That wasn't the response she expected at all.

• • • • • •

She took her family back to the airport on January 2nd. She truly hated to see them go, but there was much work to do, and it was time to get back on the grind. Construction would start on the new school in less than two weeks.

Korah met with her son on Monday morning to confirm he had hired the additional crew needed to keep their other projects going while the majority of their workforce was assigned to the school.

"I took care of it," Devin said. He sat across from her desk wearing a golf shirt with khakis, rather than the jeans he was accustomed to.

"How many men?" Korah asked.

"Twenty-five."

"You interviewed them all yourself?"

He nodded. "I did."

"Did you run background checks on everybody you're taking to the school?" Korah asked. "I don't care if they stole a piece of bubblegum ten years ago, if it's on their record, they can't go."

"I had an issue with Samuel," Devin confided. "His license is suspended for a DUI. But he hasn't gone to court yet, and he thinks he can get it dismissed."

"He can't go," Korah said bluntly.

"He's the best forklift driver we got."

Korah shook her head. "Sorry."

Devin narrowed his eyes slightly before nodding.

"How about you?" his mother asked. "Are you ready for this?"

He nodded.

"You don't seem too excited," Korah noticed.

"I'm anxious," Devin explained. "At this point, it's like sitting in jail, waiting for a parole date. Every day I wish we can get started and get it over with. But we have to wait." He sighed.

"It's not gonna be an easy job," Korah said. "We're looking at a two year projection."

"That's for the whole school," her son replied. "It won't take us that long to do our part."

Korah agreed that it wouldn't, and she understood his anxiety. She was itching to get to work as well.

"Who are you promoting, to take your place as foreman for the other jobs?"

"Baron," he said. "Baron Grant."

The name sounded familiar, but Korah couldn't picture him. "How long's he been with us?"

"Going on five years. He's the best man we have. I trust him, one hundred percent."

"I want to meet with him today," Korah said.

Devin looked like he might complain about her not taking his word for it, but he decided to keep it to himself. "Okay. I'll have him call to set up a meeting."

"You talked to Brick at the Christmas party?" Korah asked, knowing that he had. "You and him okay now?"

Devin didn't know what she expected from him. If he said anything other than, "*We're fine*," his mother might replace him at the last minute. It was clear that she wouldn't let anything interfere with the Brick House project – not even her own flesh and blood.

"We're fine, Mama. Stop worrying about that."

"Alright," Korah said, though it was clear she would continue to fret about how the two most important men in her life got along – especially now that Texas Builders' money and reputation was on the line.

"Is that it?" Devin asked. "I'm supposed to meet with the electricians in Cleburne at ten o'clock."

Korah checked her watch and saw that he had forty-five minutes to get there.

"Yes, that's it," she said. "Have a nice day."

"You too, Mama. Talk to you later."

● ● ● ● ● ●

On Friday, January 9th, Brick strolled into his Dallas office and smiled as he approached his new secretary. Susie shot to her feet with her planner in hand, ready for any question he might throw at her.

"Good morning, Mr. Avery."

"Morning, Susie." He paused long enough to make the interaction polite.

"I'll have a cup of coffee on your desk in one minute," she said. "I've spoken to all of your foremen, and I'm prepared to give you a report on your projects whenever you're ready. The forecasts are all predicting rain later this afternoon. A forty percent chance, starting at three. I'm afraid we may have to cut work short on a few projects. And the superintendent will be here to meet with Isaac at ten. You are not required to attend the meeting, but I told him you may sit in."

"Thank you," Brick said. He gave her an approving nod.

Susie was a great secretary. She was extremely detailed, always thinking ahead, and she had the memory of an elephant. She was clearly in awe of Brick, and she was intimidated by him and Isaac. Best of all Susie's bulldog features ensured there would never be any attraction on Brick's end.

Brick's business partner didn't request a homely secretary, but after the problems they had with the last girl, it seemed like a safe choice. Persia Moore had worked for the company for eight months. She was young and beautiful, with a body that made men go crazy – Brick included. She and Brick had a relationship that lasted three months and ended in disaster. He was lucky that his business came out unscathed.

Rather than head to his office, Brick continued down the hallway to say good morning to the only person he trusted enough to share his empire. Isaac looked up from a pile of unsorted papers on his desk. He mumbled something that sounded like "Good morning," as Brick took a seat.

"Morning to you, too," he said. "It's too early to be this grumpy," he teased.

"Did Susie tell you the superintendent's coming by today?" Isaac asked.

"Yeah," Brick said. He crossed his legs casually. "She said he's meeting with you – that I don't even have to be here."

"Must be nice," Isaac grumbled.

"What's your problem?" Brick wondered.

"I don't like *meetings*," Isaac said. "I like crunching numbers. I like computers. This face to face crap..." He shook his bald head. "It's not for me. You're the one everybody wants to see."

"'Tis true," Brick agreed. "But I'm sure you know that the bigger we get, the more meetings you'll have to take the lead on. It's the price of fame, my friend."

"*Fame*? I never said I wanted to be famous."

"You can groom Susie to stand in for you," Brick suggested. "But you know no one knows the accounts like you do. Hell, I couldn't even take your place. I'd look like a fool trying to decipher your spreadsheets."

"It's fine," Isaac said, organizing his papers again. "I just got a late start this morning. I'll be ready by the time he gets here."

"Did you hear anything about the Freightliner contract?"

"Yes," Isaac said without looking up. "We won that bid."

"Really?"

"Of course. And we won the Sprint warehouse, too."

"That's awesome," Brick said. His smile was bold and confident. "Why didn't you tell me?"

"When would I have time?" Isaac asked. He looked up at him and scratched his head. "Honestly, I think I forgot."

Brick laughed. It was a hearty chortle that made crow's-feet appear in the corners of his eyes. "Isn't this grand?"

Isaac shook his head. "What's that?"

"We have so much work, not only do you forget to tell me about new contracts, but when you do, you act like it's no big deal."

Isaac considered that. "Yes. I suppose you're right."

"You *suppose*? Is that the best you can do?"

"Sorry if I don't have time to strut around like the big cock on the block. But some of us have serious work to do."

"*The big cock on the block*?" Brick grinned. "Is that what I'm doing?"

"You do have a... self-satisfied air about you," Isaac noticed.

"Brick House is the biggest construction company in Texas," Brick told him.

"Well, I don't know if–"

"*And*, I am the most powerful contractor in the state," Brick continued.

Isaac rolled his eyes. "Maybe you're in the top ten."

"You mean top five..."

"*Maybe.*"

"Which means you're in the top five, too, my friend. And you deserve a reward."

Brick reached into the inner pocket of his suit jacket and produced a set of keys. He tossed them onto Isaac's desk. His partner stared at them for a moment. One of his eyebrows rose when he saw the Mercedes emblem.

"You got another company car?"

"No, sir. I got *you* a car," Brick said. "Brand new. C300. I wanted to get you a truck, but you like driving sedans for some reason."

"I, I never do any hauling," Isaac said absently. He picked up the keys and smiled for the first time that morning. "You bought me a car?"

"You earned it," Brick said. "It's parked right out front. I would tell you to take a break, take it for a quick spin, but you look like you're pretty busy in here."

"This can wait," Isaac said, rising to his feet.

"Oh, and I have good news," Brick said before his friend could rush out of the office. "Remember Persia?"

A look of dread washed over Isaac's face.

"No, it's good news," Brick assured him. "She's in jail, her and her thieving boyfriend."

"Really? Where'd you hear that?"

"I've been keeping tabs on her since she left here. I got a call from a roofing company a few months ago. She actually had the nerve to use me as a reference." Brick chuckled.

Isaac just stared at him.

"A couple of months in, she started stealing," Brick said. "Now she and her accomplice are locked up."

Isaac shook his head. "That's supposed to be good news?"

"Well, yeah. She got what she deserved. That doesn't make you feel good?"

"No," Isaac said honestly. "All it does is remind me what *you* did. We had to let her get away with embezzling forty grand because of you."

"I'd like to think some of the time she's about to serve in prison is for our money, too. The judge may not know about it, but Persia will think about us while she's on lock-down."

"What about you?" Isaac asked. "Have you learned your lesson?"

Brick chuckled. "Fine. See if I ever buy you a car again."

Isaac's features softened at the mention of his new car. He hurried past Brick.

"What color is it?" he called down the hallway.

"Black on black," Brick said with a grin. "I know what you like."

"My man," Isaac said before he disappeared around the corner.

• • • • • •

On Monday, January 12th, Brick woke up early. He couldn't sleep. His mind was racing. His heart was too. He lay on his humungous bed smiling, thinking, chuckling and even laughing out loud. He checked his alarm clock six times in forty-five minutes. Finally he got up and turned the alarm off thirty minutes early.

He strolled through his home butt-naked. He had a swagger in his step. His shoulders back, his squared chin held high. He went to the living room and used a remote to turn on the stereo. Speakers mounted throughout his home – his *manor*, that is – ensured the music would accompany him from room to room.

Cool, jazz music titillated his eardrums, but he switched to a collection of rap CD's instead. Today, Brick felt more braggadocios than Rick Ross.

He felt like Big Meech.

Larry Hoover.

He found a pair of shorts and spent the next forty minutes in his fitness center. Today he targeted his biceps, triceps, pecs and abs. He pulled on a pair of boxing gloves and gave the punching bag a few dozen blows for good measure.

Sweaty and primed and feeling two decades younger than his 45 years, Brick took a long shower. Afterwards he took his time getting dressed. By then his cellphone was jumping. One of the calls came from Korah.

"Good morning."

"Morning," he said.

"How you feeling?"

"Like fifteen million bucks."

She chuckled. "You excited?"

"That's putting it mildly."

"What are you going to wear?"

"Aren't you coming?"

"No," she said. "You hired us for construction – not as contractors. You're the only contractor who needs to be there today."

"You sure? You could stand right next to me. I'll make sure they let you get some work in with that gold shovel."

Korah grinned. It was tempting, but, "I'm sure."

"I'm wearing a three-piece Dolce & Gabbana," Brick said. "But I may leave the vest. It's wool and silk. Gray. And my hardhat."

"Sounds perfect. You gonna send me a pic, or do I have to wait to see you on the news?"

"I'll send you a pic, if you send me one."

"I'm not wearing anything special."

"You don't have to wear anything at all."

Korah smiled. A slow burn started to build between her legs.

She told him, "Go get 'em, Tiger. Congratulations."

"Thanks," he said. "We're both headed to the top."

● ● ● ● ● ●

The groundbreaking ceremony for the new high school was everything Brick dreamed it would be. The weather was a crisp 42 degrees. The sky was powder blue, with perfectly puffy clouds scattered throughout. At ten am more than four dozen vehicles converged on the scene, ranging from heavy-duty construction trucks to news vans and sedans and powerful cranes and backhoes that looked brand new.

The school district spared no expense. There were shiny ribbons and colorful balloons affixed to everything that was bolted down as well as some things that weren't. Brick shook hands and posed for pictures with so many people, his cocky, cowboy smile became frozen in place.

When the time came for the big speech, Brick saw that the superintendent for Overbrook Meadows ISD was just as excited as he was. He went on and on about how important this school was to the district, how much growth and change they'd experienced over the past five years and how confident they were in Brick House Construction.

The mayor spoke next, offering the same optimism and appreciation for the school district. She said Brick House was a shining example of the hardworking spirit of Overbrook Meadows and Texas as a whole.

When it was time for Brick to shine, he completely forgot about the speech Isaac had prepared for him. Staring out at the cameras and faces of so many people who expected the best from him, the CEO cleared his throat and spoke from the heart:

"You know, growing up poor in Lewisville, we didn't have the best schools. We didn't have computers in every room or even enough desks sometimes. But my mama always told me that if I studied hard and kept my grades up, I could be whatever I wanted to in this country.

"To be standing here today, to be selected from so many worthy candidates... This job means the world to me. And it confirms what my mama always told me." He paused, surprised that he had a lump in his throat. "I believe in education, and I believe in Overbrook Meadows, and I believe in Texas. I'm proud to be in charge of this new project. I'm humbled. And I can't wait for all of you people to leave, so we can get started!"

His joke brought laughter and applause. His good looks and his personal touch put his speech above all of the others. Isaac watched from the crowd with a huge smile on his face. Brick could be a loose cannon at times, but he always came out on top, no matter what.

Isaac was reluctant to describe what he was witnessing as *greatness*, but he knew this was probably the closest he'd ever come to it. He reached for his cellphone and set it to VIDEO when Brick hefted the shovel with the golden spade. Amidst a barrage of camera flashes, Brick scooped up a pile of prepared soil and tossed it to the side.

The crowd cheered like he scored a homer.

• • • • • •

Korah didn't hear from the great Mr. Avery again until 7 pm that night. She was not surprised that he was still living it up.

"Hey, baby. I'm taking the guys to a bar and grill down the street. You wanna come?"

"What guys?"

"My crew. We're doing a little celebrating."

"Down the street from where?"

"The new site," Brick said. "We won't be out long. You should come."

"No. Sounds like a guy's night out."

"You sure?"

"Yes. I'm sure. How was your big day?"

"It was awesome."

She could hear his smile over the phone. "You looked great on the news."

"I haven't seen it. Tell me you recorded it."

"Of course I did."

"I'll come by to watch it after I leave here."

That wasn't a request, so Korah said, "Okay," even though it was a Monday night, and her body was already itching for bed.

• • • • • •

He called again at 8:30.

"Hey, baby. You coming?"

"What?" Korah had just finished dinner, and she was washing the dishes. She wore a tank top and boxer shorts. "You said you were coming over here."

"I know, but you really should come. This place is packed. We're having a ball."

Korah frowned, listening to the lively crowd in the background.

"What time are you leaving?" she asked. "You have to work tomorrow."

"Baby, I don't know. What time is it?"

"It's 8:30."

93

"I don't know. I'll leave soon. But in the meantime, you should come and get your pretty ass over here and party with us."

His sentence structure was a little off, and Korah thought she heard a slur in his voice.

"Brick, how much have you had to drink?"

"It's a party," he said. "You're not supposed to keep track, if it's a party."

"Whose rule is that? Are you driving home?"

"No. I'm driving to your house when I leave. Unless you wanna come get me. You know what, you should do that. I know you'd hate it if something bad happened to me."

"Aw geez." Korah shook her head, but she wasn't really upset. This was probably just a ploy to get her out of the house, but she would hate it if she didn't go and something bad happened to her drunken dreamboat. "I was having a nice, quiet evening," she complained.

"And now you're having a party. Hurry up, babe." He gave her the name of the place and disconnected.

As she got dressed, Korah wondered if Brick would ever age, or if he would let her.

• • • • • •

She arrived at Southwest Seafood & Grill forty minutes later – just in the nick of time, it seemed. When she stepped into the lobby, someone shouted, "*Uh oh! You're in trouble now!*"

Korah saw that it was Brick's lead foreman, Hector.

"Your missus had to come and get you!" Hector said with a laugh.

Across the room Korah spotted Brick near the bar. He looked remarkably jovial, with a mixed drink in hand.

When their eyes locked, he shouted, "*Hey, Korah! Come on over here! Come get you a drink!*"

She brought a hand to her face to cover her smile. Brick wore the same suit as earlier, minus the jacket and tie, and the top few buttons of his shirt were open. He was dashing and clearly inebriated. Full of life. Korah was happy that he was happy. She was proud of him, despite the fact that he was overdoing it tonight.

Before she made it to the bar, his partner Isaac sidled up to her. Korah's smile widened when she saw him.

"Hey, Isaac!" She gave him a brief hug.

"Tell me you've come to get him out of here," Isaac said. He grinned like they shared a deep secret.

Korah was momentarily taken aback. It felt strange for the people in Brick's life to refer to her as his "*missus*," and think that she had any control over him. But it was also rather comforting. It solidified their *couple* status. It made her wonder what their life would be like if she actually was his wife.

"Hey, babe," Brick said. He approached and wrapped her up in a big hug. The alcohol on his breath, coupled with his public display of affection, was surprisingly enticing.

"You look beautiful," he said when they separated. "Love those pants."

Korah wore tight, white Capris with a black leather jacket over an orange blouse.

"So, your ride's here," Isaac said. "You ready to go home? 'Cause Lisa's been waiting on me for two hours. I can't babysit you anymore."

"No one asked you to babysit," Brick grunted.

"Has he been that bad?" Korah asked Isaac, her eyes bright with amusement.

"He hasn't been arrested yet," Isaac said with a chuckle, "so I guess not."

"Aw. You're full of it," Brick said. "But yes, *father*. I'm ready to go home now."

"I wish I was your father," Isaac said as he pulled his jacket on. "I'll let the fellas know the party's over. You two take it easy. And be safe. Thanks for coming," he told Korah. "It's always a pleasure."

● ● ● ● ● ●

Between Brick's constant boasting about how big Brick House was going to be and his horny hands that couldn't stay away from Korah's chest and thighs, the ride home was interesting, to say the least.

Korah didn't chide him about partying so hard with his crew or partying on a work night. She knew how monumental this day was for him. And it wasn't like he had any stressful work on the immediate agenda. The serious work on the new school wouldn't start for a few months. Until then they'd spend most of their time land clearing, which Brick could oversee without a full night's sleep.

Surprisingly, Korah liked being felt-up by a tipsy Brick. Even his absurd blabbering was a turn-on. He barely had any inhibitions before. Now his sense of decorum was totally nonexistent.

When they arrived at her home, Brick had a novel idea.

"Hey, let's build something together."

"Build something? Brick, it's nearly ten o'clock. Are you planning on going to work in the morning, or what?"

"I don't have to be there at eight," he drawled. "I'll go check on the site at ten. What about you? You don't have to be at your office by sunrise either, do you?"

Korah shook her head. "No. I don't suppose so."

"Then let's celebrate!" Brick announced. He strolled past her, on the way to the kitchen. "Do you have champagne?"

Korah scratched her head as she followed him. Surely he was kidding.

But, of course he wasn't.

An hour later they were both drunk and laughing in the living room, playing a not so friendly game of Jenga. Brick won every match. Even before Korah started drinking, she was the cause of every crumbling tower. It was so irritating! She was incredulous. And Brick was as arrogant as ever, bragging about how his constructions would always be better than hers.

At midnight Korah's eyelids started to droop. Brick apologized for keeping her up so late. He took her to the bedroom and undressed her. He turned off the lights and climbed into bed with her. He rolled her onto her back when she tried to position herself on her side. Korah's eyes fluttered open, but she couldn't see much past the darkness.

"Brick?"

He climbed over her and lowered himself between her legs.

"Yeah, baby. I'm right here."

The champagne she consumed made Korah's head spin. She closed her eyes as Brick's manhood expertly made its way to her wet center. Her toes curled as he pushed inside, inch by inch.

"Mmmmm. Brick."

CHAPTER EIGHT
FAMILY MATTERS

A month later progress at the school was going well, and Brick was standing tall as the man in charge. But his wasn't the only company thriving in the first quarter of the year. Forty miles away in Overbrook Meadows, the growth at Texas Builders was equally impressive. On Monday, February 16th, Korah met with her core crew, which now included a new foreman Devin recently promoted. With Devin's primary focus on the school, Baron Grant would oversee all of their other projects.

Baron was tall and dark, handsome and clean cut. He was down to earth. He didn't have a stellar education, but his work ethics and integrity made him shine at every site he'd ever worked on. Baron was also a lot more easygoing, compared to Devin. But his leadership skills were no less effective. Overall, Korah thought he was a great addition to the company's inner circle.

"Baron," she said. She sat at the head of the table wearing dark slacks with a peach blouse. "Where are we on the bank?"

Next to the school job, a new Bank of America tower was the biggest thing on their plate at the moment. The building was to be five stories high, with the bank on the ground floor and office space for lease on the upper levels.

"No problems there," Baron said. His voice was deep and assertive, but he looked a little unsure of himself at the conference table. "We got the windows in on all of the floors last week. Today they're bringing in the bank vault. They've limited the number of men we can have working down there, for the vault. We all had to sign confidentiality agreements. I've never done anything like that. It's kinda weird, all of this high-tech security," he said, with a nervous chuckle.

"I'll bet it is," Korah agreed. "So you have enough manpower?"

"Oh, yes, Ms. Stewart," Baron replied. "We still have ten guys working on the upper floors. The elevator crew has been staying past sunset. We got real good workers on our team, ma'am. Everything's fine."

Korah knew that as a rule construction foremen were not always honest to contractors when they encountered difficulties with a job, but she didn't think Baron was simply telling her what she wanted to hear. Despite his apprehension, he maintained eye contact and didn't stutter as he spoke.

"Did you get the amended designs for the new hangars at Love Field?"

"Yes, ma'am. I'm meeting with the owner this afternoon."

"At what time?"

"After lunch," Baron said. "At one-thirty."

"I want to come to that meeting," Korah announced. "Are you meeting at the site?"

"Yes, Ms. Stewart."

"Are the new plans going to be a problem?"

"There, um, there will be a little setback," Baron acknowledged. "But only a week or so."

He didn't look happy about that at all, which was what Korah expected of him. Even if the problem wasn't their fault, she wanted to keep all setbacks to a minimum.

"How are you dividing your time between these projects?" she asked.

Baron looked startled by the question. He didn't expect to get drilled this morning, especially in such a public setting.

"I, um..."

"He starts off at the bank every morning," Devin offered. "Once he gets–"

"Thank you, Devin," Korah said, cutting him off. Her eyes remained locked on Baron's. "You were saying?"

Devin frowned, but he wisely kept his lips sealed.

"Well, it's like Devin was saying," Baron replied. "I start off at the bank every morning, bright and early. Once I get everyone situated, and they have their assignments for the day – or for the next few hours, I'll head to the airport to check on things over there. I put Monte in charge at the airport. He's a good guy. Real smart. He gets along with the crew, but he's no pushover. They respect him, same as they would me.

"I may stay at the airport for a few hours, but usually Monte has everything under control. I'll stop by the 7-11 we're working on after that, and then I'll head back to the bank. Towards the end of the day, I'll visit all of the sites again, to make sure everything gets shut down in an orderly manner. So far everyone's been doing a great job. They know we're growing bigger and bigger. Everybody wants to step-up right now. We all feel like it's our time to shine."

Korah smiled at him.

Baron was hesitant, but he smiled as well.

"How's your wife handling all of the long hours you're putting in?" Korah asked. "I hope this isn't causing any trouble at home."

Baron looked around the room before replying. "Um, I'm not married, Ms. Stewart. No problems there. I got a dog named Pearlie. She misses me, I think..."

When a few of his coworkers chuckled, he looked down at the table, embarrassed about sharing so much.

Baron had a large nose, but it fit his face well. He sported a perfect moustache-goatee combo. His hair was styled in a short afro that was tapered on the sides and back. He was definitely handsome, with protruding pecs and a flat stomach. Korah was surprised that no woman had taken him off the market yet.

"It's okay," she said, still smiling. "We're all family here." When he regained eye contact, she said, "I appreciate everything you're doing, Baron. You have definitely stepped up at a time when we need strong leadership. We're all proud of you. Yolanda and I will meet you at the airport at one."

He nodded, his face still flushed with heat. "Yes, Ms. Stewart."

Korah's gaze finally settled on her son. "How are things going at the school, Devin?"

His eyes flashed with irritation for a moment. Korah didn't know if he was upset about Baron taking up so much of the meeting, or if it was his menial tasks at the school that bothered him.

He shook his head before saying, "It's going great. We're chopping down trees. Digging up trees. Hauling trees. I can't wait 'til we get to some actual foundation work. But so far so good."

"Great," Korah said, rising to her feet. "That's all I have for now. Let's go build something."

As was customary, they all waited for her to leave the room before they gathered their things and followed her out.

● ● ● ● ● ●

At lunchtime Korah took her daughter to Fuzzy's Taco Shop on West Berry. They got there before noon, because Korah had to book it to the airport immediately afterwards.

With all of the growth Texas Builders was experiencing, Korah found that she didn't spend as much quality time with Stephanie as she once had. Her baby was away at college, so they sometimes only saw each other at the office. But then it was all business.

After their waitress took their menus away, Korah sat back in her seat and smiled at her daughter. Stephanie had dark skin, like her mother. Her boobs were big and perky. She was shorter than Korah and more round around the midsection.

But if Stephanie was self-conscious about her weight, she never showed it. Her size 16 jeans were always tight, highlighting the curves of her hips and ass. Stephanie wore glasses and usually avoided makeup.

Korah was happy for Texas Builders' recent success, but she was also glad that their finances didn't skyrocket until Stephanie was in high school. By then she was well-grounded, unlike many of the rich kids she currently attended college with.

"How are things at school?"

"Great." She smiled brightly, displaying a mouthful of perfect teeth that were well worth the braces Korah and her late husband invested in.

"Good. Are you going to make the dean's list again?"

Stephanie shook her head. "I don't think so. I failed a test in religion yesterday."

"*Religion*? How'd you manage that?"

"It's just memorization, Mama: *Who started this thing? What year? What country?* You know I'm not good with that. I'm a creative thinker."

Korah did know that her daughter suffered with history and similar subjects, but she'd been telling her to get over it since middle school.

"Ninety percent of all classes are straight memorization," she said. "You need to stop using that as an excuse."

"It'll be alright," Stephanie said.

"Oh. And why is that?"

"It's not like I need to graduate with a 4.0. I already have a job lined up for me when I get through."

Korah grinned. "Don't let that thinking get you in trouble in the next couple of years."

"Why?" Stephanie said. "Are you gonna fire me, Mama, if I make all C's?"

"What if we go bankrupt?" Korah offered. "You might put all of your eggs in the wrong basket and find yourself looking foolish at graduation."

"*We're not going bankrupt,*" Stephanie said dismissively.

Korah agreed wholeheartedly, so she let it go. Truth be told, she wished she had a golden egg waiting on her when she was Stephanie's age.

"As a matter of fact," her daughter said, "I was wondering if you'd let me take over as CEO a little sooner than we planned."

That was so silly, Korah nearly choked on a sip of tea. "Girl, quit playing," she said after she regained her breath.

"Mama, I'm serious," Stephanie whined. "Everybody's moving up in the company but me."

"No one's moving up," Korah said with a grin. "What are you talking about?"

"What about Devin? He's in charge of the new school."

"He's always been our lead foreman."

"Baron got a promotion."

"Okay, but he's the only one."

"Nuh-uhn. What about Monte? Baron said he put Monte in charge of the airport."

"Alright, maybe him too," Korah conceded. "But you're in school. I don't need you to do any more than you already are.

Honestly, I wish you'd focus *more* of your attention on your school work, so maybe you could get an A in religion."

"Can I at least be a *senior* administrative assistant?"

"How would that change anything?"

"I could put it on my resume. It would sound better. Plus I assume a raise would come with that title."

Korah shook her head. "So you want a raise?"

"I just don't want to get left behind," Stephanie pouted. "Everybody's making moves in the company. I deserve *something*."

Korah didn't know if she was serious or not, but she had a soft spot in her heart when it came to her youngest child. "Stephanie, I..."

Her cellphone rang, causing her to lose her train of thought. Korah smiled when she pulled the phone from her purse and saw Brick's number on the Caller ID. She was grateful that everything with them was out in the open. She didn't have to leave the table to take the call.

"Hey," she said.

"Ms. Stewart, I hope you're having a wonderful day."

"It's not bad. How about you?"

"I'm feeling marvelous," he said. "Is it too late to catch you for lunch?"

"I'm at a restaurant right now," she said. "Sorry. I have to go to Love Field afterwards."

"That hangar you're building fell down, did it?"

"Ha-ha."

"Want me to send a crew to pick up the pieces?"

"You should be worried about your crappy school," Korah said. "I don't want to have to come and remodel it a month after you finish."

"Yeah right."

"How are things going over there?"

"Ahead of schedule. Couldn't be better. Exceeding all expectations."

"Mighty boastful for someone who hasn't put up one wall."

"Success comes in stages," Brick told her. "Every day I set a goal and I accomplish it. It's a good feeling."

"How about Devin? You two getting along?"

"He, um, I don't think he likes to see me coming," Brick said. He didn't sound upset, but still, his comment made Korah's heart sink.

"Why do you say that? What happened?"

"He's got an independent streak," Brick explained. "He knows his stuff, and he likes to be left to it. I understand that, but, you know, that's my site. If I want to come and stare at my future football field, I'll do it. Whenever I please. We haven't talked much, but I get the sense that he doesn't like people standing behind him, looking over his shoulder. And that's, uh... That's unfortunate, 'cause I ain't going nowhere."

Korah swallowed another sip of tea. This one was needed, because her mouth was completely dry. She wondered if this was a problem she needed to get involved in. Brick didn't sound like he was irritated, so hopefully this was simply a case of men being men.

"When are you going to come check out the site?" he asked.

"From what I hear, it's just a bunch of dirt," Korah replied, happy for the change of subject.

"Yeah, but it's *my* dirt. I made a complete forest go away."

She chuckled. "A *forest*? I don't think it was that bad."

"I still want you to come," he said. "I got lots of tools laying around. I think I can even scrounge up a jackhammer."

Korah blushed at the memory of their encounter with a jackhammer at Brick's home in Dallas. After a beautiful picnic in his backyard, Korah spotted the power tool and begged to use it, even though it was nearly eleven pm on a weeknight. Brick gave in and found himself spellbound and then turned on by the sight of her wielding the heavy machinery.

"I'm not a breast man," he'd said, *"but I've never seen breasts jiggle like that. And your ass..."*

"We should come at night," Brick said. "I wanna see you drive a forklift. You down?"

"I'm with my daughter," Korah said, hoping she didn't look as heated as she was starting to feel.

"Oh, well I'll stop trying to get you wet," Brick said, which didn't help matters at all. "Tell Stephanie I said hi."

"Okay. I will."

"Talk to you later."

"Alright. Bye." Korah put her phone away and then frowned at her daughter's expression.

"What's that look for?"

"What did he say to make you have to tell him you were with me?" Stephanie wondered.

"Obviously it was something I don't want you to know about."

"Ooh, Mama."

"Girl, shut up. What's going on with your love life?" Korah asked, hoping to deflect attention from her own.

"Nothing," Stephanie said with a slight shrug.

"How are you and...? What's that boy's name – the one you brought on Christmas?"

"Exactly," Stephanie said. "Old *What'shisname*."

Korah chuckled. "Y'all broke up already?"

"No. But I don't think it's going anywhere. I think he knows it, too."

"I'm sorry to hear that. Do you know what it is you don't like about him? I thought he was cute."

"He is," her daughter said. "He's cute, and he's smart."

"But..."

"Just not for me."

Stephanie looked unsure of the reason herself, so Korah decided to let it go.

"You know who *I* think is cute?" Stephanie asked.

Korah almost didn't want to know. "Who?" she asked with a guarded smile.

"Baron."

"Oh, hell no."

"What?"

"Don't even go there."

"Why, Mama?" The girl's eyes were spirited again. "I just said he was cute."

"I don't need any more crushes – and certainly no more *relationships* in the company."

"Why you being so negative? Everything's working out with Devin and Yolanda dating."

"So far," Korah acknowledged. "But things could still go south for them at any moment. They don't even seem as close as I thought they'd be, since they came clean. They barely talk at work. I don't see them smiling at each other, or touching."

"They're probably trying to play it cool," Stephanie guessed. "They know you don't really want them to date."

"I didn't say that. I'm okay with their relationship."

"But I can't go out with Baron?" Stephanie pulled the straw from her tea and chewed on the tip.

"Girl, are you serious?" her mother asked with a frown.

"Why not? He said he was single. Just him and his dog Pearlie..." She giggled.

"What exactly do you like about him?" Korah asked, sensing this wouldn't blow over.

"He's tall and strong," Stephanie mused. "He's a hard worker, and he's a little shy. Everybody respects him. Doesn't he remind you of Daddy?"

That comment made Korah's heart twitch. Yes, Baron was all of those things, just like Korah's late husband.

"I think Baron has a lot on his plate right now," she said honestly. "Do you really want to sidetrack him with a crush? And besides, you don't know anything about him, aside from what we discuss at our meetings. How many times have you met him? Once? Twice?"

"How many times did you meet Brick, before you realized you had feelings for him?"

Korah didn't have to think about that. It only took one encounter. Brick wanted to meet with her, for what turned out to be a strange business proposal that turned into something completely different. Korah thought she hated him, but at the same time, she wanted more of him. It was an intriguing conflict.

"Are you in love with him?" Stephanie asked.

Korah shook her head. Her daughter knew she was lying, but before she could call her on it, Korah's cellphone rang again. At the same moment, their waitress arrived at the table with their lunch.

"Mmmm, this looks good," Stephanie murmured as the woman deposited the plates on the table.

Korah retrieved her phone and saw Yolanda's name on the Caller ID. "Hello?" she said, turning away slightly.

"Ms. Stewart, something's wrong." Yolanda's voice was rushed and grief-stricken. "Ms. Priscilla fell down. *She won't wake up.* I called 911 already."

Korah's eyes widened. A dark chill enveloped her whole body. Her heart stopped beating for a few moments. When it started again, it kicked so hard, Korah nearly lost her grip on the phone.

"Where, are, are you at the office?" she stammered.

"Mama, what's wrong?" her daughter said.

"*Yes, she's on the floor in her office,*" Yolanda wailed. Her panic made her sound much younger than her 34 years.

"I'm on my way," Korah said, scrambling to her feet.

"*Please hurry, Ms. Stewart. I'm scared.*"

Korah brought a hand to her mouth to stifle a scream. Her eyes welled with tears.

"I'm on my way," she breathed and disconnected.

"Is everything alright?" their waitress asked.

Korah shook her head. She stared at the waitress like she had no idea who she was or where they were.

"I'm, I'm sorry. We have to go," she managed.

Stephanie shot to her feet and rushed to her mother's side. "*Mama, what's wrong?*" Her voice was pleading.

"Priscilla fell down," she said, moving away from the table. "Yolanda called 911."

"*Oh no!*" Stephanie's mask of anguish and dread now matched her mother's.

Even the waitress looked pained as she watched the women rush out of the restaurant.

CHAPTER NINE
JACKSON MEMORIAL

Korah arrived at the Texas Builders' headquarters just as an ambulance was pulling out of the parking lot. The emergency vehicle had its lights and sirens on. Korah had to pull over to yield for it. As she did, she stared with her mouth agape, her eyes wide and fretful. She knew her good friend was in that ambulance. If the driver planned to blaze through traffic and traffic lights to get her to the hospital as quickly as possible, then Priscilla's condition had to be grim.

Rather than follow the ambulance, she continued to the office to pick up Yolanda. Korah thought she and Stephanie were having a breakdown, but Yolanda was much worse for wear. She was the only other person in the building when Priscila went down. Korah hated to imagine what Yolanda must have gone through in the past ten minutes.

On the way to the hospital, Korah had to put her own grief on hold to contend with Yolanda's. Stephanie sat in the passenger seat bawling as well.

"Baby, calm down," Korah told her assistant.

"*I'm trying, Ms. Stewart.*" Yolanda sat up in the back seat. Her fair skin was swollen and red around the eyes. She wrung her hands together in her lap, fiercely gripping and tearing a soggy paper towel.

"Sit back," Korah told her. "And put your seatbelt on."

Yolanda shook her head, but she did sit back. She reached blindly for her seatbelt, until her trembling fingers made contact.

"What'd they say?" Korah asked. Her eyes moved quickly from the freeway to the rearview mirror. Her features were pulled into an interminable grimace, but she tried to sound strong, for the sake of the others. If she gave in to her emotions, none of them would be able to speak coherently by the time they made it to Jackson Memorial.

"*They, they think it's a stroke*," Yolanda said. She wiped her nose fiercely. "I didn't, I didn't think she was breathing. But she was. *Ms. Stewart, it was so scary*. It was so bad."

She brought a hand over her mouth and began to sob again.

Korah looked over at her daughter, who looked very spooked. She reached and took hold of her hand. She squeezed hard. Eventually her daughter made eye contact and squeezed back.

"She's gonna be alright," Korah told them. "Priscilla's strong. *She's so strong*. She'll make it through this."

Her voice sounded more confident than she felt, but she believed what she said, and she was able to draw solace from that. Priscilla was strong. She was *a tough, old bird*, as her husband Hiram was fond of saying. She'd been with Texas Builders for twenty-five years. Korah didn't even consider her an employee anymore. Priscilla was family.

She would pull through. She had to.

● ● ● ● ● ●

At the hospital, the ladies didn't find relief from their worry or any quick answers. An ER nurse directed them to the waiting area, saying they were working to stabilize Priscilla, and outside of family members, no one could see her right now.

Korah forced herself to take a seat. After watching Stephanie pace the floor, she implored her to do the same.

"Did you call Hiram?" she asked Yolanda.

The girl nodded. "Yes. He's on his way."

An uneasy silence fell upon them as they contemplated the fright he must be feeling. Korah was reminded that Hiram wanted Priscilla to retire on her 60th birthday. She'd remained employed for six more years, partially because she preferred to have something meaningful to do with her days, but also because Korah didn't want her to leave.

As she sat in the waiting room, her eyes wet, her hands trembling, Korah couldn't believe she'd been so selfish. She knew the stroke probably would've happened anyway, even if Priscilla was home with her family. But it didn't. It happened at work. Korah felt somewhat responsible. She wondered if Hiram would feel that way, too.

When he arrived, Hiram looked haggard. His face was drained of blood. He walked into the ER with a feeble stagger in his step that Korah had never noticed before. His worried eyes darted to and fro. The girls rushed to his side and escorted him to the nurses' station.

"This is Priscilla's husband," Korah told them. "Is she okay? Can we go back?"

"Only the husband for now," the nurse said. She came around the counter and took hold of Hiram's arm. The two of them disappeared in a crowd of scrub-clad employees, who all moved about with varying stages of urgency.

Korah turned and looked at her girls. She gave them a slightly reassuring smile before heading back to their seats in the waiting room. The moment her back was to them, her expression shattered into a fierce scowl. But she pulled it together again by the time she sat down.

● ● ● ● ● ●

For the next hour the ladies sat and stood and paced and initiated depressing phone calls while waiting to get word on Priscilla's condition. At two o'clock, Stephanie was the first to give in to her stressed body's needs.

"I have to get out of here for a minute. I think there's a cafeteria. Do you want me to bring you something?"

Korah shook her head. She wasn't crying anymore, but dark bags under her eyes bore witness to her sorrow.

"Do you want anything?" Stephanie asked Yolanda, as she rose to her feet.

Yolanda shook her head as well, but Korah said, "Go with her. Did you eat lunch yet? You need to eat something."

Yolanda sighed before saying, "Okay."

"I'ma bring you a sandwich," Stephanie told her mother as they walked away.

Korah nodded absently.

"Call us if you hear *anything*," Yolanda urged.

Korah told them she would.

Thirty minutes later a nurse finally called her name. Korah hurried to the nurses' station, her stomach tightening, the contents shifting.

"Hi, I'm Sheldon," the nurse told her. He was tall with dark brown skin. His eyes were compassionate. "I spoke with Priscilla's husband, and he said I could speak with you about her condition."

Korah nodded quickly. She was very grateful to hear that.

"You were told she suffered a stroke?"

She nodded again. "Yes, but that's all I know. Is she okay?"

"She's stable," the nurse said. "She had an *ischemic* stroke, which is the result of lack of blood flow to the brain. In this case it was due to a blood clot. The good news is there is a very small window in which a stroke patient must get to a hospital, and Priscilla made it here well within that time range."

Korah squeezed her eyes closed and thanked the Lord. Her eyes welled with tears again, even though that was good news.

"But all strokes are damaging," the nurse went on. "The doctors were able to remove the clot and restore blood flow to the brain, but Priscilla's suffering from partial paralysis. She is breathing on her own. And she passed the swallow test, which is another good sign. Now we have to wait to see how much her brain will recover. It's too early for a prognosis at this time."

All of the information bombarded Korah, like she was being stoned.

Stroke
Blood clot
Paralysis
Brain
Recover

She couldn't imagine her dear friend in such poor condition, but she didn't hesitate when the nurse asked, "Would you like to see her?"

"*Yes.*"

He led her down the hallway and then to a row of elevators. They got off on the second floor and walked for what felt like a long time. By the time they reached another set of elevators, Korah had no idea what part of the hospital she was in. They went to the third floor this time, and she found herself on an intensive care unit. Priscilla's room was straight ahead, on the right.

Korah entered and nearly gasped at the sight of her mother-figure lying motionless on a hospital bed. There was an assortment of high-tech equipment surrounding her and attached to her. Korah thought the room would be filled with medical personnel, but there was only Hiram. He sat on a wooden chair with padded seats. He had his legs crossed, both hands in his lap. He stared straight ahead, possibly at Priscilla, possibly at a distant memory that may have been happy or sad.

Korah approached him first. She put her arm around him and then dropped to her knees so that she could fully hug him. He did not reciprocate, but Korah thought she felt him lean into her a little.

When she backed away, he locked eyes with her for a moment before his gaze returned to whatever he was looking at before. He didn't look upset, but it was clear that he'd been crying. His jaw moved back and forth rhythmically, but his teeth didn't grind hard enough to make a sound.

Korah walked to the bed with her heart in a vice. She stared down at a frail body that barely resembled her friend. It was strange how transformed she was, without her makeup or hair styled, stripped down to the bare essentials. Priscilla's cheeks were sunken. Her eye sockets were too. She looked pale. Very small. Her paper-thin chest rose and fell slowly. The machines around her glowed and beeped, like an alien cockpit.

Korah reached down and took hold of her friend's hand. Priscilla felt so cold. Korah cradled her hand with both of hers, subconsciously trying to warm her. She stood there and cried quietly for an unknown amount of time before her cellphone rang, shattering the tranquility of the setting.

Korah left the room as she took the call. It was Stephanie. Korah had to ask a tech where she was, before she could relay the information to her daughter.

She felt a lot better when the girls arrived to lend their support.

• • • • • •

By six pm the waiting room on Neuro ICU was filled with Priscilla's friends, family members and well-wishers. She was limited to three visitors at a time, so they took turns rotating. Hiram was the only one who never left her side.

Priscilla had awakened by then, and she could communicate. The doctors were impressed with her abilities so far, but there was clearly much work to be done. The first time Korah saw her after she regained consciousness, Priscilla looked exhausted, but she smiled weakly for her worried boss. The smile did not register on the left side of her face, which broke Korah's heart all over again.

But her eyes remained dry for her friend. Her own smile didn't falter.

"I think you're gonna surprise all of these people," she said. "You'll be chasing the grandkids around in no time."

Priscilla squeezed her hand slightly, and then she closed her eyes and went back to sleep. Korah returned to the waiting room with the glow of hope warming her chest.

At six-thirty Devin entered the waiting room. He would've come sooner, but Korah implored him to stay with the crew at the school until it was time to shut down for the day.

"How's she doing?" he asked as he approached his family.

"Better," Korah said. "She's sleeping right now, but I talked to her when she was awake. The doctors say she's doing good. She's going to get better."

Devin leaned down to hug his mother and his sister. He did the same for Yolanda, but Korah thought their greeting would be a little different. A little warmer. He sat next to his girlfriend and reached to hold her hand. Yolanda looked up at Korah before looking into her man's eyes. Her expression softened as she leaned into him and rested her head on his shoulder.

At seven p.m. Brick arrived at the hospital. He wore a suit, which was his standard attire these days. Korah left her seat and hugged him in the middle of the waiting room. His big, strong body made her feel like he could protect her from anything, even this. It was frightening, how much she had come to depend on him.

112

"How is she?"

Korah led him to a large window that provided an impressive view of the hospital district. She gave him the latest information on her condition.

"How are you doing?"

Korah's lips quivered as she stared up at him. Brick wrapped his arms around her, and she buried her face in his chest.

"Baby, it's okay," he said, speaking softly into the top of her head.

"I feel like it's my fault," Korah confessed aloud for the first time.

"Why? Why do you say that?"

"She, she wanted to retire," Korah cried. "But I wouldn't let her. Her husband wanted her to stay home. I know he's mad at me. *I know he is.*"

"It doesn't sound like working gave her a stroke," Brick reasoned. "You can't blame yourself for that."

"I know I shouldn't, but, but I can't help it."

He rocked slowly with her. "I talked to Priscilla at the Christmas party," Brick said. "She loves working with you. She told me it gave her something to do with her time, and she'd go crazy if she retired."

Korah knew that to be true, because Priscilla told her the same thing.

"Her husband's not mad at you," Brick said. "He's upset and he's afraid, but he's not mad. If he didn't want you to be here, they would've asked you to leave by now."

Korah knew that was true as well. Plus it was Hiram who told the nurse it was okay to share his wife's medical information with Korah. That was something he did not have to do.

"Are you hungry?" Brick asked when she quieted down. "Have you eaten?"

"My daughter brought me a sandwich."

She didn't tell him that the sandwich was still wrapped and untouched. Korah hadn't eaten since breakfast, which consisted of only a peach and a granola bar. She knew that hunger was contributing to her stress and muddled mind state, but she didn't have an appetite.

"How long are you staying?" Brick asked.

"I don't know. You don't have to stay with me. I have my family here."

"I just got here," he said. He kept his arm around her as they returned to the others. "Stop trying to get rid of me."

● ● ● ● ● ●

At 8pm Korah told her daughter, "You need to go home. Y'all too," she said to her son and Yolanda.

"I'm staying with you," Stephanie protested.

"I wanna stay too," Yolanda said.

"You have school tomorrow," Korah told Stephanie. "And somebody needs to open the office in the morning," she told Yolanda. "We still have a lot going on, and I don't know if I'll make it in tomorrow."

Yolanda's eye flashed with dread. She almost asked her boss what she could possibly do without Priscilla in the building, but she bit her tongue. She knew there were no easy answers to that question. And the last thing Ms. Stewart needed right now was more things to worry about.

"Devin, take her home," Korah told her son.

Devin rose to his feet without argument, partially because his mother was right about them needing rest and also because he wasn't comfortable with Brick in their family circle. Their relationship was moving too fast for his taste.

He helped his sister and then Yolanda to their feet.

Stephanie looked like she was about to pass out from exhaustion, but she didn't want to leave her mother there. If Brick wasn't staying, she wouldn't do it. But he gave her a reassuring nod and reached to hold Korah's hand.

Stephanie gave her mom the cold sandwich.

"I know you're not going to eat this now..."

"I will," Korah lied. She stood and walked her group down the hall. She hugged and kissed each one of them before they got on the elevator.

When she returned to their seats, she saw that Brick had the sandwich now. He gave her a *tsk-tsk* look when she sat down.

"I forgot I didn't eat that yet."

"No, you lied to me," he said. "I would punish you," he said under his breath, "but there are too many people around."

114

Korah smiled. It was her first real one since lunchtime. She remembered the last and only time Brick ever *punished* her. That was for trying to stop an intruder with her car, without taking into account that he had a bigger, badder car.

"Let's go get something to eat," he said.

He stood and helped Korah up. She didn't complain because he always knew best.

• • • • • •

When they got back to the waiting room, it was after ten, and most of Priscilla's family had gone home. Korah and Brick went to her room and found her sleeping soundly. Hiram dozed as well, in a recliner next to the bed. Korah and Brick backed out and returned to the waiting room.

"Are you going to spend the night here?" he asked when they settled into their seats.

Korah yawned and shrugged. "I don't know. I want to be here if something changes. But you don't have to."

"I'm not leaving you," Brick said. "I told your daughter I would stay."

"Really? I didn't see you two talk."

"We had a quick chat."

"Korah, you should go home."

They both looked up and were startled to see Hiram standing there. Korah shot to her feet and went to him. Priscilla's husband was in his early seventies. His silver hair was thin and sparse, but not completely bald on top. His posture was noticeably stooped, his skin dotted with liver spots.

He wore an old pair of glasses that were big and bulky. Korah remembered that Priscilla told her it was a chore to get Hiram to visit the optometrist. Whenever he did get a new prescription, he'd insist on using the same frame from a pair of glasses he got twenty years ago.

"Mr. Levin, I thought you were asleep."

"It's hard to sleep, with so many people coming in and out," the older man said. He spoke with a heavy Yiddish accent.

"I'm sorry," Korah replied. "We didn't mean to disturb you."

"Not just you guys. There's doctors and nurses. A lot of people."

While Priscilla had always been outgoing, Korah knew that her husband was quite the opposite. A hospital can be an awful place for a recluse.

"How are you holding up?" she asked him. "Is there anything I can do for you?"

"Yes. Go home," Hiram said. He took hold of her hand and looked into her big, brown eyes.

"You've been very helpful, and I know Priscilla appreciates it. But there's no reason for you to stay this late. There's nothing you can do. Go home. Get some rest."

Korah sighed. She reached and pulled him in for a hug. It was startling how small and delicate he felt.

When they separated, she relented. "Okay. We'll go home."

The old man smiled and then patted her on the shoulder. He turned and shuffled towards another group of hold-outs. Before Korah and Brick walked away, they heard Hiram telling them the same thing.

CHAPTER TEN
HIRAM THE GROUCH

Over the next week Priscilla exhibited strides in her recovery that made her doctors upgrade her overall prognosis on a daily basis. Korah spent so much time at the hospital, she could bear witness to her friend's progress. But what she saw wasn't enough to alleviate her worries over how much work Priscilla had left to go.

The day after her stroke, Priscilla was able to sit up in bed and manipulate objects with her right hand. She could move her right leg as well, but the other side of her body was weak and barely responsive.

When Korah visited her that day, she was surprised to find Priscilla's spirits high, her attitude upbeat.

"I'm so sorry for all of the trouble I've caused."

Korah frowned and leaned closer to the bed, because her friend could barely raise her voice above a whisper.

"What? Did you just apologize for having a stroke?"

Priscilla nodded and smiled. Her smile was still one-sided, which hurt Korah's heart every time she saw it. Priscilla also had to wear a patch over her left eye, because it wouldn't blink at normal intervals, and the doctors didn't want it to get too dry.

Korah took hold of her hand. She was delighted when Priscilla squeezed back. It was just the two of them in the room at that moment, which was a rarity. Hiram rarely left his wife's side.

"I'm glad you still have your sense of humor," Korah told her. "But don't let me hear you apologizing for your stroke. If anything, I should apologize for making you work so hard."

Priscilla swallowed and grimaced. Her one good eye remained locked on Korah.

"It's not your fault," the older woman managed.

"Maybe not," Korah acknowledged. "But I keep thinking about it, and I know I was wrong. Your husband wanted you to stay home with him, but I wouldn't let you retire. I feel so bad about it."

"Stop, stop that," Priscilla said. "You're being silly."

"Has Hiram said anything about it?"

Priscilla sighed, and Korah knew that he had.

"He's always upset about something," Priscilla said. She took another slow breath. It was clear that this conversation was exhausting her. "I came to work because, I wanted to," she managed.

"We don't have to talk," Korah said. She took a seat in one of the chairs next to the bed. "You need to get your rest."

Priscilla sighed and took another slow breath. She turned, so that she could continue to watch Korah. "I, I also talk when, whenever I want to," she said.

Korah giggled. Her eyes glistened with tears. "I see why Hiram couldn't make you retire. I never noticed you were this stubborn."

"We only have one life, one life to live," Priscilla told her. "It's too short to spend it, doing what other people want, want you to do."

Korah took those words of wisdom to heart, and she didn't try to restrict her friend anymore when Priscilla wanted to talk, laugh, or even try to get out of bed on the third day.

By then the doctors had removed her eye patch, which did a lot to improve her disposition. It was also around this time that Korah noticed Priscilla could smile with both sides of her face again. When she visited her on Thursday, her friend had another big accomplishment.

"Look," Priscilla said. She reached for the television remote and put the sound on mute.

Korah waited, expecting her to say something. After several seconds of silence, she asked, "What's up?"

"You didn't see?" Priscilla asked. She was all smiles that morning.

Her bright mood made Korah grin as well. "No. What'd I miss?"

"Just tell her, for God's sake," Hiram called from his recliner in the corner of the room. He had been posted up in the seat for so long, he looked like he was at home. He had several newspapers scattered about and his house shoes tucked under the chair.

"Shut up, you old fool," Priscilla told him.

Korah laughed at their banter.

"Watch again," Priscilla said. She reached for the remote again, this time changing it to a different channel.

Now Korah's attention was drawn to the television mounted above the bed. She looked back with a confused expression.

"She did it with her left hand!" Hiram barked.

Korah's eyes brightened. That feat made her so happy, she didn't mind being yelled at. She hurried to the other side of the bed, so she could hold her friend's left hand. Priscilla's grip wasn't as strong as her right hand was, but she was definitely on the mend.

"*Oh my goodness*! This is awesome," Korah gushed. "When did this happen?"

"Over the last couple of days," Priscilla said. "But I didn't want to show you, until I knew it was for real."

"What did the doctors say? Are you gonna fully regain movement?"

"They won't say that for certain. But they're optimistic."

"You sound so much better," Korah noticed. "Almost like your old self."

"Some things are still a little fuzzy," Priscilla admitted. "But I do feel like I can do more than what they think I can do. To be honest, this place is too touchy feely. I can't wait to go home."

"*Home*? They're not talking about letting you go, are they?"

"Are you kidding? They send people home in worse shape than me. My doctor would like it if I could walk out of here on my own, but that's not a prerequisite."

"She doesn't have to walk," Hiram grumbled. "They could put her in a wheelchair, let me take her right now."

119

"Sounds like *someone's* tired of the hospital," Korah said without looking his way.

Priscilla rolled her eyes. "Check this out," she said.

She reached down and pulled her sheets up to her knees, exposing pasty white legs Korah didn't think she'd ever seen before. Other than the EKG leads, she didn't see anything special. But then Priscilla wiggled her toes, all ten of them.

"Wow! Are you serious?" Korah didn't think she'd ever been so happy to see another woman's toes. "How long's this been going on? Are you keeping secrets?"

Without responding, Priscilla raised her left foot off the bed and then bent her leg at the knee. Korah was blown away. Priscilla lowered her leg gingerly. Korah saw that the slight exercise caused a few beads of sweat to blossom on her forehead.

"What are you gonna do next, show her your bloomers?" Hiram wanted to know.

"Now you see why I didn't want to retire," Priscilla said with a shake of her head. "Could you imagine being around that grump all day?"

Korah wished she could remove herself from the conversation and the room at that moment. She knew Priscilla probably didn't mean any harm by the comment, but Korah thought it would lead to a confrontation she'd been avoiding.

Rather than condemn Korah for making his wife work against his will, Hiram lifted one of his papers and grunted as he buried his nose in the business section. Korah still wanted to get the hell out of there, but she decided to stick it out, for Priscilla's sake. It was the least she could do.

● ● ● ● ● ●

Three days later, Priscilla had regained even more of her mobility, and her doctors determined it was safe for her to be discharged. The news made Korah very happy, but it also left her a little worried. Priscilla's wit was not as quick as it once was, and her left side was still at a clear disadvantage.

But she could feed herself and dress herself and even make it to the bathroom on her own. She had to rely heavily on a walker for the journey across the room, but she could do it. The rest of her healing would take place at home and at rehab.

On Sunday, February 22nd, Korah visited her room at Jackson Memorial for the last time. When she got there, Priscilla's family had all of her things packed up. Her son had just left to bring his SUV from the parking garage to the discharge area. Korah was delighted to see her friend sitting on the edge of the bed under her own power. She sat next to her, and they immediately held hands like sisters.

"So, today's the big day..."

"Yes, it is," Priscilla said.

Her smile was big and hopeful. She even had a sparse coat of lipstick and eyeliner on. She looked so much like the woman Korah worked alongside for the past fifteen years, it was hard to imagine that she couldn't walk or speak at all six days ago.

"I know you're happy."

Korah reached and brushed the hair away from her friend's eyes. It was interesting how close they had gotten over the past week. Prior to the stroke, the women rarely had cause to touch this much. Now it seemed completely natural.

"I am," Priscilla beamed. "How are things going at work?"

Korah's smile faltered. Hiram was lounging in the recliner behind them. She could almost feel his eyes glaring at the back of her head.

"It's fine," she said. "Everything's great."

Priscilla gave her a knowing look. "Are you sure? I've been worried sick about how I left your books."

Korah felt her heart rate increase. The bookkeeping was a huge cause for concern. Korah and Yolanda had tried to make sense of it, but they couldn't even get into certain files without Priscilla's passwords. The files they did have access to quickly overwhelmed them. Korah never realized so much of her work was dependent on one person until tragedy struck.

"We don't have to talk about that now," she said. "We'll get by."

"Nonsense," Priscilla said. "You're a great contractor, Korah. But most of that stuff is outside of your job description."

"I don't mind adding to my job description."

"You shouldn't have to do that."

"Yolanda's helping me. Stephanie too. Everyone's pitching in."

121

That comment only deepened Priscilla's skepticism. Yolanda never went to college, and Stephanie hadn't made it through her sophomore year. Neither one of them had the accounting background to make financial decisions for the company.

"I'm obviously going to have to retire – *for real this time*," Priscilla said with a smirk. "But I'll help train my replacement."

Her comment left Korah conflicted. She fully agreed with Priscilla's retirement now, and she certainly needed help training a replacement. But there was no way Priscilla was up to it. Even if she only assisted by phone, it may be too much of a strain for her recovering body.

Before she could reply, Hiram spoke up. He'd been grumpy since Priscilla got admitted to the hospital. Now that they were about to leave, he held nothing back.

"She will *not* help train a replacement. She's retired. That's the end of it."

Korah's eyes widened. She was sick of him eavesdropping on their conversations, but she understood how he felt. She turned on the bed, so that she could face him.

"That's fine, Mr. Levin. I know she needs time to recover."

"I'm fine," Priscilla argued, drawing Korah's attention back to her. "Well, maybe not my body, but my mind is. I can help train my replacement," she said adamantly

"No means *no*." Hiram was just as defiant. "The doctor said you need rest. Work is not rest. Work is the *opposite* of rest."

"Hiram, you don't understand anything about those computers," Priscilla argued. "I can't just leave them out in the cold like that. I designed most of their spreadsheets. I'm the only one who understands them."

"That is not my problem," her husband growled.

She blew him off. "You're being unreasonable. There's no way–"

"Don't tell me what I already know!" he bellowed, growing more upset. "Korah, if you truly value her friendship, you will let her rest. She doesn't know what's best for her. She never has."

Korah's face burned with embarrassment. She didn't think Hiram was completely right about his assertions, but she knew he wasn't completely wrong, either. Overall she wanted to get out of this conversation. The Levins had been arguing about the same thing for years. Texas Builders may be the focal point, but Korah's company was not the root of their problem.

Thankfully a member of the hospital's patient transport team appeared in the doorway at that moment. He pushed a wheelchair into the room and looked from Priscilla to her husband. They were both dressed in street clothes.

"Um, which one of you is being discharged?"

"*Do I look like a damned patient*?" Hiram bellowed.

It took a couple of seconds for him to rise from his chair, which would've made his last comment sound comical under normal circumstances, but Korah's face remained deadpan. She shot to her feet as well.

"Looks like your ride's here," she said to Priscilla. "Is there anything you need me to take down for you?"

"No, dearie. My son's here. He took everything already."

"Okay," Korah said. She leaned closer to give her a hug. "I guess I'll talk to you later then."

"I'll call you," Priscilla promised. "Don't worry. We'll get everything figured out."

Korah locked eyes with Hiram again before she left the room. The look in his eyes made her feel like none of that was guaranteed, not even the phone call. Korah forced a smile before she turned and stepped quickly down the hallway.

● ● ● ● ● ●

Later that day Brick came over for dinner. He brought takeout from a new Italian restaurant downtown. They ate quietly in the kitchen. Korah's thoughts were all over the place. Brick hated to see the look of worry in her eyes, especially with so much good fortune on his side of the table.

Afterwards they went to the den and sat together on the sofa. Korah felt comforted with his arms enveloping her. She felt secure. She didn't know if he'd stay the night, but she wanted him to. Tonight she was more stressed than when Priscilla first went to the hospital.

"How is she doing?" Brick asked, knowing what was on her mind.

"She's doing well," Korah said. "Surprised a lot of people. She's talking like her old self. She can't move around very well, but she is moving. She can get dressed and make it to the bathroom.

"But she has a long way to go. It hurts to see her like that. She was always so fast on her feet. And her brain... Brick, she could do things with numbers that I never even tried to keep up with. She was a genius. She still is. She just, she's not herself yet."

"Did you ever get a chance to talk to her husband?"

"Oh yeah," Korah said with a sigh. "Things went about how I figured they would."

"He blamed you for her condition?"

"No. But he's definitely upset about her continuing to work for so long. When Priscilla offered to help train her replacement – I didn't ask her to – Hiram jumped down her throat. He said he didn't want her to do any work *at all*.

"I mean, I agree with him. She does need to heal. But if I have a few questions about one of our accounts, I think she's well enough to answer. She certainly sounds like she wants to help. But I feel selfish for thinking that way. Maybe Hiram's right."

"What kind of questions do you need answered?"

"I don't know," Korah said. "I haven't been to the office very much this week. I'll have to get with Yolanda tomorrow to figure things out. I know she said she couldn't even get into certain accounts. The ones she could look at went right over her head. I'm sure I'll understand those reports more than Yolanda does. But I'm not an accountant, either."

"Do you want me to have Isaac stop by and take a look at your books?" Brick offered. "He's the best in the business. I don't think there's much of a difference between your contracts and ours. I'm sure he could make time to get your books in order. He might be able to suggest a replacement for Priscilla as well."

Korah thought about that for a moment before saying, "Brick, I can't do that. But I do appreciate the offer."

Startled, he asked, "Why not? It won't be a problem. I assure you."

Korah sat up, so she could look him in the eyes. His were sandy brown and sincere.

"Even though we're working together right now," she said, speaking softly, "we are still competitors. I can't..." She frowned. "I don't think I can open up my company's finances to you.

That's... You wouldn't do that for, someone like Industrial Works, would you? And I'm pretty sure they wouldn't let Isaac go and fix their books, either."

He grinned slightly. "But I'm not dating Industrial Works. What's wrong? Don't you trust me?"

"Of course I do. But I can't give all of our accounting information to one of our major competitors."

"*Major competitor?*"

"We were neck and neck on the school bid," Korah reminded him. "As far as I'm concerned, you're still the ones to beat."

He chuckled, but his smile faded when he realized she was serious.

"Do you think I would use any of the information Isaac obtained from your files for my competitive advantage?"

Korah shrugged. "I don't know. What if you found out we're using cheap materials?"

His frown deepened. "You're using cheap materials?"

"No," Korah replied with a smile. "We would never do that. But if we did, I wouldn't want my competition to know about it. Surely you can understand that."

Brick did understand, but he felt like she should have a little more faith in him.

After a few more minutes of talking and snuggling, he checked his watch and saw that it was after nine.

"Hmmm, I gotta go," he said, rising from the sofa.

Korah stood as well. "Really? I was hoping you would stay the night."

The need in her eyes and voice moved him. But he said, "I have a meeting tomorrow morning. I need to stay sharp, especially since I have Texas Builders gunning for my number one spot."

Korah chuckled. "I don't know about *number one*, but you're in the top fifty, for sure."

"Ooh. The lady's got jokes. Well, if I'm in the top fifty, that must mean you're in the lowly eighties."

Korah's eyes widened. She slapped him playfully on the arm. "Whatever."

She wrapped her arms around his midsection and held him tightly. Brick returned the gesture.

125

"So, you're not mad?" she asked.

"No. About what?"

She shook her head. "Nothing."

She felt Brick's hands sneaking down her back until they encountered and quickly claimed her ass. She smiled, hoping he'd changed his mind. But he released her and took a step towards the door.

"I really enjoyed dinner," he said. "We should have Italian more often."

"I can make lasagna," she said as she walked with him. "Next time you're in the mood for it, let me know."

"I will."

He kissed her softly in the foyer. "I'll see you later."

"Alright."

He opened the door and stepped out into the cool February air. He looked back and told her, "Good luck, with everything at the office."

"Thanks," Korah said, knowing she certainly needed it.

CHAPTER ELEVEN
KICK START

On Monday morning Korah still didn't have a solution for her dilemma, but she left the house with her head high, her brain wired from a strong cup of coffee. Texas Builders had experienced setbacks before. Their current problem was nearly catastrophic. But wallowing in grief would not provide a solution, so she had no intention of doing that.

When her late husband was diagnosed with prostate cancer in 2001, he had only five months to teach her all he knew about contracting before Korah had to take control of the company. After his death, she and Priscilla ran Texas Builders together until Korah got her degree in construction management a few years later. In those early years, Korah thought there was no way the company would survive without Devin Sr. at the helm.

But they did survive, and under Priscilla's tutelage and Korah's direction, Texas Builders began to thrive. They were now leagues ahead of her late husband's most hopeful projections. Korah was determined to keep pushing forward. As far as she was concerned, Priscilla's ailment was a mere speed bump along their road to success, rather than a complete roadblock.

When she got to the office, she called her core team to the meeting room for a brainstorming session. Other than Korah, her core team had now dwindled to just Yolanda and Stephanie. They were both bright-eyed and anxious. They looked to Korah for guidance, and she did not show weakness.

"Looks like we've got a bit of a problem on our hands," she said. She sat at the head of the table looking sharp in a new skirt suit. She wore her shoulder-length hair down and layered. She looked from her daughter to Yolanda. Her assistant was the first to respond.

"Yes, it's pretty bad, Ms. Stewart."

"Is Priscilla coming back?" Stephanie asked.

Korah shook her head. "No. She's officially retired."

After letting that sink in, Yolanda asked, "Will she be able to help train her replacement?"

Again Korah shook her head. "No. It doesn't look like it. Hiram wants her to stay home, and that's understandable. Priscilla is willing to help. And, to me, she sounds like she's up to it. But I'm not going to defy her husband on this."

Yolanda looked even more troubled. "Will she be able to answer a few questions at least? I don't even have the password to get into some of her files."

"I'm sure I can get that information for you," Korah said. "What else do you need?"

Her eyes widened. "What do you mean?"

"If you and I take over Priscilla's job – well mostly *you*," Korah said, "what resources would you need?"

"I, I don't even know where to begin, Ms. Stewart." It hurt Yolanda to confess her shortcomings, but there was no way around it.

"What about me, Mama?" Stephanie asked.

"I'm sure we'll need your help as well," Korah said. "But I don't know if bookkeeping is your thing."

"Why not? I don't want to be left behind."

"I'm not leaving you behind," Korah assured her. "This is *your* company. It always will be. But I don't have time to placate you right now. I'm looking for solutions, not whining."

Stephanie was stunned by the chastising, but she took it like a champ. "Sorry, Mama."

"I don't think we can do what Priscilla did," Yolanda said, "not without a lot of training."

"Are you willing to go back to school?" Korah asked her.

"Yes," Yolanda said right way. "Whatever you need me to do."

"I can pay for your courses," Korah said. "I don't think you need the whole bachelor's degree. An associate's should be fine. But if you do want to pursue a full degree, you can. The only thing is you still need to be here every day."

128

"I understand," Yolanda said. The thought of a promotion made her blood race. She had always felt like a valuable part of the company, but this news solidified it. Korah was about to turn her *job* into a *career*. This is what she'd always hoped for.

"In the meantime," Korah continued, "we have contracts on the table, bids that need to be submitted, invoices that need to be paid and accounting that needs to be documented. No one at this table has the expertise for any of that, so it looks like we're going to have to bring in another person."

The girls nodded in agreement.

"I need someone who knows their stuff, but they also have to be willing to train you as they go," Korah said to Yolanda. "They have to understand that it would be a temporary position. But most importantly, they have to know their stuff."

Yolanda nodded.

Korah returned her attention to her daughter.

"Stephanie, I need you to start looking–"

"Wait," Yolanda said. "I think I know somebody."

Korah was all ears.

"It's a friend from high school," Yolanda stated. "He went to college in Atlanta, at Morehouse. He's a financial lawyer with a strong accounting background. He just returned to Overbrook Meadows a few months ago. His mother is sick, and he wants to start his own practice here. I think he'd be willing to come and help train me. He can definitely get our books in order. I don't think he would charge much."

Korah's eyes lit up. "Really? Wow. Sounds like a godsend. How soon can you find out for sure?"

"I can call him right now."

"Go ahead," Korah said.

Yolanda shot to her feet and hurried to her desk. Korah waited until she was out of sight before she turned to her darling daughter.

"What is it you would like to tell me?"

"Nothing," Stephanie pouted. "I don't want to *whine*."

Korah grinned. "It's okay to whine now. It's just you and me."

Stephanie folded her arms over her chest and sighed. "Mama, you know I wanted to take over Priscilla's position. Why are you passing me up?"

129

"I thought you wanted to take over *my* position."

"I do."

"Last year you told me you wanted to take over Yolanda's position."

"Mama, you know what I mean."

"Why are you so worried about being left behind?" Korah wondered.

"Because Devin's the head of construction, and now Yolanda's going to be the new vice-president. And when you retire, you'll probably let her take the CEO spot – or you'll give it to Devin. What will that leave me?"

Korah shrugged. "I don't know. *Owner*?"

"*Part* owner," Stephanie complained. "I still have to share with Devin."

It would've been easy to blow her off, but Korah understood that her daughter was ambitious, and her worries were valid.

"How did you become so power-hungry?" she wondered.

"I'm not power-hungry."

"You just want to run things..."

"I think that's what Daddy would want."

"Yes," Korah said with a smile. "You're right. That's what he would've wanted. And I'm happy to announce that you will take over my position as CEO when I retire – not Yolanda and not Devin, either."

Stephanie's mouth fell open. "Really? When did you decide?"

"This morning."

"But, but I thought Devin would get first shot at it."

Korah shook her head. "I think Devin's doing fine where he is. He likes construction, and he likes being a foreman. His leadership skills work for that environment, but I can't imagine him sitting at this table yelling at people. It's not a good fit."

"Did you tell him yet?"

"No. But I can assure you Devin doesn't want to work in this office. He likes to be on the sites, riding around in his truck. He likes to get his hands dirty. But I will tell him, next time we talk."

"Awesome," Stephanie said. Her smile was ear to ear. "So, when do you plan on retiring?"

"Not until you're out of school," Korah said with a chuckle. "Maybe a little longer than that. My plan is to stay on until I turn sixty."

"*Sixty*? Mama, that's over ten years!"

"Patience, grasshopper."

Stephanie shook her head but didn't say anything.

"Anyway," Korah said, "Priscilla's absence will cause a lot of changes here – most of which are a long time coming. With Yolanda moving into bookkeeping, I'll need you to step up and be her replacement. That will give me some time to groom you and teach you everything I know."

"Okay, that sounds cool. But you know I have school in the morning on Tuesdays and Thursdays and in the afternoon sometimes."

"Yes, that's why I'll need another assistant to pick up the slack when you're not here. I need you to find someone as soon as possible."

"You want me to hire a new secretary?"

"I'll interview her. But, yes, if you could find a few people, that would be great."

"Okay, Mama. I can do that. Do they need to be a college grad?"

"No, I don't think so. Yolanda did a great job, and she never went to college."

"Yolanda's a rarity."

"I know," Korah replied. "I'm going to miss having her right next to me. She's really Johnny-on-the-spot. Please don't think I'm going to take it easy on you, just because you're my daughter."

"I know, Mama. I've been watching her for years. I can do it."

"Good, because we need to get moving. I need five resumes on my desk before lunchtime."

"I'm on it," Stephanie said as she pushed away from the table. "You can count on me, boss."

"Don't call me boss."

"Okay, Mama," Stephanie said with a smirk and continued on her way.

When she was alone in the meeting room, Korah took a deep breath and allowed herself to bask in the comforting warmth of hope – just for a moment – before she too had to return to her office for more pressing matters.

• • • • • •

Korah spent the next hour returning phone calls before she had to leave to run a few errands. She stopped by her daughter's desk on her way out.

"How's it going?"

"Great," Stephanie said. "I got three people already. Do you care if it's a male or female?"

Korah hadn't considered that. "No," she said. "As long they have a good work history."

"So you don't want anyone without experience? 'Cause, you know, everybody gotta start somewhere."

"Use your best judgment. I'll look at the resumes when I get back."

She stopped by Priscilla's office next and found Yolanda neck deep in paperwork.

"How's it going in here?"

"Fine."

Korah could see that wasn't the case, but she appreciated her positivity.

"Did you get in touch with your friend?"

"Yes," Yolanda said. "He said he can stop by this afternoon."

"That's great. Did he say what he'd charge us?"

"No. He wants to see how much work we have first. But it won't be that much. I told him we're in a bind, and I've known him since high school. It won't be anything unreasonable."

"That's great," Korah said. "I'll be back after lunch time. I look forward to meeting him."

"I'm sure he'll be here by then."

"What'd you say his name was again?"

"I didn't," Yolanda said. "But it's Tyson. Tyson Tellis."

"Is there anything you need me to ask Priscilla? I'm going to stop by her house before I come back."

"The first thing I need is the password to all of her programs. After that, I'm not sure. I was going to wait until Tyson got here to let me know what else."

"Alright. I'll be back."

"Good luck."

"Thank you," Korah said, thinking of how Priscilla's husband might react when he opened the door and saw her standing there. "If I don't come back, tell the police Hiram did it."

Yolanda was confused by the comment, but Korah left without offering an explanation.

• • • • • •

Luckily Hiram did not answer the door at Priscilla's modest home on the north side of town. The woman of the house answered herself. Priscilla leaned heavily on a walker for support, but Korah thought she looked great. It brightened her spirits to see her dear friend in her regular clothes, with her hair and makeup done like usual.

"Korah, come in!" she said. "Aren't you a sight for sore eyes!"

"I was just thinking the same thing," Korah said. She entered the home and then looked around warily.

"Oh, don't worry. He's not here," Priscilla said, reading her mind. "I sent him to the store to get me some tea. I made sure to pick the kind they only sell at the Whole Foods in Arlington," she said with a wink.

"That's nice of him to go so far," Korah said as she took a seat on the sofa.

"He's been very good to me," Priscilla replied as she worked her way to the couch.

Korah itched to help her, but she knew that her friend craved independence. Plus moving around on her own was part of her rehab. She almost helped anyway, because of the way Priscilla's arms trembled as she lowered herself to a sitting position. But she made it just fine, and she looked proud to have done so by herself.

"I don't know if I'll be able to get up anytime soon," Priscilla said with a sigh. "So I hope this will be a long visit."

"Sorry," Korah said. She gave her an encouraging smile. "But I have a tight schedule. And I don't want to be here when Hiram gets home."

"Oh, don't worry about him. He's all bark."

"I'm not taking any chances," Korah told her. "Anyway, how have you been? I see you're moving around a lot better."

"I feel good," Priscilla said. "I get tired a lot quicker than I used to, but I feel myself getting stronger."

"That's great. I know you can't wait to be done with that walker."

"It's not just the walker I'm getting sick of," Priscilla said. "To be honest, I wish I could go back to work."

"Oh hell no. You're not getting me cursed out."

"I know," Priscilla said. "I know I can't, but I really would like to. Everything I worried about is here now. I already feel like this *retired life* is going to drive me crazy."

"It's only been one day," Korah said. "Give it some time. Have you started rehab yet?"

"Today's my first day. My therapist is coming to pick me up at one. I can't wait to get out of the house."

"Don't worry. Things will get better," Korah assured her. "Once you get to moving around more, you'll see that there's a whole world outside of this home and outside of my office."

"Yeah? Like what?"

"I don't know," Korah said. "Haven't you ever wanted to travel or become a photographer or skydive?"

A quaint, little smile brightened Priscilla's eyes. "I would love to *skydive*."

"I was just kidding about that one."

"It would drive Hiram completely nuts!"

"I knew you were egging him on on purpose all these years," Korah said with a sly smile. "You like for him to worry about you."

Priscilla didn't respond, but her smile remained.

"Is it okay if I ask you a few questions," Korah said, "about the work you left at the office?"

"Sure. What do you need to know?"

"Well, for starters we can't log onto your computer, because we don't have your password."

"It's hiram1969. That's our anniversary."

"Awww. You *do* really love him."

"Eh..." She shrugged. "I'm stuck with him, at this point."

"I'm bringing in a new accountant," Korah said. "And I'm sending Yolanda to school, so she can take over your position at some point."

"That's good," Priscilla said. "She's a smart girl, very dedicated to the company."

"Is it okay if I call and ask you questions sometimes?" Korah asked. "I might have to bring some papers here for you to explain to us. Do you think that would be a problem with Hiram?"

"No, of course not."

Korah gave her a look, and Priscilla added, "If it is, I'll just send him out for more tea."

They both laughed.

Korah reached and touched her face softly. She traced a finger from her left temple to her chin, happy that her friend had regained sensation on that side.

"I'm glad you're doing better."

"Me too," Priscilla said. "And please don't worry, child. Everything's going to work out fine. You'll see."

• • • • • •

Priscilla lived near Brick's new worksite, so Korah decided to stop by before she returned to the office. She'd driven by the area before, but not during the daytime, when construction was in full swing. As she pulled into the makeshift parking lot, which was nothing more than huge, unpaved field, she was impressed with the progress thus far.

All of the trees on the property had been cleared. An assortment of bulldozers, backhoes and forestry mulchers moved in all directions, making quick work of the remaining vegetation. It wouldn't be long before the pipeline contractors came to create an elaborate network of underground plumbing and Devin was ready to start the foundation for the football field.

Korah grabbed her hardhat and pushed it down on her head before she exited her SUV. There were more than fifty vehicles in the parking lot and twice as many construction workers on the premises. The morning temperature was a cool 42 degrees. Korah wished she'd worn pants rather than her skirt suit, but the grumbling sounds from the engines of the heavy-duty construction vehicles warmed her whole body.

She felt excited all of a sudden and eager. The enormous construction site looked and smelled like money to her. Millions and millions of dollars.

She enlisted the help of a Brick House employee to find her son. He told her to hop aboard his ATV, which thankfully was a two-seater. He maneuvered the site expertly, though there were no trails or sidewalks, and soon Korah saw a huge TEXAS BUILDERS sign in the distance. As they got closer, she recognized her company trucks as well as the men with TEXAS BUILDERS emblazoned on their shirts and jackets.

Her driver dropped her off next to a trailer that also belonged to her company. As she approached the entrance, her son stepped out into the bright morning sun. Korah thought Devin looked commanding in his work uniform. His jeans fit him nicely. His father's tool belt hugged his hips with a slight tilt on the right side. He wore a long-sleeved button-down that couldn't hide his strong chest and shoulder muscles. His dark eyes brightened under the bib of his hardhat when he spotted his mother.

"Good morning," she told him.

"Morning." He stepped closer and hugged her briefly.

Korah stole a quick kiss on the cheek before she backed away.

"How's everything?"

"Great," he said, looking out onto his portion of the property. "We're almost done with the land clearing. We'll have the field ready in no time."

"Where is it going to be?"

"The middle will be right about there," Devin said and pointed, "where those two backhoes are. The training center will be on that side..." He gestured towards another area about a hundred yards away. "And the bleachers should make it all the way to... about where we're standing."

Korah continued to grin at him. "How you liking it?"

"It's a good site," he said. "A lot of people here, but everything's going smoothly – so far. It'll probably be different when the other contractors show up. And then we'll have the electricians, glass companies, welders... It's gonna be busy. I've never worked on anything this big. It'll be something to see."

"You worried about working with so many people?"

136

"Nah. I'm only worried about what goes on in my section. Whatever drama they got going on over there," he shot a thumb in the direction of where the new school would be, "is not my concern."

Korah was a little put off by his exclusive attitude, but she didn't think it would hurt the project, so she didn't mention it.

"What are you doing here?" he asked.

"I was just in the area. Thought I'd stop by."

"How are things going at the office?"

"Getting better," she said. "I just left Priscilla's."

"Really? How is she?"

"Pretty good, actually. She sounds like her old self. Still has a little trouble moving around, but she'll be fine. I'm so proud of her."

"What about her husband? Did he run you off?"

"He wasn't there," Korah said with a chuckle. "But he probably would have, if he knew I was coming."

"What are you gonna do about her replacement?" Devin wondered. "Yolanda says y'all can't even log onto her computer."

"I'm taking care of that. I got her log-in information, and Yolanda's bringing in a friend of hers to help with the accounting."

"Oh yeah?"

"Yeah, some lawyer named Tyson. She said she went to high school with him. Do you know him?"

Devin shook his head.

"Yolanda says he knows his stuff, and he'll be willing to help us without charging an arm and a leg. I hope she's right."

Devin nodded. "That would be sweet."

"*And*," Korah said, "I'm sending Yolanda to college. She's going to study accounting for a couple of years. Hopefully she'll be able to take over Priscilla's job, at some point."

Devin raised an eyebrow. "Yolanda's gonna be your vice-president?"

"If she can do it. Don't you think that's a good idea?"

"Yeah," he said. "She's real smart. And she loves the company. I know she's happy about that."

"She is," Korah confirmed. "Oh, and one more thing: When I retire, I'm trying to decide if you or Stephanie will take over for me. You're the oldest, so I wanted to give you first dibs, but—"

"I don't wanna work in an office," Devin said. "I like it out here. I don't care if Stephanie is the CEO, so long as she doesn't make more than me."

"That's what I figured," Korah said, still smiling.

"When did you make all of these decisions?"

"This morning."

"Are you thinking about retiring?"

"No. Not any time soon. Just planning for the future."

"What abou–"

"Hey, Devin!" someone shouted, cutting him off.

They looked back and saw a construction worker approaching. Korah didn't know his name, but she knew that he worked for their company. The worker's face went white when he looked from Korah to the look of disdain in his foreman's eyes.

"Man, don't you see me over here talking?" Devin snapped.

"I'm sorry, sir. I'm sorry, Ms. Stewart. I'll, I'll be, over here..." He backed away with his head down, eyes averted.

"Take it easy," Korah advised her son. "Save your temper for when you really need it."

Devin took a deep breath and relaxed visibly, but Korah didn't know if he would heed her warning or not.

"I gotta get back to the office," she told him.

"Alright, Mama. Talk to you later."

As she walked away, Korah made eye contact with the man who interrupted them.

"You guys are doing a great job," she told him.

He was hesitant to return her smile. "Thank you, ma'am. I'm sorry for interrupting y'all."

"It's okay," Korah told him. "No harm done. Keep up the good work!"

· · · · · ·

By the time she made it back to the parking lot, her pumps were caked with dirt, but her outlook was bright. She was initially offended when one of the guys called out, "*Hey, sexy lady*," but as she turned to confront the creep, she recognized the voice and found that it was not a creep at all.

Brick stood twenty feet away looking dapper in another new suit. This one was oyster gray. He wore it with a white shirt and striped tie. Brick's copper-colored skin seemed to glow under the morning sun. He leaned against his truck with one hand in his pocket. He was GQ smooth, even without trying.

"Morning," Korah said.

"What can I do for you?" Brick asked as he stepped towards her.

The sway of his walk made Korah's stomach tighten. His chiseled features took her breath away.

"I was just stopping by," she said. "I wanted to see how things were going with Devin."

"Oh, you didn't come to see me?" If he was offended, it didn't show.

"Sure I did."

His head cocked slowly. "Then why were you about to leave?"

Korah didn't think she would ever get used to the bass in his voice, the way *Texas* dripped off his tongue and from his pores.

He reached and took hold of her hand. "Why don't we step into my office, and talk about this," he suggested.

Korah felt like she had a million places to be, but at the moment, she couldn't remember where any of them were.

"Okay," she managed.

Construction trailers are similar to trailer homes, except they're designed for work rather than living. Brick's trailer was twice the size of Devin's, and Korah was not surprised to see that the inside was immaculate. There was a large table near the back that was surrounded by padded office chairs. Korah knew that he entertained important guests there, and apparently Brick spared no expense. Most trailers were lucky to have folding, metal chairs.

He closed and locked the door once they were both inside. He grinned at the curious look in Korah's eyes.

"So, what do you need?" he asked as he closed the distance between them. He reached and lifted the hardhat off her head.

"I, um, I need more money," Korah said.

"Really?" He placed her hardhat carefully on a counter. "How much more do you need?"

He reached and touched the side of her face. The slight contact made Korah gasp quietly. His fingers slipped behind her head, and he urged her to come closer.

"Ten million," she whispered a moment before their lips touched, igniting a firestorm in her belly.

Brick pecked her top lip and then the bottom. He sucked it into his mouth and tugged it gently with his teeth. Both of his hands moved to her ample hips.

He told her, "I love it when you wear jeans. But your skirts make me hard."

The disclosure made Korah's eyes widen. A tingle between her legs settled on her clitoris and drummed pleasantly.

"I can give you ten million dollars," he said. He took another step, until his body pressed against hers. His hands moved slowly towards her ass. He gripped both cheeks tightly and drew her even closer.

The pleasant sensation between Korah's legs suddenly burst into flames, causing her nipples and pubic hairs to stand erect. Brick kissed her again. This time he slipped his tongue past her lips. He tasted her, until her blood flowed like lava.

"Brick, I gotta go," she panted between succulent kisses.

"What about your ten million?"

Korah cried out when he hiked her skirt up and fondled her ass through her panties. She felt her body immediately become moist for him. Her juices were hot and sweet. She wanted him to taste her. She wanted to climb on top of him – right then and there – but this was a little too kinky, even for them.

She reached and pulled her skirt down. Brick reluctantly allowed her to do so.

"We, we'll have to finish this later," she told him as she backed away.

Her legs felt as weak as blades of grass, but she had to get away from him. At that moment she didn't know why she'd want to escape such a fine specimen of a man, but she knew the reasons would come to her once she was no longer within range of his mind control.

Brick turned to watch her, but he didn't follow. His right hand moved to adjust his erection – or so Korah thought. As she watched, he began to rub the bulge in his pants. His eyes remained glued to hers.

"You're a freak," she told him.

"Only for you," he said.

Korah was surprised by how happy that declaration made her feel.

"You promise?"

He nodded, his face dark with desire.

"Yeah, baby. I promise."

CHAPTER TWELVE
TYSON

Love Field was in the opposite direction of the office, but Korah decided to make an unexpected visit when she left Brick's site. She stopped by Starbucks to get a few things to snack on during the 45 minute trip.

When she got there, Korah was pleased to see three brand new aircraft hangars nearly completed. Her TEXAS BUILDERS sign was prominently displayed for all to see. There were three company trucks on the scene as well as one of their old equipment trailers. The trailer was damaged last year when another contractor attempted to delay their progress with random acts of vandalism, but today it was in perfect shape.

The new foreman on the site, a tall brother named Baron Grant, hurried to greet Korah when she stepped out of her SUV. He was dressed similarly to Devin, complete with a leather tool belt that hung casually on his hips.

"Good afternoon, Ms. Stewart." His smile was quick, his mood bright.

When she first met him, Korah thought Baron's nose was too big. But now she saw that it fit smoothly with the shape and contours of his face. She could understand why her daughter was developing a crush on him, though she still wasn't fond of the idea. Between her and Brick and Devin and Yolanda, there was enough love in the air already.

"Hi, Baron. How's it going?"

"Awesome. Things are going so well, I was about to leave it to Monte for the day. I'm glad you caught me, before I took off."

"You headed back to the bank?"

142

"Yes, ma'am. That's my biggest priority right now. We'll be done over here by Thursday."

Korah admired the hangars they had built from the ground up. Neither was big enough to house more than one aircraft at a time, but they were very impressive.

"Show me the alterations you had to make for the new designs."

"Absolutely!" Baron said. "Wait here, and let me go get the cart..."

He hurried off and returned a minute later driving a golf cart. Korah climbed aboard, feeling a lot safer than she did on the ATV at Brick's site.

Baron gave her a tour of the three hangars, making sure to point out all of the intricacies the architect requested as well as a few areas they had problems with. Korah paid close attention to everything he said. This was the first time they had spent any one-on-one time together, and she had to admit he was rather charming.

She also kept a keen eye on his interactions with their workers. The group seemed to be a lot happier than Devin's usual crews. Korah knew that could be because they were so close to completing the job. But Baron's exchanges with them also played a big part in it.

The few times he had cause to speak to his crew during Korah's tour, he didn't raise his voice, and his smile never faded. Korah noticed that he didn't bark orders wantonly. Every instruction he gave the men had, "Could you," at the beginning, but he was no less effective than the way Devin went about it.

By the time he brought her back to her car, Korah was thoroughly impressed with Baron. She would do everything she could to keep her daughter away from him, but as far as her jobs were concerned, she was comfortable with him as the lead foreman.

"Thank you very much," she said as she hopped off the golf cart.

"Anytime, Ms. Stewart. You should stop by the bank later on today, if you really wanna see something special..."

"I might just do that," Korah said. Her smile was genuine as she reached to shake his hand. "Thanks again, Baron. Glad to have you on the team."

143

• • • • • •

When she got back to the office, Stephanie rushed her before she could make it to her desk.

"Mama! Where you been?"

Korah frowned. "Working. Why?"

"Oh, my God! What happened to your shoes?"

Korah looked down at her pumps and shook her head. "I got dirty at Brick's site."

"You got *dirty* at Brick's site? Hmmm. Do tell..."

"Shut up, girl." Korah bent to pull her shoes off before continuing to her office. "Here."

Her daughter took them, but she wasn't happy about it. "Ewww. What am I supposed to do with these?"

"Put them in a bag, so the dirt won't get everywhere. And I need you to get me another pair in the next hour. And I need you to get the floor mat out of my car and shake it off. It's filthy." She handed over her car keys.

"Wait," Stephanie complained. "Why do I have to do all this?"

"Because Yolanda is Priscilla now, and you're Yolanda."

"Speaking of which..." Stephanie said. She had to struggle to keep up now. Her mom was surprisingly nimble without shoes on. "I got those resumes you wanted."

"Great," Korah said. "The sooner you get me a fulltime assistant, the sooner you can get off shoe duty."

She took a seat behind her desk and bent to rub her feet. Tomorrow she planned to wear her work boots for sure. They had double insoles that made her feel like she was walking on feathers.

Stephanie hurried out of the room and came back with the resumes. She placed them on her mother's desk and took a seat while she looked them over. Korah took less than three minutes to make her decision.

"Okay. Call this guy."

Stephanie took the resume from her. "Really? Malcolm?"

"Yes. Why do you sound surprised?"

"I didn't think you'd pick the guy."

Korah frowned. "Why'd you bring me his resume, if you don't think he's a good choice?"

"I didn't say he wasn't a good choice. I just didn't think you'd pick a guy."

"Well that's very sexist of you."

"No, I like his resume," Stephanie said. "And I think a guy would be a good choice. This office has been dominated by women for a long time. Now we'll have *two* men."

"*Two* men?"

"Oh yeah, Yolanda's lawyer friend is here. They've been in Priscilla's office for over an hour."

"Really? Well, I'd like to meet him."

"*Yes, you would,*" Stephanie said with a sly grin.

"What is that supposed to mean?"

"Mama, he's *gorgeous*."

"I... really don't care what he looks like."

"Yes, you do. I'll go get him."

Korah still had a frown on her face when Yolanda appeared in her doorway a few moments later with the newcomer in tow. The frown melted away when she saw Tyson Tellis. Korah subconsciously pushed her bare feet under her desk and sat up a little straighter in her chair.

"Hey, Ms. Stewart," Yolanda said. "This is my friend Tyson. Tyson, this is Ms. Stewart, the owner of Texas Builders."

Korah rose from her seat as he approached to shake her hand. His grip was strong but not uncomfortably so.

Tyson was tall, at least six foot-three. His skin was dark chocolate. His hair was longer than Korah's. It was styled in thick dreadlocks that were tied behind his head. He wore dark slacks with a cream-colored button-down. He was slim, and his clothes fit him nicely. His face was clean-shaven, his eyebrows thick. He had a thin, European nose, full lips, and a squared chin. He was the perfect blend of urban professionalism.

Stephanie was right about him being a looker. The last time Korah saw a man this handsome, she was staring at the homepage on Brick's company website.

"Good afternoon," he said. "Nice to meet you."

"Thank you for coming," Korah said. "Have a seat."

Yolanda continued to stand in the doorway while Korah and Tyson sat on either side of the desk. Yolanda looked a bit apprehensive. Tyson wasn't nervous at all.

He looked into Korah's eyes and said, "I've heard a lot about your company. I'm impressed with everything I've seen thus far." His voice was smooth and deep.

"Thank you," Korah said. "Tell me a little about yourself. I understand you're from Overbrook Meadows?"

"Yes, born and raised," he said. "I graduated from Finley High with Yolanda. I got my law degree from Morehouse in 2002. I specialized in accounting and finance. I went straight to work for Temple and Fisher in Atlanta and made junior partner four years later. I went back to school, Emory this time, in 2007, while still litigating cases for the firm. I got my master's degree in 2011.

"I'm currently on a leave of absence from the firm, due to my mother's sudden illness. I'll be in Overbrook Meadows for at least four more months. I haven't decided if I will return to the firm or start my own practice here. So this is actually a good time for me to help with the situation you have here. I can make myself available on a daily basis – outside of days I have to attend to my mom."

Korah was very impressed. Tyson's credentials surpassed what they needed.

"Did you speak with Yolanda about our long-term goals?" she asked.

"Um, yes. She says you need someone to help with your accounting until she's sufficiently trained to take over the job herself. She says she's going to start school in the fall."

"The summer, actually," Yolanda interjected. "I looked into it and found some classes at the community college. Tyson said he could help set up my curriculum," she told Korah.

"You two have looked at our books?" Korah asked Tyson. "What are your thoughts so far?"

"Everything is in excellent order," he said. "The woman you had before, Priscilla, I believe she is a financial wizard. Her work is easy to follow. Excellent record keeping. Of course I will have questions about specific accounts, and I'm afraid I don't know the construction biz very well. Would Priscilla be available for me to contact, when I have questions that Yolanda can't answer?"

"Not... really," Korah admitted. "It's a delicate situation. For now, her husband wants her to stay as far away from work as possible. And I understand his concerns. In the meantime, you'll

146

have to gather your questions and let me take them to Priscilla. Hopefully I can do that a few times a week."

"That should be fine," Tyson said.

Korah was glad he was so agreeable and confident. It was refreshing to come across a young brother who was this smart and upstanding. It sounded like he put a very promising career on hold to care for his ailing mother. That said a lot about his character.

"As far as training Yolanda," she said, "how long do you believe it would take before she can do this job? If you do decide to return to Atlanta in four months, she will still be an undergrad."

"It depends on the workload," he said. "As far as the bidding process, as I mentioned, I don't know enough about that yet to ascertain how difficult it is. But the bookkeeping, I believe Yolanda could learn to do that within three to four months – if she's dedicated and doesn't mind moving numbers all day."

"I am dedicated," Yolanda said quickly. "I'll do my best to learn as much as possible as quickly as possible."

"If she has any questions after my time here is done," Tyson continued, "I'll still be available for a conference call – or she could fax me a contract, so I can look it over for her. I'll also introduce her to a few of my associates in the area. Good resources are just as important as know-how these days."

Korah looked from Yolanda to Tyson. So far this sounded like a dream come true. There was only one more thing she was concerned about.

"How much would you charge for this?"

"I offered to do it as a favor for an old friend," he said. "I've known Yolanda since the eighth grade. She told me her company is in a bit of a bind, and it happens to be my area of expertise. So, you know, no biggie."

Korah was stunned. "I can't have you working here for free, especially when you came back to the city to care for your mother."

"My mother has brain tumors," he disclosed. "On most days she's fine, but this is a huge ordeal. She doesn't need 24 hour care – not yet, and hopefully she never will. I wanted to be nearby to help with her medical needs. Her first surgery is in a few weeks."

"I'm sorry to hear that," Korah said. "What you're doing is very admirable. I wish more young men were like you. But that doesn't mean you should work for me without pay."

"Okay." He shrugged. "You can pay me."

Korah didn't know how to respond. She wanted to offer a rate that was fair, but she didn't want to go overboard, especially if he didn't really want it.

"Ten thousand a month?"

"I'll take five," he said.

Korah raised an eyebrow. "Okay," she said.

"Great." Tyson stood and reached to shake her hand again. "I have already started a list of questions I would like to ask Priscilla. I'll have them to you by the end of the day. I also have a few invoices you need to sign off on. Is it okay if we get back to work?"

Still stunned, Korah nodded. "Yes, that would be great."

"Thank you," he said and left the office.

Yolanda gave her boss a big grin before she turned and followed him down the hall.

Ten seconds later Stephanie rushed back into the room. She took the seat Tyson just vacated and asked, "So what'd you think?" she asked with a hushed tone. "That man is *fine*, right?"

Priscilla's office was down the hall and around the corner. Korah wasn't worried that Yolanda or Tyson would hear them, but she glared at her daughter.

"Why aren't you at school?"

"I took the day off," Stephanie said, "for the family business."

"No one asked you to take a day off for the family business."

"Whatever, Mama. You know you needed me here. And we got a lot done today, too."

They did accomplish quite a bit. However, "If I need you to take a day off, *for the family business*, I'll let you know. Until then, you need to keep your butt in school."

"Fine," Stephanie said. "So what'd you think of Tyson?"

"He seems very capable," Korah replied. "Where are my shoes?"

Her daughter snorted and bent to remove her own pumps. "Here. Just use mine."

They were compatible with her outfit and roughly the same size, so Korah accepted them.

"I'll be glad when Malcolm gets here," Stephanie said. "You might be a little *too* bossy for me."

After being mesmerized by Tyson, Korah nearly forgot they had also selected a new assistant.

"You got in touch with him?"

"Yes. He'll be here for an interview at nine a.m. I won't be here. I'll be at *school*. So I hope you hire him, or you'll have to be your own assistant tomorrow."

"Thank you."

"Malcolm sounds like he looks good, too," Stephanie added.

"Girl, what is wrong with you? Why are you so boy crazy all of a sudden?"

"I'm just saying... Lately, we've had a lot of fine mens up in here."

Yes, we have, Korah thought.

"Have you talked to Baron lately?" her daughter asked.

"No," Korah lied. "That man is far too busy, even for me."

Stephanie's eyes narrowed for a moment before she smiled and left the office.

"Bye, Mama."

• • • • • •

By five p.m. Stephanie was long gone, and Korah was ready to call it a day herself. On the way out, she stopped by Priscilla's office and found her new team hard at work. They sat on either side of the desk with a couple of dozen papers scattered between them.

"How's it going?" she asked.

They both looked up at her with different expressions; Tyson looked slightly bored while Yolanda was clearly frustrated.

"Fine," they both said.

"Are you staying late?" Korah asked her former assistant.

"Not much longer," Yolanda said. "I'll lock up."

Korah nodded and then yawned. "Alright. I'll see y'all in the morning. Thanks again for agreeing to help out," she told Tyson. "You really came around at the right time."

"Don't mention it," he said. "This is a walk in the park, compared to my usual stuff. I still feel like I'm on vacation."

He smiled. Korah did too.

"Glad to hear it. Alright, goodnight, y'all." She rubbed the small of her back as she continued down the hallway.

"*Goodnight, Ms. Stewart!*" Yolanda called before she returned her attention to the task at hand.

An hour later she and Tyson were almost ready to go home. Yolanda's eyes were fatigued from reading so much. The prospect of doing all of this on her own one day was completely terrifying. Even still, she was thrilled about the opportunity.

Her cellphone rang, interrupting the momentum they had going.

"Hold on a second," she told her friend before she answered it. The Caller ID told her it was Devin calling. "Hey... Yeah, I'm leaving soon, in a few minutes... Alright, I'll see you later."

She disconnected and told Tyson, "Sorry about that."

"Do you have to go?" he asked.

"Yeah. It's after six."

"Was that the boyfriend?"

She smiled. "Yes, that was him."

Tyson leaned back in Priscilla's plush executive chair. With his elbows on the armrests, he brought his hands together and rubbed them together. His fingers were long and smooth. There were no callouses on his palms. Tyson was a hard worker, but not the kind Yolanda was accustomed to.

"Alright," he said. "I think we're about through here. When do you think Ms. Stewart will speak with Priscilla again? Tomorrow I can't come in until after noon. Do you think she will talk to her before then?"

"I'm not sure," Yolanda said. "I'll let her know first thing in the morning. I know this is a priority for her, so we should have some answers by the time you get here."

Tyson nodded. "I was wondering: Are you worried about working with me, with so much mutual attraction between us?"

Yolanda's eyes widened. She laughed. "Yeah right."

Tyson continued to smile. His dark eyes were fixed on hers. "Seriously, though. I can feel the way you've been watching me."

Yolanda shook her head. "You're kidding, right?"

"You don't find me attractive anymore?"

"I like your hair," she said. "I'm glad you let it grow. I can't believe they let you wear it like that at a law firm."

"My resume speaks for itself," Tyson said. "And every law firm needs a black face in the upper echelon. I'm sure I helped them reach their dreadlock quota."

Yolanda giggled. "So you were a token?"

"Maybe at first. I don't know. I know how much the position paid, so I never cared. Still don't. I think people give tokens a bad name – unless they're underqualified. That's different."

"I'm proud of you," Yolanda said honestly. "You really went and did it."

"I'm proud of you, too."

She smacked her lips. "For what?"

"You're going to college. Taking over this position. When I left, you didn't have this much ambition. Now you're a certified company-man."

"Everybody's got to have something."

"And you've got the boss' son, too."

She nodded. "Yeah."

"He's cool with you and me working together?"

"Why wouldn't he be?"

"Did you tell him I'm an old flame?"

"Flame?" She chuckled. "We only went out for three months. And that was over fifteen years ago. As far as Devin's concerned, you're an old friend from school. Nothing more."

"We went to prom together," he reminded her.

"Yeah, and you broke up with me right after because I wouldn't give it up."

"That's not why we broke up."

"Oh yeah, it was because I didn't have any *ambition*. How did I forget?" she asked sarcastically.

"You didn't want to go to college," he recalled. "It was my mom who said you didn't have any ambition."

"You must've agreed. But then again, you started dating Julie Wilkerson right after. And she didn't have any ambition either, except for her goal to sleep with every basketball player."

151

Tyson laughed. He had slight dimples in his cheeks that appeared when he smiled. "She was a ho, wasn't she?"

"Biggest one I've ever met," Yolanda agreed. "Which can only mean you broke up with me because I wouldn't give it up after prom."

"Not true," he insisted.

She shrugged. "Doesn't matter."

After a few moments, he asked, "So you're completely over me?"

"Yes, and you're over me, too. Stop playing."

He said, "Alright," but he didn't sound fully convinced.

"Do you think I'd bring you here, if I still had feelings for you?" she asked. "I'm dating my boss' son. For me to cheat on him with you would be the dumbest move I could make. I may not be the brightest apple, but I'm not that stupid."

"You sound like this is *your* family business."

"They make me feel like family." She nodded. "Yeah, they do."

"And if you marry what's his name, you'll be family for real."

"Yes, that's true too."

"*Or* you could come work for me when I start my own practice," Tyson offered. "I'll need a pretty, young bookkeeper, like yourself."

"Sorry. I have too much time invested here," Yolanda replied.

"That's cool. In the meantime, I'll do my best to suppress my attraction towards you," Tyson said. "But you have to do the same."

She rolled her eyes. "No problem there. You ready to go?" she asked as she rose to her feet. She ignored the way Tyson's eyes swam over her body as he stood.

"Yes," he said. "I suppose I am."

CHAPTER THIRTEEN
TWO BULLS

On Tuesday, February 24th, Devin was having a wonderful day at the school worksite. It took nearly two months, but the trees and vegetation had finally been cleared from his workspace, leaving nothing but rich, dark soil for hundreds of yards in all directions.

At 10 a.m. he stood in the center of what would be his new football field. The air was pure, the sky baby blue. The sun was bright and warm on his face and arms. The temperature was a pleasant 49 degrees. The expected high today was 62, which was ideal, compared to the blistering heat summer would bring.

Devin took a deep breath, a slight smile lighting his eyes. He loved all aspects of construction, but this was a special moment. He felt like an artist staring at a blank canvas. Most of the working world never got to experience the delight of creating something from absolutely nothing. In a couple of years they would have high school football games and soccer matches on the very spot he was standing. None of the kids would be aware or even care to know how many men it took to transform this piece of land into something totally different.

But Devin would know. He would come to at least one of their games and sit in the stands he built and admire the field and training center. He would look around at the excited faces and know that they owed part of their happiness to him and his company's efforts. And *that* was actually worth more than any paycheck he received. Not many people would understand, so Devin rarely shared his thoughts with others. There were a lot of things that stayed hidden away in his heart and soul.

When he turned and saw Brick's work truck rounding the corner, approaching his workspace, a dark cloud suddenly blocked the beautiful sun rays he was just admiring. Devin wasn't sure why, but Brick's presence always gave him a sinking feeling, deep down in his gut. He hoped Brick House's CEO would continue driving to a different part of the site, but no such luck.

Brick parked his lavish work truck right next to Devin's trailer and hopped out wearing a dark gray suit that looked too expensive for someone who'd be working around dirt all day. Brick reached back into his truck for a hardhat, but the accessory didn't alter Devin's opinion of him.

As he stood watching and waiting, Devin understood that he was looking at a man who had grown too big. Brick was too successful to dress like and associate with the common worker. That may have been the reason he and Devin would never get along. Or maybe that wasn't it at all. All Devin could say for sure was there was definite animosity between them, and Brick continuously gave him reasons to dislike him.

When the boss-man spotted him on the field and began to take deliberate steps in his direction, Devin knew that he would soon have another reason to loathe Brick. It was unlikely his mother's boyfriend was coming with good news.

"Morning," Brick said when he was within speaking distance.

Devin nodded. "Morning."

Brick watched as Korah's son folded his arms over his chest in a defensive manner. When they were closer, Brick noticed that Devin always wore a guarded look around him. He assumed it was because he was still upset about his mother's relationship. But how long does it take to get over something like that?

Brick had let Devin's attitude slide for the past couple of months because he didn't need his workers to be sociable. He needed them to work. But his pride-man began to stand tall whenever he was in Devin's presence. He knew it was only a matter of time before they had it out. Brick also knew that he had the upper hand, so he wasn't concerned about when or why it finally happened.

"What you got going on over here?" Brick asked, looking out at the vast stretch of land Devin and his crew was assigned to.

Devin didn't know if that was a trick question or a stupid question. It was obvious what he had going on over here. Rather than respond, he gave Brick a look of confusion.

His expression rubbed Brick the wrong way. When a man asks a question, you should answer – or at least that was the way Brick was raised. But he caught himself. This was Korah's son. He didn't want there to be any friction between them. Maybe his question wasn't as clear as he thought it was.

"Those guys," he prompted. "What are they doing on my site?"

The words *my site* were not lost on Devin. It was something he wasn't used to hearing. Everywhere he'd worked up to this point was always *his* site. His nostrils flared slightly, and he tried to keep his voice neutral as he responded.

"Those are my surveyors," he said, referring to the six men in florescent orange construction vests who were currently setting up their equipment at strategic points.

Their assessment would tell Devin everything he needed to know about the land he was about to start work on. Of course Brick knew that already, so Devin wasn't sure why he was being questioned.

"I saw a truck back there," Brick said, gesturing towards Devin's trailer. "Are those guys from Blue Mound?"

Devin nodded. His broad chest rose and fell slowly.

"The thing is," Brick said, moving his hands to his hips, "I've already decided which surveyors are working on this site. Did you get the memo?"

Devin clenched his jaws tightly, lest he say something out of line that he'd later regret. He got plenty of faxes and memos from Brick. The bastard seemed to have a new one every day. Some of that crap was worth reading. Most of it was not.

"I don't think I got that one," he finally replied.

"That's a shame," Brick said. "I'd hate to think you brought those guys out here for nothing."

Devin's nostrils flared again. He took another slow breath. "I've been working with Blue Mound for years," he replied. "They survey all of my properties. They do great work."

"That's great," Brick said. "But the thing is, this isn't your property. And I've already decided that Red Eye is doing all of the surveying here. You should've let me know that you were ready for the surveyors, and I could've set everything up for you."

"I don't need you to set anything up for me." That comment slipped out before Devin could stop it. He was surprised that it brought a smile to Brick's face.

"Well, I can't tell," the contractor said. "You did it on your own this time, and look what happened. You gotta pay these guys for nothing."

"They're already here," Devin countered. "Might as well let them finish."

"In your world, I'm sure that makes perfect sense," Brick said. "But this is *my world*. I already gave Red Eye the whole site. They're expecting to survey this field, and I'll be damned if I have to call and tell them Blue Mound is already here."

His smile was gone by then.

"So I need you to tell those boys you made a mistake," Brick advised. "Honestly, I don't care what you tell them. Just get them off my property."

He waited a few seconds to see if Devin had another retort. He did not. Brick didn't want to talk to Korah's son in this manner, but Devin had a lot to learn about respect and opportunity. If he didn't recognize how big this job was for Texas Builders, that was his problem. But if he wanted to couple that ignorance with lack of respect, that was intolerable.

"I'm going to send my faxes directly to your main office from now on," Brick told him. "I don't want any more misunderstandings like this."

Devin couldn't believe what he was hearing. Did this man just threaten to tell his mama on him? But it was the thought of Korah that made it possible to continue suppressing his anger. This job meant the world to her, and apparently so did *Prick* Avery. If it was up to Devin, he'd tell Brick to get the hell away from him and take his funky surveyors with him. But he knew that would break his mother's heart.

"I'll send these guys home," Devin said. "And you can continue sending your faxes to me. Sorry for the misunderstanding."

Brick could tell it hurt him to apologize. He knew that he shouldn't derive any satisfaction from Devin's suffering, but he did. A boy's got to know his place in a man's world.

156

"That's fine," Brick said with a nod of his head. His smile was back in place. "You have a good day, now."

He turned and strolled casually back to his truck.

Devin shook his head and turned back to his surveyors. He was so angry, his whole body trembled. The guys from Blue Mound did great work, but poor management had left them nearly bankrupt last year. Devin had known the owner since high school, and they were still good friends. He knew how badly they needed this job. He didn't want to send them home after an hour's work, when they planned to be here all week.

"Fucking asshole," Devin muttered as he waved at their lead man. "Bad news," he shouted when he got the guy's attention. "Y'all gotta pack it up..."

• • • • • •

Twenty miles away at the Texas Builders' headquarters, Korah's morning was going completely different. Not only did her interview for a new assistant go remarkably well, but the new guy, Malcolm Nevels was ready and eager to start.

Korah pulled Yolanda from Priscilla's old office so she could get his tax and insurance paperwork filled out. Yolanda then spent the next hour with Malcolm, giving him a rundown of the company and the expectations Korah would have for him. By eleven o'clock, Malcolm was ready to go. Yolanda brought him back to Korah's office with a glowing report.

"He's very smart. Soaks up everything like a sponge. I think he's gonna work out fine."

"That's great," Korah replied. "How are things going in Priscilla's office?"

"Well... I was hoping I could move my stuff in there," Yolanda said. "That is gonna be *my* office, right?"

Korah felt a tug at her heart. For as long as Texas Builders had been in operation, the office down the hall was Priscilla's. She knew Priscilla wasn't coming back. Allowing Yolanda to move in and change the name on the door would further reinforce that.

"Or I could stay at my desk," Yolanda said, noticing her inner turmoil.

"No," Korah said. "That's your office now. Please box-up all of Priscilla's personal items, and bring them to me by the end of the day."

"Okay," Yolanda said trying not to let on how giddy she was.

"Is Tyson coming in today?" Korah asked.

"Yes. He should be here any minute. He couldn't come earlier, because he had to take his mom somewhere."

"That's fine," Korah said. "Are you okay working by yourself?"

"Um... I think I'll just keep answering the phone until he gets here – or until you get Malcolm situated."

Korah nodded. "Alright."

Yolanda left the room. Korah's new assistant took a seat and looked up at her expectantly. Malcolm was young, no more than 22. His skin was fair, like Brick's. His short hair had a red tint to it. He wore a big pair of nerd glasses, which was the fad these days, and he was clean-shaven, except for a tuft of hair on his chin. Despite his small stature, both height and width, Korah thought he was attractive. She was glad her daughter wasn't there to ogle him all day.

"Priscilla sounds like she was irreplaceable," Malcolm said, cutting into what had become a prolonged silence. He had a sweet voice. It was almost effeminate, but he didn't come across as gay.

Korah stared at him for a moment before saying, "Yes. She is."

"What happened to her – if you don't mind me asking?"

"She had a stroke."

"Oh, that's sad. When I was a kid, I had to get a new dad."

Korah's eyes narrowed. She wasn't sure why he was sharing.

"My first dad was great," Malcolm went on. "He used to take us to the mall and let us play with all of the toys. And we'd go to the park, and he'd push us on the swings at night. He had a lot of parties. We met a lot of interesting people, when I was little."

Korah's frown deepened. "That's... nice."

"Actually it wasn't," Malcolm revealed. "My mama later told us that Daddy was a *crackhead*."

Korah's eyes widened.

"It's okay," Malcolm said. "It doesn't run in the family. Or if it does, I didn't get it."

Korah wasn't sure how to respond to any of this.

"Turns out all of those trips to the mall," Malcolm said, "Daddy was just using us as a distraction while he was *stealing.*"

"No."

He nodded. "Mmm hmm. And our good times at the park; Daddy was hooking up with his connect in the middle of the night."

Korah's jaw dropped.

"And all of those parties..." Malcolm went on.

Korah shook her head.

"Yep, *crack parties,*" Malcolm said. He laughed.

Korah was reluctant to show her own amusement.

"When my mom found a new daddy for us, I hated him," Malcolm revealed. "But after a while, I found that there were things he did better. Like, he gave us an allowance, and he never asked for it back. And when he took us to the mall, he actually bought us stuff. He moved us out of our apartment, too. Sometimes I go back and look at where we used to live, and it's really bad. It's a shame. But I didn't notice it, when I was little."

Korah was glad things turned out well for him. She sensed there was a point to this story.

"So change isn't always a bad thing," Malcolm said. "Sometimes things will turn out a lot better, when you have someone new in your life."

"Is this about Priscilla?" she asked.

He nodded. "Yes, Ms. Stewart. You looked so sad a moment ago. I didn't want you to be upset – not on my first day."

Korah smiled. "Thank you. That's very considerate."

"So, what would you like for me to start on?" he asked, ready for work.

"Well, if Yolanda's officially moving into Priscilla's – I mean *her* new office, then you should get settled into her old desk. But I don't know how she'd feel about you messing with her stuff, so you'd better ask first. It's almost lunchtime," Korah said, checking her watch. "I'm going to visit Priscilla at one. Before that, I was thinking about going to Chili's. You wanna come with?"

"Yes, ma'am. That would be awesome! After all I've heard about Priscilla, it would be nice to meet the living legend in person."

"Great. I'll let you know when I'm ready to leave."

• • • • • •

At noon Korah stopped by Yolanda's office before she and Malcolm left for lunch. As she approached, she wasn't surprised to hear laughter coming from the room. But it did give her pause. When she entered, she found Yolanda and Tyson engaged in conversation that didn't sound work-related. But they didn't look suspicious. They greeted her with big smiles – which was refreshing, considering how the office still made Korah's heart ache for Priscilla.

"Hey, Ms. Stewart," Yolanda said.

"Good afternoon," Tyson added.

Today he was dressed more casually in a short-sleeved button-down that wasn't tucked into his black slacks. But he still looked professional. And his work was above reproach. Yesterday he presented Korah with three detailed invoices that were flawless. If he wasn't so overqualified for the position, she would love it if he stayed with them permanently.

"I'm going to stop by Priscilla's house after lunch," Korah told them. "Yolanda said you had some questions?"

"Yes," Tyson said, rising to his feet. He approached and gave her a few papers. "My questions are on the top. And here's a statement she created for one of your customers. I highlighted the transactions I'm not sure about. If she could write a brief explanation in the margins, that would be all I need for now."

"Alright," Korah said. She handed the papers to Malcolm, who was waiting in the hallway. "How's Yolanda's training going?"

"Just fine," Tyson reported. "She's a quick learner. It's going a lot better than I expected."

"It would probably go faster if he'd quit bringing up old school stories," Yolanda said with a chuckle. "I feel like I'm at Finley High all over again."

"No, that's her," Tyson said as he returned to his seat.

They were both in good spirits.

"Try not to have too much fun," Korah said before she left them alone.

"We won't," Yolanda promised. "Don't worry, Ms. Stewart. I won't let you down."

• • • • • •

Devin wasn't a caveman when it came to things like dinner being ready when he got home, but Yolanda did feel guilty about not being there when he got off work. They had been shacking-up since early December, ever since Korah confronted them about their relationship, and they got everything out in the open.

At the time, Yolanda thought she'd be happy about making their relationship public. After sneaking around with Devin for nearly a year, she was starting to feel like a mistress. But moving in with him exposed a new set of issues that may have been there all along; she was just too blind or too much in love to see them.

Instead of going straight home that day, she stopped by Panda Express to pick up a to-go order. She knew that was one of Devin's favorite restaurants. Hopefully he wouldn't be upset about her working late if she came home with a meal already prepared.

When she got home, her boyfriend seemed dark and brooding. He sat in the living room with a beer in one hand and the television remote in the other. He still wore his work uniform and his work boots, which were caked with dried mud. Yolanda saw that he had tracked muck from his boots throughout the living room. But she wasn't one to complain. She did try to keep the place as clean as possible, but technically she was merely a visitor in Devin's home. If he wanted to ruin his carpet with this slovenly behavior, that was his choice.

Yolanda deposited her purse on the couch and stopped briefly to give her man a kiss before she went to the kitchen to prepare his dinner.

"Hey, baby."

"Why you working so late?" he muttered.

"You know I'm doing double duty since Priscilla got sick," Yolanda said without stopping. "It's hard work, and I'm doing the best I can. I'm sorry. I'll try to leave at five tomorrow."

Devin remained seated, his eyes glued to the television. "What's for dinner?" he called after a few moments.

161

"Panda Express. Do you want to eat in here, or you want me to bring it to you?"

"You can bring it," he said.

Yolanda kicked off her pumps as she took a couple of plates from the cupboard. The food was still warm, and it smelled delightful. Her stomach started to growl when she returned to the living room to set up Devin's tray stand. He avoided eye contact, which could have meant a number of things. Yolanda decided to keep quiet, until he was ready to say what was on his mind.

A few minutes later, they were both eating quietly, watching the First 48. Yolanda hated that show. She didn't like how it broadcasted the worst black people had to offer the country. But it was one of Devin's favorite programs, so she didn't ask him to change it.

When she was nearly done eating, she asked, "So, how was your day?"

Devin shook his head and sighed, and she knew she'd hit a nerve.

"That bad?" she ventured.

"I got into it with Brick," Devin said and then took a long drink of his beer.

Yolanda was reluctant to hear his grievance. The bad blood between Devin and Brick was obviously not going away, and it was doubtful that she could do anything to help the situation. But she cared for Devin. If it was in her power to help him feel better, she certainly wanted to try.

"What happened?"

"He's all in my shit," Devin said, his eyes still on the TV.

Yolanda felt a sinking feeling in her gut. She placed her food on the coffee table and asked, "What'd he do?"

"Made me send my surveyors home," Devin said. Just thinking about it brought back all of the anger and embarrassment he'd experienced earlier today. He felt hot blood racing through his veins, making the hairs stand on his forearms.

"Why would he do that?" Yolanda asked.

"'Cause he wants to control every little thing," Devin explained. "He said we can only use *his* surveyors. I swear I wanted to break his jaw, the way he was looking at me and talking to me."

Yolanda's heart skipped a beat. A cold numbness enveloped her whole body.

"You, y'all had an argument?"

He shook his head. "No. We didn't argue. He just told me to send my surveyors home, and I stood there and took it."

"Did, was this the first time he said something about using only his surveyors?"

Devin turned slowly and glared at her. The look in his eyes gave Yolanda a lump in her throat.

"So, you wanna take his side?"

"I'm not taking anyone's side. I just asked a question."

"He sends a lot of fucking memos," Devin spat. "That's all I get in my fax machine; a bunch of dumb-ass memos."

"So... are you not reading them?" Yolanda dared to ask.

"Why you taking his side?" Devin asked again.

"I told you; I'm not taking anyone's side. I just asked if he told you about the surveyors before. 'Cause if he did, then you are wrong. You should've did what he told you to."

"Ain't no reason for it," Devin snapped. "What difference does it make if it's my surveyors or his? His ain't no better than the ones I always use."

"It matters because he said–"

"Because he wants to stick his nose in everything! I don't need that nigga stomping around my site, like he's running shit."

"That's not your site, Devin. That's *his* site," Yolanda said, growing irritated herself. "And I don't need you yelling at me."

"Then why can't you ever be on my side?" he wondered. "No matter what I tell you about him, that nigga's always right. You supposed to be my woman, but you don't never have my back."

"I'll have your back when you're *right*," she said. "But if you're wrong, I have to tell you. What kind of person would I be if I let you walk around thinking you're doing right when you clearly aren't?"

"This some bullshit!" Devin's eyes rolled back to the television.

"This job is more important than you not liking Brick," his girlfriend told him. "Your macho attitude is going to cost you millions of dollars, if you keep it up."

Devin brought his beer can to his lips and grimaced when he realized it was empty. He crushed the can in his big fist and stood so quickly Yolanda recoiled in fear. Devin had never laid a hand on her – no matter how angry he was. But when dealing with a temper as bad as his, there's always a chance for violence. Or at least that's what Yolanda's sisters had been telling her.

"I'm finna go," Devin said. He snatched his keys from the kitchen bar on his way to the front door.

Yolanda didn't leave her seat, but she asked, "Go where?"

"Get something to drink."

"It's almost eight o'clock," she told him. "Are you going to the store or to a bar?"

"Just need some fresh air," he said.

That didn't answer her question, but she appreciated the fact that he wanted to take his anger elsewhere. He usually came home drunk and apologetic after these episodes. Yolanda knew that was only a temporary fix, but she accepted it.

She accepted a lot from Devin. Sometimes she wasn't sure why.

When he didn't return in twenty minutes, she knew he hadn't gone to the corner store. Devin's house was big and lonely, but it was also much more peaceful without him there to gripe about his daily grievances.

Yolanda was about to bathe and get ready for bed when she heard the text message chime on her cellular. She dug the phone from her purse, expecting to see a message from Devin that would indicate where he was. But it wasn't him.

It was Tyson: I'm not going to make it to the office tomorrow. Could you let Ms. Stewart know?

Yolanda texted him back: Yes, I can. Is everything okay?

He said: Yes. Just got some dates mixed up. Gotta take mama somewhere

Yolanda typed: Oh. That's fine. I'll tell Ms. Stewart

She sat on the couch for a few minutes, hoping he'd keep the conversation going, but her phone didn't chime again. She gave it serious thought before she sent him another text: What are you doing now?

Tyson responded quickly: Nothing. Aren't you with your boyfriend?

He's mad. Went to get drunk

Sorry to hear that. You okay?

Yolanda knew she shouldn't, but she typed: No. Can you talk?

Tyson asked: Is it okay to call?

Yolanda swallowed hard before responding: Yes

Thirteen seconds later her cellphone rang. Yolanda stood and headed for the bedroom as she answered. If Devin returned suddenly, she'd hear him enter the house and have time to end the call before he made it back there.

"Hey," she said.

"You sound stressed," Tyson noticed.

"I am. I'll be alright."

"I don't like to hear you like this," her old crush said. His voice was calming, almost therapeutic. "You should be happy. You don't deserve to be treated badly..."

CHAPTER FOURTEEN
TOUCHY FEELY

Over the next few months things progressed smoothly at the new school as well as the other sites Texas Builders won contracts on. Baron and his team completed work on the aircraft hangars at Love Field, which received stellar reviews from the property owner and the pilots who leased the space.

Their next biggest job for Bank of America was also going great. Korah didn't know much about Baron prior to the school job, but by spring of 2015 he was her right hand man. He attended most of the morning meetings at the Texas Builders' headquarters, which pleased Stephanie immensely.

She promised her mother she wouldn't talk to him outside of business matters, but that didn't stop her from flirting ferociously. So far Baron was polite but seemingly uninterested, which suited Korah just fine.

She hoped Stephanie's affections would move on to one of her classmates, but she didn't fault her daughter for being attracted to Baron. He was an honest, hardworking brother. A natural leader. Korah knew he would make some woman very happy one day, if he ever decided that his love life was more important than the blueprints that consumed most of his time.

In March Korah surprised everyone by announcing her new assistant was their very first "Employee of the Month." She even hung a framed picture of Malcolm in the lobby for everyone to admire. Yolanda stepped into Korah's office that day, her eyes green with envy.

"Ms. Stewart, I'm not mad or nothing. But I was your assistant for more than *ten years*, and you never made me employee of the month."

"I know," Korah said with a smile. "And I'm sorry. If the perk was active when you were my assistant, you would've won it many times over. You know that."

"What made you start it up now?" Yolanda wondered. "I know Malcolm ain't all that."

"It's not just him. We've been growing so much, I'm trying to come up with different ways to show my appreciation for everything everyone's doing. You know I went to that management seminar last week..."

"That's what they told you, to start naming an employee of the month?"

"That's one of the new ideas I'm going to implement."

"Tell me the truth, Ms. Stewart. Is Malcolm better than I was?"

"No," Korah said. "But he does go above and beyond."

"I'm listening..." Yolanda pouted.

"Girl, stop. It's not a competition. I love all of you equally."

"Where's your employee of the month now?" Yolanda wondered.

Korah shook her head. "Well, if you must know, he went to pick up a few outfits I had at the cleaners. But he called and said my car was past due an oil change, so he might be doing that. And he's bringing lunch when he gets back."

"So you're running that boy ragged," Yolanda deduced.

"I barely ask him to do anything," Korah said. "He takes *over-achiever* to the next level."

"I guess," Yolanda said. "But I still think I deserve some *retroactive* recognition. And it's not like I'm slacking now. I work real hard, every day."

"Perfect," Korah said with a grin. "So it works."

"What works?"

"Not being named Employee of the Month makes you work harder."

Yolanda's eyes narrowed as she gave that some thought. "You ain't slick."

Korah shrugged. "Keep up the hard work, and maybe next time it could be you."

Yolanda laughed as she left the office, but Korah knew that her spirit of competition had just kicked into overdrive.

● ● ● ● ● ●

On Wednesday, May 13th Korah was going over a new contract with Malcolm when Yolanda and Tyson returned from lunch. The two friends were in a good mood; their boisterous laughter made it all the way to Korah's office. She was a little concerned about how close the two had become since Tyson came to help with their bookkeeping, but Korah didn't feel any real dread until Stephanie poked her head into her office a moment later.

Stephanie was about to say something, but she looked from her mother to Malcolm, and her mouth snapped shut. Her eyes pleaded for privacy, and Korah read them well.

She told Malcolm, "Could you excuse us for a moment?"

He nodded and shot to his feet. "Yes, ma'am. Is it okay if I take this contract to my desk, to look over it a little on my own?"

"Yes," Korah told him. "That would be fine."

Malcolm quickly left the room. Stephanie entered and closed the door before she took the seat he vacated.

"What's wrong?" Korah asked.

"Mama, it's something going on with them two," Stephanie reported.

Korah had a good idea what she was talking about, but she asked, "Who?"

"Yolanda and Tyson." Stephanie spoke with a hushed tone.

Korah had been thinking the same thing, but she was reluctant to voice her opinion. "What makes you say that?"

"You see how close they are," Stephanie said. "They were damned near holding hands just now when they came in here."

Korah felt like she got kicked in the gut. She couldn't believe Yolanda would do something that stupid so blatantly. "What do you mean *holding hands*? And watch your language."

"They weren't really holding hands," Stephanie backtracked. "But they were all up on each other; real *touchy feely*. You know how a guy will touch you, like, in the middle of the back, when y'all walk through a door?"

Korah did know how that felt. It was something Brick did every time they went out.

"But it's not just today," Stephanie said. "They act like that every day; always laughing and flirting with each other."

"You saw them flirting?"

"*I* call it flirting," Stephanie said. "If a man says something funny, and you reach out and touch his arm while you're laughing, that's flirting, right?"

Korah had to agree that it was, but she didn't respond.

"I know you've seen some of this yourself," her daughter said. "I think it gets worse when you're out of the office. But it still happens when you're here."

"I have noticed how close they are," Korah admitted. "But I don't know what kind of friendship they had when they were in school. Are you saying a man and a woman can't be good friends? What about that boy you were friends with; the one you kept saying was your play-brother? Y'all were close like that, and nothing happened."

"Sorry to break it to you, but me and Tony ended up sleeping together."

Korah's eyes widened.

"It was a *long* time ago," Stephanie said.

"How long ago could it have been?" Korah wondered. "You're only twenty."

"This ain't about me. Are you turning a blind eye to what's going on with Yolanda and Tyson on purpose?"

Korah shook her head. "No. I just don't want to think about it. I don't want to make any accusations."

"Did she break up with Devin?"

Korah continued to shake her head. "No. I don't think so."

"Don't you care about what she does to him?"

"Of course I do. I told them not to start dating in the first place," Korah reminded her. She felt a mellow throbbing behind her eyeballs that had the making of one hell of a headache. "I hope she's not crazy enough to cheat on him in front of everyone, but that's their problem. *Dammit!*" She rubbed between her eyebrows but couldn't reach the source of tension.

"I'ma confront her," Stephanie decided.

"No, you're not."

"Well, I'ma tell Devin, then."

"You're not doing that, either," Korah said. "I'm telling you to stay out of it."

Stephanie was seething, but she respected her mother enough to be obedient to her wishes. "Could you at least get rid of Tyson?" she asked with a grimace, "so I don't have to watch them disrespect Devin like that?"

Korah blew out a pent-up breath. If Stephanie was right about the two of them, then they did have a serious problem on their hands. As much as she hated to get involved, confronting Yolanda was the only way to get to the bottom of this.

"Go back to your desk," she told Stephanie. "I'm going to call Yolanda in here. Do not say anything to her, and do not come in here while I'm talking to her. You got it?"

"Yes," Stephanie replied, happy to be closer to a resolution. "But if I hear y'all arguing, I'ma come in here and whoop her ass."

"If you lay a hand on her, you're fired," Korah threatened. "You hear me?"

"Mmm hmm," Stephanie said on her way out of the office.

Korah didn't know what that meant exactly, but she decided to let it slide. She pressed a button on her phone and waited a few beats until Yolanda came to the line.

"Yes, Ms. Stewart?"

"Could you come to my office, please?"

"Yes, Ms. Stewart."

A moment later Yolanda appeared in the doorway, looking as bubbly as ever.

"Have a seat," Korah told her. "Close the door first."

Yolanda closed the door and sat down with a confused expression. "Hi. Is something wrong?"

"Look," Korah said with a sigh. "I don't want to get involved with any of this. I truly don't. Whoever you like and decide to go out with is your business."

Yolanda's frown intensified.

"But when you and Devin decided to start a relationship," Korah continued, "you brought me and the whole company into it. That's why I didn't want any of my employees to date each other. Things can get complicated..."

170

"Ms. Stewart, I... What's wrong? Did I do something wrong?"

Korah cursed herself for having to play mediator for this foolishness.

She started by asking, "Are you and Devin still seeing each other?"

"Yes," Yolanda said cautiously.

"Y'all still live together?"

Yolanda blushed before nodding. "Yes, Ms. Stewart."

"Is everything okay? Are you having problems?"

Korah watched as her new bookkeeper's eyes darted to and fro.

"We, I guess we have problems like any other couple," she said. "Devin, I mean, you know how he is..."

Korah shook her head. "No, not really."

"He has a bad temper," Yolanda said. "But we still love each other. We don't argue a lot. But it doesn't take that much to piss him off. Sometimes I feel like I have to walk on eggshells, when I'm around him..."

Devin's temper was nothing new, but Korah never considered how it affected his relationships. She assumed he only behaved that way at work. But now that she thought about it, it made sense that he brought some of his stress home with him.

"I'm sorry to hear that," she said.

"It's not that bad," Yolanda insisted.

"Do you want to break up with him?"

She shook her head adamantly. "No, ma'am. I love Devin. I hope we get married one day."

That was the first time Yolanda had mentioned wedding bells. On any other day, the news would've delighted Korah. But there was still the matter of Tyson.

"What about your friend?" she asked. "You and Tyson seem to be very close. I mean, *very* close."

Yolanda smiled. Korah watched as her tension melted away.

"He's just my friend," Yolanda said.

"I know he's your friend, but I'm a little worried about how close you guys are. You're always laughing and having a good, old time. Y'all do get a lot of work done – don't get me wrong. And I like that you're happy while you're working. But I have to say,

Yolanda, if I didn't know any better, I'd think you and Tyson have something going on."

The girl continued to smile innocently, which made Korah feel like she was being honest.

"Ms. Stewart, I would never do anything that stupid. If I was going to cheat on Devin – *which I wouldn't* – I certainly wouldn't do it right in front of you."

Korah felt the same way. That would be a terribly senseless thing to do.

"Tyson is like my play-brother," Yolanda said. "I've known him since middle school."

The words *play-brother* made Korah tense up again, but she had to give her the benefit of the doubt. She always prided herself on being able to tell when someone was lying to her. She didn't feel like Yolanda was being deceitful.

"Alright," she said. "Well, I'm sorry for bringing it up. But you should know that most people take what they see at face value. If you're staring into a man's eyes, and you're giggling, that looks like flirting. If he holds the door open for you and touches you as you pass by, that makes him look like your boyfriend. You can't expect people to understand the complexities of your relationship with Tyson, so you might want to be careful. I'm sure you know what Devin would think, if he saw the way the two of you are carrying on."

Yolanda nodded. "You're right, Ms. Stewart. I'm sorry if I gave anyone the wrong impression."

"How much longer do you plan on training with him?"

"I start school next month," Yolanda said. "Honestly, I'm almost ready to fly solo right now. But I'll definitely be ready by then. You said I can start calling Priscilla directly, right?"

Korah nodded. "Yep. Hiram finally understands that he can't keep her under lock and key. Priscilla threatened to come back to work for us full time, if he kept trying to stop her from helping out when we get in a bind."

Yolanda's mouth fell open.

"Don't worry," Korah said with a smile. "She's not coming back. You're our bookkeeper, Yolanda. Keep up the good work, and you'll be our vice-president soon."

The girl's smile came back in full flair. "Thank you, Ms. Stewart." She rose to her feet. "Is that all?"

Korah nodded. "Yes, and sorry for asking you all of this personal stuff."

"No, it's fine," Yolanda said. "I'm glad we got everything out in the open."

Thirty seconds after she exited the office, Malcolm returned, but Stephanie pushed past him before he could enter.

"Hold on a second, Mr. Employee of the Month."

She closed the door on his startled expression.

"What'd she say?"

"I know you didn't close the door on my assistant," Korah said.

"He'll be alright," Stephanie replied. "What did Yolanda say?"

"She said she and Devin are still together, still living together, and she and Tyson are *just friends*. She's known Tyson since middle school, and they're very close. She said he'll be done training her next month."

Stephanie folded her arms over her stomach, clearly not ready to let go of her suspicion. "You believe her?"

"Yes, I do," Korah said. "And I can't believe you slept with *Tony*! You'd better not let me find out it happened in my house."

"Why you trying to flip it on me? I was just being honest."

"Get out of my office," Korah told her. "And don't you dare slam a door in Malcolm's face again. He's the only person in this building that I like right about now."

"Mama—"

"*Security*!" Korah shouted.

She was kidding, but Malcolm opened the door a second later. "Is everything okay, Ms. Stewart?"

Korah laughed, while her daughter turned and gave him the evil eye.

"*Move*!" Stephanie barked as she stormed out of the office.

Malcolm gave her a wide berth. "She's, um, she's a feisty one," he said when she was out of earshot.

"She's all bark," Korah assured him. "You don't need to worry about her at all..."

● ● ● ● ● ●

At the new school site, Devin was happy to finally have real construction underway. But he found that nothing was easy for him on a Brick House site. The surveyors Brick forced him to use were professional, and Devin grudgingly admitted they did as good a job as the guys he tried to bring in.

Since the little *incident* between him and Brick, Devin made a sincere effort to be more professional himself. He checked the fax machine in his trailer a few times each day to make sure he didn't miss any important memos from the man in charge. And, in an attempt to avoid another frustrating confrontation, Devin sent Brick a memo himself in regards to the architectural designs for the school's training center.

He thought that would keep the asshole out of his hair, but no such luck. Before lunchtime that Wednesday, Devin looked into the horizon and saw the Brick House CEO's work truck rumbling towards his trailer, kicking up dust in the afternoon breeze. Devin prayed he would keep on rolling by, but Brick pulled to a stop on the outskirts of the work area and hopped out of his truck wearing another suit; this one was tuxedo black with a white shirt and black tie.

"Yo, he's coming for you," one of Devin's workers joked. "What you done did this time?"

Devin couldn't think of anything, and the mean look he fixed on his employee made it clear that he didn't find any of this amusing. Lately he'd been engaged in an inner conflict that left him increasingly angry and mentally drained. On one hand, he appreciated the school job and was grateful for the opportunity to lead such an important project. But on the other hand, Devin hated Brick, and he wished his mother hadn't put him in such an uncomfortable situation.

Did Korah really expect him to play nice with her boyfriend for the next year and a half – or however long it took them to finish this godforsaken field? If so, why hadn't she told Brick to do the same? The football field was not physically connected to the school. It shouldn't be that hard for Brick to keep his ass over *there*, and let Texas Builders do the job he hired them to do over *here*.

Brick plucked a hardhat from the bed of his truck and pushed it down on his head as he made his way towards his future training center. He had a single sheet of paper gripped in one fist.

Devin turned and stared at him, rather than make any move to meet him halfway.

He concentrated on his breathing, making sure his breaths were slow and steady. Yolanda told him that if he felt himself getting angry, he could thwart it with this breathing exercise. Devin didn't know if that was true, but he knew he had a temper problem, and he appreciated his woman's attempts to help keep him levelheaded.

When Brick was close enough to speak without raising his voice, he said, "Howdy," with a casual nod of his head.

Devin wasn't expecting him to be friendly. It took him a moment to return the greeting. "Morning. What can I do for you?"

Brick grinned. He had the swagger of a bull rider and the arrogance of the only sheriff in town. Devin forgot that he was supposed to be monitoring his breathing. He clenched his jaws closed, rather than ask what the hell he was smiling at.

"Got your memo," Brick said, showing him the piece of paper in his hand.

Devin typed it up himself, so he had no cause to read it again.

"Looks like you wanna bring in another construction company," Brick continued.

So there it was. The control freak wanted to micromanage again. No surprise there.

"I sent the memo, so you'd know about it ahead of time," Devin said. "Isn't that what you asked me to do?"

"Yes," Brick said. His brown eyes were filled with cunning and confidence. "But I'm curious about why you want to bring in another company," he said. "Seems like if I hire you for a job, *you* should do it. If I wanted some other company to do it, I would've hired them."

Devin shook his head. "No offense, Mr. Avery, but I think you're a little *too* involved in our work over here."

Brick cocked his head slightly. "Is that right?"

"I'm only bringing in Victory Construction to do the roof of the training center," Devin said. "We're doing everything else ourselves; the field, the bleachers and the rest of the training center. That's all us."

175

"But why do you need Victory to do the roof?" Brick wanted to know. "Why can't you do the roof?"

Devin closed his eyes for a moment and remembered his breathing. In and out. Slow and sweet. When he opened his eyes, Brick was still standing there waiting for an answer. But he wasn't really, because he already knew.

According to the school designs, the main building would have a unique, curved roof that, while beautiful, was too complicated and time-consuming for Texas Builders to reproduce. The problem with that was, the designs called for the roof to be duplicated on a smaller scale for the training center.

It was not uncommon for a construction company to bring in another team to handle designs of this nature, even if the first company was subcontracted themselves. So why was Brick in his face about this? Devin didn't have to rack his brain to figure it out. The bastard wanted to keep his thumb on every little thing taking place on the property. But he was a fool if he thought Devin would continue taking his shit.

"I sent you a memo," he said flatly. "You said you wanted to know ahead of time, and I told you. So what's your problem now? You only want me to use your people for that, too?"

Brick continued to smile when he said, "Son, I don't think you like me."

"I'm not your son."

Devin regretted his words the moment they left his mouth. But he also felt liberated. In most cases a bully will back down if you stand up to him. And that's what this was all about, wasn't it? Brick was flexing his muscles because he had all of the good cards in his hand.

As predicted, the boss-man's smug smile slipped from his face. He stood up straighter and seemed to puff out his chest as he stared at his girlfriend's son. Not to be outdone, Devin straightened his back and matched his animosity pound for pound. They were nearly the same height. Brick's brawn was concealed by his suit, while Devin's toned muscles stretched the fabric of his golf shirt.

"Who do you think's building the roof on the school?" Brick asked. Before Devin could answer, he said, "Me. *Brick House.* That's who. I wish I had known you'd have a problem with such a simple design."

That was a low blow. Texas Builders could build the roof just as well as his company. Devin's decision to subcontract was based on time and manpower. The sooner he finished his work there, the sooner he could get away from Brick and avoid senseless skirmishes like the one he was currently embroiled in.

"Alright, we'll build the roof ourselves," he said. "Is that what you want?"

"That's what I wanted when I came over here," Brick acknowledged. "But now I want to know why you think I have to tolerate your attitude. Far as I can tell, I never did a goddamned thing to warrant the aggression I get every time I look your way. You mad 'cause I'm dating your mama? That what it is? That what's got your panties in a bunch?"

The muscles in Devin's right shoulder twitched. In his mind's eye, he saw himself take a swing at the old man. The vision was so clear and so wonderful, Devin had to take a step back, to make sure he didn't do it for real.

"Alright, well let me break it down for you," Brick said. His voice was deep and grumbling. He spoke so loudly, a few of Devin's crewmembers stopped what they were doing to watch the argument.

"You're here because I want you here," Brick barked. "When I decide I don't want you here, then your ass ain't here no more. From here on out, you don't subcontract nothing but glass, electrical and plumbing! If you can't build the roof on that training center, then I'll build it my goddamned self. And if you got a problem with that, then I'll build all of this shit. You can pack up your rinky-dink crew and hit the highway right now!

"This is not a 7-11. This is the biggest job site you've ever been on. So you'd better learn to show some appreciation. Act like you want the work, and stop trying to bring in other people to do it for you. And when the contractor shows up at your trailer, don't forget that's the man who's writing your checks. *I'm the man writing your checks!*" Brick shouted, jabbing a thumb at his own chest.

"Don't forget that shit, Devin. And you'd better stop eyeballing me, boy."

The men continued to stare each other down while the workers looked on in shock and the beautiful birds of May flitted about the skies above them.

Brick was the first to look away. He turned, actually, and marched back to his truck, leaving Devin standing on the soft, brown earth that would soon be transformed into a football field. Devin took pride in the fact that he won the *stare down*. But it was a fleeting victory, because he knew that it had come at a great cost.

He did not look forward to seeing his mom or his woman today. He could barely look his workers in the eyes when he turned to give them their new assignments.

CHAPTER FIFTEEN
SUNRISE

Brick didn't bother calling ahead. He strolled into Korah's main office one hour after his spat with Devin and didn't slow down for the young man who sat at Yolanda's old desk.

"Excuse me," Malcolm said, rising from his seat. "Excuse me. Sir!"

By the time he caught up with him, Brick had stepped into Korah's office. Malcolm rushed past him with a harried expression, as if he'd allowed the Mongols to penetrate the Great Wall of China.

"Ms. Stewart, I tried to stop him!"

"It's alright," Korah said, looking from her assistant's eyes to Brick's. The latter looked as angry as he did when he tracked down Korah's vandals last October. She couldn't imagine anything she had done to warrant his fury, but Brick obviously wasn't there for a social visit.

"Could you leave us alone for a moment?" she told Malcolm. She tried to remain poised and confident, but she didn't feel that way at all. Brick made her feel weak on a normal day. The way he was staring at her now made Korah want to wilt like a tulip.

"What's going on?" she asked when Malcolm excused himself.

Brick thrust his hand forward, and Korah noticed for the first time that he had a sheet of paper squeezed in his fist. He'd been holding it for so long, the memo was nearly indecipherable. Korah took it from him, and she recognized her company

179

letterhead. She read the note carefully. Her hands were moist with sweat when she looked up at Brick again.

He didn't sit down, which put Korah in a position of inferiority. She wanted to stand as well, but she feared her knees would buckle.

"Did you know about this?" he asked her.

"Why are you so upset?" she replied. "What's going on?"

"You didn't answer my question."

"I didn't write it. No. If that's what you're asking."

"But you knew about it?"

Korah was hesitant to respond. She didn't know if Brick already discussed this with Devin or whether Devin said she approved it or not. Brick was her boyfriend, but she couldn't allow him to divide her company.

"Why don't you sit down," she suggested, "and tell me what's wrong? Why are you upset?"

"I'm upset because I'm sick of arguing with your son," he spat. "I'm sick of him trying to outsource work that I gave to *you*. Did he tell you about the surveyors?"

Dammit. Korah knew she was already on the losing end of this. She could continue avoiding his questions, or she could admit that Devin had kept her in the dark. She chose to be honest. Brick was clearly not in the mood for more bullshit.

"No. What about the surveyors?"

"He brought in another company, even though I told him we would only use Red Eye."

Korah took a deep breath and blew it out slowly. "I'm, I'm sure it was an oversight," she offered.

"Is that what you wanna call it?"

"Brick, I don't know what else it could be. I know he wouldn't purposefully go against your wishes."

"No, I think that's exactly what he did," Brick said. "You only have to talk to him for two minutes to see that he doesn't give a damn about me or my rules."

"I'm pretty sure that's not the case."

"No? Well maybe you should've been there an hour ago when he stared me down, acting like he wanted to throw a punch."

Korah's pulse was racing. Her mind was too. She knew Devin still had issues with Brick, but she thought he had enough sense to put the job first.

"Devin would never do that," she said. "I think you're overreacting."

"I'm overreacting? Is that right? You think I don't know when a man wants to take a swing at me? I don't know when some little punk is mouthing off, being disrespectful? This is all in my head?"

Oh, God. Korah's body went cold and numb. She knew her son well enough to know that everything Brick said was probably true. But it was still hard to believe.

And though she did love the man standing in front of her, she loved her son more. That would probably always be the case. The five million dollar contract was important to her company, but not if it came at the expense of tearing her family apart.

"Listen," she said, trying her best to remain professional, rather than sound like an angry mama bear. "I don't like the way you're talking about my son. If you were as rude to him as you're being right now, that's probably why he reacted to you the way he did. Devin knows what he's doing. And you know he's not completely comfortable with you. I'd hate to think you initiated this confrontation, just to egg him on. I think the three of us need to sit down—"

"Did you know he wanted to outsource the work on the roof of the training center?" Brick demanded, completely ignoring her.

"No," Korah said. "No, I didn't. Okay? But that's not a big deal. Why are you so upset about it?"

Brick stared at her for a few seconds, and then it hit him. He shook his head, like she was the biggest disappointment he'd ever seen.

"You didn't build the roof on your mother's church, did you?"

That question seemed to come completely out of left field. Korah knew exactly what he was referring to, but she couldn't help but ask, "What are you talking about?"

"Your mother's church, on the south side," he said. "It's on the intersection of Illinois and Hattie. You remember that church?"

Korah seethed. She knew the church very well, and she didn't appreciate the tone Brick used while referencing it. Her mother fell in love with Sunrise Baptist shortly after they moved from Chicago in 1980.

A few years after her mother's death, Korah remodeled the church from the ground up. The finished product was one of her most notable constructions. It was also the only job that put her in the red, but she didn't do it for money.

The most notable aspect of the new church was a horn-shaped roof that was nothing short of an architectural masterpiece. The first time they met, Brick told Korah he visited the church and was extremely impressed with her work.

"I never said we built that roof," Korah said. She spoke with a defeated tone that did not acknowledge the powerhouse she had become.

"Yes, you did," Brick said. "When I asked you about the church, you said you built that roof. I asked you about it specifically."

"Brick, when you asked me that, we were competing for a job."

"So you lied?"

"No, I didn't lie. I just didn't tell you we outsourced it. If you wanted to believe we built it, that was fine with me. But like I said, we were in different places then. If you had asked again before you wrote up the papers for the school, I would've told you we didn't build the roof."

They stared at each other for what felt like a very long time. Korah watched his chest rise and fall as he took slow, deep breaths. She felt like a total failure, although she knew that wasn't the case. There was nothing wrong with outsourcing the roof work on the church, and there was nothing wrong with Devin outsourcing work for the training center. She suspected Brick's grievance had more to do with Devin than the job they were hired to do.

"Do you want us to finish at the school?" she finally gathered enough courage to ask.

Her heart didn't beat at all in the few seconds it took Brick to respond.

"We have a contract. I'm not going to breech it."

That didn't sound like he wanted them there, but it was good enough. Korah quietly blew out a sigh of relief.

"Do you want me to remove Devin from the site?"

"Do you have someone to replace him?" Brick asked right away.

"Yes," Korah said, thinking of Baron. "I can have a new foreman there tomorrow morning."

"That'd be fine," Brick said.

He turned and left the office without so much as a *Goodbye,* but that was better than how Korah expected their conversation to end, so she had to count her blessings.

Malcolm appeared in her doorway a moment later, looking like a terrified sheep who barely managed to evade the big, bad wolf.

"Ms. Stewart, are you alright?"

Korah closed her eyes and tried to steady her breathing. She nodded. "Yeah."

"Wasn't that your boyfriend?"

Korah opened her eyes, and he saw how much the conversation took from her. Five minutes ago she was on top of the world. Now she looked completely frazzled.

"No," she told him. "That wasn't Brick, the boyfriend. That was Brick, the contractor."

"Oh." He gave that some thought. "I don't like Brick, the contractor."

Korah smiled weakly. "I don't either. But with Brick, you gotta take the good with the bad."

"Hmmm. Well, I hope there's more good than bad."

"Of course," Korah said. This time her smile was genuine. "Brick's a big, old teddy bear."

"What about your son?" Malcolm asked. "When are you gonna give him the bad news?"

"After work. Might as well let him finish the shift..."

● ● ● ● ● ●

Devin was surprised when he didn't hear from his mother for the rest of day. He didn't hear from Brick, either. But he knew it wasn't over. He checked his phone at five-thirty, when he told his men to pack it up for the day. He noticed that he had missed a couple of text messages.

The one from Yolanda said, What did you do now?

183

The one from his mother said, Stop by the office on your way home

Devin's features darkened as he returned the phone to his pocket.

When he made it to the Texas Builders' headquarters an hour later, he saw that his mother's car was the only one still there. Inside the building, the place seemed eerily quiet. Devin walked slowly to his mother's office, his mind racing, plotting and scheming.

When he rounded the corner, Korah looked up and stared at him through her open office door. Her dear son looked tired and stressed, beaten by the world. Devin saw his memo on her desk as he approached. It was badly wrinkled, as if Brick had it gripped tightly in his fist during the whole ride from Dallas.

If he took the time to bring it, rather than simply call, then the Brick House CEO was surely fuming. Devin looked from the memo to his mother's eyes, and he was momentarily transported back in time. He was thirteen years old again, and she had his eighth grade report card. He had four C's and three low B's. On that day, his mother had told him he'd never amount to anything, if he settled for mediocrity.

"Have a seat," she said.

Devin thought it had been a while since his mother looked this commanding. He was suddenly glad he was her son. If anyone else had behaved so badly, they would probably get a pink slip. But his familial bond would save him.

He shook his head. "Mama, I just want to stand."

"I said sit down."

Her voice was stern. Authoritative. Devin knew there would be little recourse for his insolence. It wasn't like she'd pull off her belt and commence to whoop his ass. But he quickly planted his butt in the seat, just in case.

She asked, "Why didn't you tell me about the surveyors?"

Devin rolled his eyes before saying, "It wasn't a problem. He said he didn't want my guys there, so I didn't use them. That's all there was to it."

"You didn't have a problem with Brick saying you couldn't use your guys?"

"Do *you* have a problem with it?"

"Why would I? I'm way over here in the office."

"Then I don't have a problem with it, either."

Korah stared at him for a second before asking, "What about Brick? Is there something you want to say about him?"

Devin shook his head. "Nope."

"You don't think he's controlling?" Korah asked. "You didn't have a problem when he said you couldn't bring in this roofing company, either?"

She pushed the crushed memo across the desk.

Devin didn't look down at it. "If you already talked to him, why you asking me?"

"I want your side of the story."

"I don't like him," Devin admitted. He knew that was hurtful for his mom, but it felt good to get the burden off his chest. "But I don't have to like him to do this job."

If Korah was offended by his comment, she hid it well. "Yeah, that's what I thought, too. I thought you were level-headed enough to get in there and do the job, despite your personal grievances."

Devin's nostrils flared as he sucked down a deep breath.

"You don't like the way Brick is on the site, or you don't like him because I'm with him?" his mother asked.

"Neither one," Devin said, a slight sneer wrinkling his nose.

Korah shook her head. She brought a hand up and slowly rubbed her temple.

"Mama, why you with him?" Devin wanted to know. "You know he's a player. He's just gonna hurt you."

"He has never mistreated me," Korah stated. "I hoped you would get over your childish attitude by now. Brick and I have been together for eight months. When is he supposed to do this awful thing you're waiting for? He's a good man. He hired us to work on his school–"

"We don't need his job, Mama. We don't need his handouts."

"*Handouts*? Since when is a contract a handout? Even with only a third of the school, this is one of the biggest jobs we've ever had. The exposure we're getting is immeasurable. But we don't need it, just because you don't like Brick? Do you realize how ignorant that sounds?"

"I knew you were gonna take his side," Devin grumbled. "I'm your *family*. Did you forget that?"

185

"No, I didn't forget. That's the only reason you're in my face right now. If it was anyone else, I would've had you escorted off the school site the moment Brick left my office."

Devin's sneer intensified. He exhaled roughly.

"This isn't about him against you," Korah said, not realizing her volume was steadily on the rise. "This is a *business decision*," she stated. "Because this is a *business*! And today you made a *bad business decision*. You've been making them, every time Brick comes your way."

"I didn't—"

"Everybody knows the construction foreman bends over backwards for the contractor!" Korah shouted. "Everybody knows that. You paint a smile on your face. You tell him everything is great. And if he says you have a problem, then you apologize and fix it!"

"I'm not kissing his ass," Devin stated.

Korah nodded. "Yeah. I know. That's why you're not going back to the school."

Devin was stunned silent. He couldn't hide his surprise. Korah continued speaking, while his mouth hung open.

"Starting tomorrow Baron is the lead foreman at the school. You can take over his role as the lead on our other sites."

"You gonna kick me off the school job?"

It hurt her to treat him this way, but she didn't have on her Mother hat right now. Korah's voice was without sympathy when she said, "You left me no choice."

"I'm not going back to those little jobs," Devin decided. "This ain't right, Mama! You don't even care about what that man has been doing to me."

"Well here's your chance, Devin! Tell me what *that man* has been doing to you. Tell me right now!"

When he came up empty, Devin doubled-down on his threat. "I'm not going back to those little jobs. I don't have to work at all."

Korah's heart kicked like a woofer, but she made her next executive decision without hesitation.

"That sounds like a good idea. I think you do need some time off, to get your head on straight. Call me when you're feeling better, and we'll talk."

Devin saw red behind his pupils. His whole body felt scorching hot. He didn't think he'd ever been this angry. "*My head is on straight,*" he growled.

"Thank you for stopping by," Korah told him. She purposefully swiveled her chair to the right, until she was facing her computer. She willed her hand to stop shaking as she reached for the mouse and resumed her work.

Her son remained seated, his breaths now audible. Korah did not look his way again.

"I said thank you, sir. Could you please leave my office?"

She didn't think he would, but Devin pushed away from the desk and made a show of storming out of the building. When she heard his work truck start and speed out of the parking lot, Korah finally gave in to her own emotions.

But only for a few minutes.

After that she wiped the tears from her eyes and got her breathing under control as she tidied up her work area. She locked up the office and resisted the urge to call Devin during the drive home. As she navigated the interstate, she ran their conversation through her mind over and over again and kept coming up with the same thing. She knew that she did what had to be done.

But that didn't mean it was an easy thing to do.

CHAPTER SIXTEEN
DID YOU EVER?

*Alone without vision or moonlight. The dark
Is overwhelming. I'm cowering. I'm floundering. I'm stark
Naked. This place is beyond freezing. My shivering
Bones are Morse code, quickening. I'm withering
Away. I'm decaying. I'm rotting. I'm rotten
I'm blinded by the signs. All warnings forgotten*

Korah called Brick before she undressed or cooked dinner that evening. The look in his eyes the last time they spoke was all she could think about. She didn't want to talk business anymore. She was tired of arguing. She wanted to speak to him as his girlfriend. She needed him to comfort her and tell her everything would be alright. But before they could push work to the side, she had to let him know about the changes she'd implemented.

When Brick answered, she thought he still sounded irritated. "Hey."

"Hi," she said. "You made it home yet?"

"No. I'm on the road."

"I wanted to apologize again for what happened on the site today – for what's been going on between you and Devin. It's not right, and you don't deserve it. He has been replaced as the lead foreman. Baron Grant is taking his place. He's been with us for five years. He's very professional. Knows his stuff. I'm positive you won't have any problems with him. And Devin won't be on your site at all."

Brick grunted and said something she didn't hear.

"What was that?"

"I said I don't deserve the shit your son's been giving me."

"I know," Korah said. She sighed. "I agree with you."

"Did you talk to him?" Brick asked. "Did he say what his problem is? Aside from lying to him when we first met, I have always treated him with respect. But he doesn't respect me. I've never been treated like that by someone who is *working for me*."

Korah closed her eyes, shaking her head slightly. It hurt her to see that he was still holding on to his anger. She felt like her world was being torn in half, with Devin on one side and Brick on the other.

"I never should've allowed him on my site," he continued. "I knew how he felt ahead of time. I don't know why I thought it would be any different."

"He has problems with his temper," Korah explained. "Some of his issues have nothing to do with you."

"Really? That's another nice piece of information I could've used, before I invited him to my site. I'm, this whole thing was something that could've been avoided."

"What whole thing? Hiring us to work on the school?"

"Well... yeah, Korah. This is why I don't like to mix business with pleasure. Once feelings get involved, people make bad decisions. Don't think straight."

Korah couldn't believe what she was hearing. She sat up on the couch, her eyes wide, her brows furrowed. "What are you saying?"

"I'm saying if I had been in a more rational mind state, I... Maybe I would've made better choices. You, I mean, do you think you would've been my first option, if we weren't in a relationship?"

"No, Brick. I don't think that. But are you saying you regret it?"

"I don't know. Maybe. I know I would've done more research."

"What?" She couldn't believe he was on the verge of insulting her company. "What the hell are you talking about?"

"*Research*, Korah." He was growing more heated by the second. The gridlock traffic he was stuck in didn't help any. "I would've checked to make sure I got along with the foreman," he said. "I would've checked to see if you really built the roof on your mother's church. I certainly would've taken those problems you had with the Harden Shopping Center into consideration."

Korah's mouth hung open. How long was he going to harp on that church roof? And did he really bring the shopping center into this? That was nearly a decade ago, and they didn't have their own construction company at the time. The company she hired was the one who screwed up the shopping center, and Brick knew that.

"I did not ask to work on your site," she breathed. "You asked me. You asked me more than once before I agreed to it."

"Yeah, and I just told you why."

"Because of your feelings?"

"Yeah. That's what I said."

Korah couldn't stop her frustration from building momentum as the argument escalated. "If you want us off the property, we'll leave. I won't cause any trouble over the contract. I'll write up a new one, as a matter of fact, absolving you of any wrongdoing."

After a moment, he said, "I'm not kicking you off the site. I'm just, I think this is getting too problematic; trying to juggle our work and our relationship."

Korah shook her head again. She closed her eyes a moment before they blurred with tears.

"So if you're not kicking us off the site, what are you saying? You don't want to be in a relationship anymore?"

When he hesitated, she said, "You're just using this as an excuse. We didn't do anything wrong on your site, and you know it. I took care of your problem with Devin. So what more do you want?"

No response.

"You don't know what you want, because it's not about work," she breathed. "You never see any relationship through. You've probably been looking for an out for God knows how long."

Brick finally found his voice. "I don't – I didn't say I wanted to end it. I just don't think I can deal with our relationship while this school work is going on. When I argued with your son today, I felt hindered by our relationship. Everything I wanted to say or do, I couldn't, because he's your son."

"You're going to be working on this school for two years," Korah said. "Are you saying you want to put our relationship on hold for *two years*? Is that what you're saying?"

She heard him sigh roughly, but that was all the response he gave.

Korah opened her eyes, and the tears spilled freely. She blew warm, moist fumes from her nostrils. "Did you ever love me?" she managed to ask without her voice trembling.

Brick heard the pain in her question and it weakened him. Some of the things she said were correct, while others were not. She didn't seem to understand how *restricted* Devin made him feel this afternoon. Brick was at the top of his game. He was rich and single and in charge. There were few people he had to answer to. But because of Korah, he was somehow constrained. But it wasn't just her. All relationships came with that. Brick sensed that's why he generally shied away from them.

Relationships.

Was it not possible to be with a woman without giving up any part of yourself? When is a woman worth the limitations that piggybacked every commitment? If ever there was one, Korah was it. But was she, really?

He didn't think it took him more than a couple of seconds to respond, but when he opened his mouth to speak, he found that Korah had already disconnected.

● ● ● ● ● ●

As distraught as she was, Korah only allowed herself a moment to dwell in self-pity. She still had a company to run, and she had an obligation to fulfill. Maybe Brick couldn't separate his work and his feelings, but Korah certainly could. The Brick House CEO was her least favorite person in the world right now, but she intended to remain professional with the work they were doing for him.

She called Baron Grant. She cleared her throat and rubbed the tears from her eyes while his phone rang.

"Hello?"

"Hi, Baron? This is Korah." Her voice sounded perfectly normal.

"Uh, oh, Ms. Stewart? Hi. Um, sorry – you caught me eating. What can I do for you?"

"Sorry to disturb your dinner."

"Oh, uh, no. It's no problem. What's, what can I do for you?"

191

"I need you to take the lead at the school job, starting tomorrow."

"You, um, tomorrow?"

"Yes, sir."

"What about Devin?"

"He's taking a leave of absence."

"Oh, is, is everything okay?"

"Yes, everything is fine. I need you to promote someone to be lead foreman at the bank site, and promote someone else to lead the other jobs."

"Me? You want me to do it? What about Dev–"

"Devin is taking a leave of absence," she repeated. "You are my lead foreman, while he's away. If you can't do it, I need to know now. I know this is short notice, but I need you to get on the ball. Time is of the essence."

"Okay. Yes, ma'am. I can do it."

"Do you have someone in mind for the other jobs?"

"Uh, yes. Yes ma'am."

"Alright. I want to meet with all three of you in my office tomorrow morning. I need y'all to be there at seven, because you still have to get to the other jobs by eight. Please contact the other two men now, to make sure they get enough sleep. If you have any trouble, or you're not able to get in touch with both of them, call me back tonight."

"Yes, ma'am. I'll take care of it."

"Okay, thank you, sir. You have a good evening."

"Yes, Ms. Stewart. You too, ma'am. Thank you, ma'am."

● ● ● ● ● ●

Twenty miles away, in a quiet, north side neighborhood, Yolanda sat on the living room couch nibbling on her fingernails. Nail-biting was a bad habit that she was able to overcome in her early twenties. But every now and then she had a relapse. Today her stress level was shooting past manageability. She needed a release, and her poor fingernails paid the price. She stared at the TV and then the clock and then the TV again. Gradually her attention returned to her nails, which didn't look great after being worked over by her teeth.

At seven o'clock Devin still hadn't called. She was reluctant to call him, because she knew he was probably meeting with his mother. She worried about what his mindset would be after the meeting. She didn't want to be there to experience it, but she felt obligated. She was his woman, wasn't she? They had been dating for over a year, yet he hadn't proposed to her. She figured that was probably for the best, but she was still his woman.

Devin finally lurched through the door at 7:15. He had a beer in hand. It was a 24 ounce can of Colt 45, a *tall boy*, as her brothers would call it. The beer can was sheathed in a skinny paper bag, which made Devin look like a wino. He closed the door and regarded his girlfriend sheepishly. Yolanda's expression was a mixture of pity and weariness.

"You drinking and driving now?"

He shook his head. He made his way to his easy chair and sat down slowly. Yolanda watched as the weight of his disappointing day began to unravel, causing his shoulders and head to slump. He looked beat-down, like a heavyweight throwing in the towel at the beginning of the twelfth round.

"I didn't open this until I got here," he said, referring to his beer. He brought the can to his lips and took a long, slow pull.

Devin was known to be a casual drinker, but bringing alcohol home was something new for him. Yolanda tried to remember when it started. She knew that Brick had been the catalyst recently.

"What happened at work?" she asked. "Did you talk to your mom?"

He nodded, his eyes rolling towards the television. "Yeah. I talked to her."

Yolanda waited for more, but that was all he offered.

"What did she say? What happened between you and Brick?"

"He's fucking with me," Devin explained. "And Mama took his side. She always takes his side."

From experience, Yolanda knew there was probably more to it than that.

"What did he do?"

Devin turned and stared at her. There was something strange about his expression that gave Yolanda a chill down her back. That was new, too. He never made her feel like that before.

193

"He got mad because I wanted to bring in another crew to do the roof on the training center," he said. "He asked me to let him know ahead of time, if I was bringing another company in. When I did, he jumped down my throat. Talked to me like, like I wasn't nothing."

The chill Yolanda felt a moment ago now enveloped her heart as well. Korah didn't tell her much about Devin and Brick's confrontation, only that they had an argument. This sounded like something much worse.

"You said something back?" she asked.

He nodded. "I stood up for myself. And if he would've took a swing at me, I was ready to defend myself from that, too."

Yolanda's eyebrows bunched together. "Y'all were gonna fight?"

"Whatever," Devin said. His eyes rolled back to the television.

His girlfriend's face was a mask of confusion. There was too much missing from his story.

"Why would he get mad about you bringing in another company?"

"That's what I told Mama. He didn't have no reason to bitch about that. He just wants to control everything. He stays on my ass."

"Well, how did he tell you?" she wondered. "He just walked up and started yelling at you?"

"He brought my memo back, all balled up in his fist. He was pissed. He was talking down on our company; talking about why can't we build the roof ourselves, and did we need him to build it for us. He was out of line. But Mama don't think so. She said I can't go back there. I can't go back to work at all."

Yolanda's eyes widened. Her mouth fell open as well. "*She suspended you?*"

"Yeah," Devin said, glad to finally have someone in his corner. He regained eye contact. "She took his side over mine. She wouldn't even listen to what I tried to tell her."

Yolanda brought a hand to her face. She continued to stare at him in shock as she scratched the side of her head. That didn't sound like Ms. Stewart at all. The school contract meant a lot to their company, but she wouldn't suspend Devin if Brick was totally in the wrong, would she? Yolanda had to remind herself that there are always two sides to every story. So far she had only heard Devin's, and it didn't make any sense.

"Did, couldn't you have told Brick, '*Okay*,' when he talked to you, regardless of what he was saying?"

Devin's eyes flashed with anger, and she knew that she had stumbled onto something.

"Why should I bow down to him? He ain't no better than me."

Yolanda felt she was treading on thin ice, but she couldn't placate her boyfriend, not this time.

"But he's the *contractor*, Devin." She spoke softly, hoping to soften the blow. "If the contractor wants the building to be green, and you already painted it red, then you apologize and repaint it. You're supposed to do whatever the contractor says. You know that. I don't think that's bowing down. That's just business. He hired you."

Devin shook his head in wonderment. "So you're siding with him, just like Mama?"

Yolanda sighed. "If your mother told you to treat Brick like he's your boss, then yeah. I am siding with her. Because on that site, Brick is in charge. Sounds like you're letting your personal beef with him get in the way of business."

"Man, fuck this shit!"

Devin stood so quickly, a slight scream shot up Yolanda's throat.

"*Why you always gotta side with her*?" he bellowed.

He stood over his girlfriend, leaned over her. She brought up both arms in a defensive motion.

"*You're supposed to be my woman! Why can't you ever be on my side?*"

"*Because you're wrong!*"

The volume of Yolanda's voice somehow rivaled his. She wasn't sure where she found the strength or courage to stand up to him. But as her heart thundered, flooding her bloodstream with adrenaline, she was able to rise to her feet as well.

"You let your temper get in the way of everything!" she shouted. They were nose to nose now. The smell of beer on his breath made her nauseous. "You need help!"

"You supposed to be my woman!" Devin said.

He couldn't believe she didn't have his back on this one. He felt betrayed and alone. The enormity of his dilemma and the overwhelming lack of support he received depleted the last of his resolve. He backed away from her. He was tired of arguing. Tired of explaining himself. Tired of everyone.

"I'm finna go," he said, heading for the door.

"Go where?" Yolanda turned to watch him. Her fair skin was red about the eyes and cheeks. Her breaths were quickened, causing her chest to rise and fall noticeably.

"What difference does it make?" Devin said. "We ain't got shit else to talk about."

Yolanda disagreed. They had a lot to talk about. They had a shitload of things that needed to be addressed. But this was Devin's way, wasn't it? He let his temper get the best of him *yet again*. His mouth wrote a check that his ass couldn't cash, and now he wanted to run from it. When it came to real life drama, he had the scruples of a scared, little boy.

"If you leave, I'm not gon' be here when you get back," she threatened.

Devin stopped and stared at her. He didn't know what that meant exactly. Would she really leave him? If so, where would she go? Probably to her mother's house, or to complain to her loud-mouth sisters. Devin decided that was probably for the best. If she wasn't going to be there for him, then he didn't need her there.

He opened the door and stepped out into the dwindling sunset.

• • • • • •

Yolanda did not go to her mother's house, or to complain to her loud-mouth sisters. Instead she called Tyson when she got on the freeway. He said his mother was staying with her sister in Houston for the rest of the week, and she was welcome to come over. Selecting Tyson as a confidant wasn't something Yolanda planned. It was something that was ingrained in their friendship since they were teenagers.

When she first met him, Tyson was a bright, skinny adolescent with a mind for math and reading, which were two subjects Yolanda did not excel in. They hung out in different circles until high school. During their freshman year, they happened to be seated right next to each other in Dr. Carroll's class. One afternoon Tyson caught Yolanda attempting to copy answers from his Algebra exam.

An offer to tutor her blossomed into a rewarding friendship that continued to flourish past their senior year at Finley High, until Tyson moved to Atlanta to start his studies at Morehouse. As teenagers, Tyson constantly challenged Yolanda. He wanted her to be brilliant, to make balanced decisions.

Their relationship was platonic, so they freely talked about the boys and girls they liked. They frequently discussed their plans for the future, which were always grander on Tyson's side. Yolanda knew he would do great things in life. His mother and father would allow nothing less.

Their friendship didn't suffer until they started dating towards the middle of their senior year. Suddenly Tyson's ambition made Yolanda feel inadequate. He never chided her, but he did encourage her to pursue a higher education. She filled out a few college applications, but she wasn't the strongest student. She considered her SAT scores an embarrassment. She found a couple of universities that would take her, but they weren't offering any tuition assistance.

Disillusioned, Yolanda decided people like her should simply get a job after graduation and start building a life of some sort. And that's what she did.

When Tyson returned to Overbrook Meadows to care for his ailing mother, he reached out to a lot of old friends, Yolanda included. It took her a week to build up the nerve to call him back. Once she did, they quickly resumed their friendship and the roles they once played in each other's lives. Tyson began to push her again. He pushed her to learn the accounting required to keep Texas Builders afloat. And he pushed her to want better for herself, in all aspects of her life.

Devin was often a topic of conversation.

Lately, usually during her drive home from work, Yolanda began to ask herself if she deserved a man like him; a man who was quick to anger, slow to apologize. A man who rarely considered the repercussions before he spoke.

Of course Tyson was the exact opposite in every way. But Yolanda didn't want to be with him, either. Their friendship was perfect, just like it was in high school. They complicated things back then; made it all the way to third base once. But they were smart enough to see the error of their ways and resume their friendship afterwards.

As for Tyson's current flirting, Yolanda didn't think he was serious. He was a sexy man. No doubt. Smart, funny, successful and sweet. He told her the time they'd been apart changed both of them. He thought that if they tried to date again, as adults, they would fit perfectly this time, like two long, lost puzzle pieces.

Yolanda knew that it was dangerous to visit a man who felt that way. But right now she was broken. Tyson always knew what to say to make her feel better.

She knocked on his door as the last traces of sunlight disappeared from the evening sky. A moment later, he answered. Yolanda was surprised to see him dressed casually in shorts and a tee shirt. But that was silly of her. Just because he dressed so crisply at work did not mean he didn't unwind at home like everyone else.

Yolanda saw that he wasn't so skinny anymore. He didn't have Devin's size or definition in his muscles, but Tyson filled out nicely. He had strong arms, beautiful dark skin.

Noticing her wet, swollen eyes, his expression immediately registered empathy. He reached and took her hand. His hand was soft, where Devin's had rough spots and hard calluses.

There were so many differences.

Yolanda's throat caught as she followed him inside. Tyson reached and closed the door behind her.

She felt like she was sealing her fate as he turned the knob on the dead bolt, effectively locking her inside.

CHAPTER SEVENTEEN
COUNSEL

A week later everything was looking peachy at the Brick House empire. The man sitting on the throne leaned back in his executive chair as he looked over the reports his partner prepared for him, detailing their first quarter earnings. When he first started the company twenty-five years ago, Brick was fresh out of college, and he would've gone crazy over numbers like these.

His office was big and masculine, decorated with a stylish western theme. Brick wore a slim, navy blue wool suit that fit him perfectly. His hair was recently trimmed, his face clean-shaven. His straw-brown eyes were soft and contemplative. He looked like a million bucks, and he should have felt like it too. But he didn't have the smile Isaac expected to see when he stopped by his office and noticed him looking over the reports.

Isaac was eager to get home to his wife, but he stuck his head in the door and asked, "Hey boss. You working late tonight?"

Brick looked up at him, and he did smile then. He shook his head. "Nah. I'm right behind you."

"What do you think of those numbers?" Isaac asked.

He was a short man, not too round about the waist, but a few more servings of his wife's beans and cornbread might get him there. He was a brilliant man. Brick had known him since their college days at Texas A&M. He brought Isaac in to balance the books and prepare contracts the day Brick House was founded. Since then, Isaac had become a full-fledged partner. Brick could win clients over with a warm smile and a strong handshake, but it was Isaac's skills with numbers that ensured every contract was profitable.

"I think we're doing great," Brick said to him. "Keep up the good work."

His old friend shook his head, but his smile remained. "Keep up the good work? I don't know if you actually read that damned thing, but we made more in the first quarter of this year than we did all of last year. I'd say that deserves a little more than '*We're doing great*.'"

"Yeah," Brick said. He nodded and pushed his smile a little wider.

Isaac shook his head as he entered the office. He took a seat across from his friend and sighed.

"Alright, man. Tell me what the problem is."

"Go home, old man. Don't you have plans with Lisa?"

"I got a few minutes to spare."

"Don't waste them on me," Brick told him. He placed the report on his desk and moved to turn off his computer.

"Susie tell you we got the new Dole plant?"

"Uh, yeah," Brick replied. "I think she said something about that."

"Alright, now I *know* something's wrong," Isaac said. "A month ago, that bid was all you cared about. Industrial Works beats us every time. You said you'd dance a jig the day we finally won a contract over them."

Brick chuckled. "Dance a jig? I said that?"

"Clearly those were happier times," Isaac deduced. "What gives, boss? You still upset about what happened between you and Korah's son?"

Brick's smile disappeared, and his friend's did as well.

"What do you know about it?" Brick asked.

Isaac never visited their sites. This didn't seem like the kind of gossip that would make it all the way back to him.

"You had the man replaced," Isaac said. "That's kind of a big deal."

Brick looked down at his desk in embarrassment.

"How's the new guy working out?" Isaac asked.

"Baron? He's great," Brick muttered. "No problem there."

"You and Devin got over your little rift yet?"

Brick frowned. He shook his head. "I don't think that's gonna happen."

Isaac was quiet for a few seconds. "How has this affected you and Korah's relationship?"

Brick grimaced slightly. He shook his head again.

Isaac lowered his bald head and rubbed his forehead. "You run her off too, didn't you?"

"I'm not the one who ran her son off," Brick said. "If you know so much, then you should know what he said to me."

"I heard he wasn't showing you enough respect."

"More like none at all."

"And that's important..."

"Hell yeah it is."

"So instead of trying to work it out, you run him off the site..."

"He ran hisself off the site. Don't put that on me."

"They say you confronted him about a memo he sent you."

Brick kept quiet.

"They say he did everything you asked him to, but you still threw a fit."

"Who the hell is *they*?"

"Doesn't matter."

Brick shook his head in frustration. "I was upset because he couldn't build the roof on the training center."

Isaac kept his tone neutral when he said, "People subcontract work all the time, Brick. I don't see what the problem is."

"The problem is I thought they could do it. I didn't know I was hiring amateurs."

"Wow. Now that's harsh. You were singing Texas Builders' praises last year."

"Well, that was last year."

"Before you found out they couldn't build that roof."

"Yeah, that's right." Brick was getting more annoyed by the second. "If you got something to say, you need to say it."

"Alright." Isaac looked him in the eyes. "I think outsourcing work on a roof is not uncommon, for any company. Which means you didn't have a good reason to confront that boy. You did it because you don't like him."

"He didn't like me first." Brick snorted when he realized how childish that sounded.

"And please tell me what Korah has to do with you and Devin's foolishness?"

Brick reached to scratch his temple. "What do you mean? That's her son. If I'm with her, then I gotta be around him. I can't have one without the other. What are we gonna do, avoid each other at family gatherings and shit?"

"So you broke up with her?"

"We're on a break," Brick clarified.

"And that's the best excuse you could come up with, because you don't get along with her son?"

"I told her the relationship is interfering with work."

Isaac stared at him for a second before saying, "But we just agreed that you don't have a problem with Texas Builders on our site. I know they haven't done much yet, but they haven't messed up anything, either."

Brick shook his head. He took a deep breath and blew it loudly from his nostrils. Arguing with Isaac always made him feel stupid.

"So what the hell is your point?"

"I think it's pretty clear you're trying to sabotage your relationship."

"I don't have a reason to do that."

"You've been single so long, it's all you know," Isaac continued. "You got no stick-with-it in you, Brick. No working it out. No compromise. Even if her son did piss you off, you could've found a way to work with it."

Brick soaked in his friend's words, and he thought he might have a point. He was forty-six years old, and he hadn't had to compromise much in his personal life since he moved out of his mother's house. Since then, he'd grown comfortable with the man he'd become. As a matter of fact, his life was great. If something or someone in it went against the grain, all he had to do was remove that person to get things rolling smoothly again.

He hated to think of Korah's son as a malfunctioning cog in his perfect life, but it really was that simple. Brick chose to remove the cog, while Isaac thought he should *try to work it out*. Brick scoffed at that notion. The only people he would try to work it out with were folks who were paying him for a job – not the other way around.

Of course Korah was a casualty in his selfish way of thinking. That did hurt. It hurt a lot. But Brick made plenty of painful decisions as he grew into the man he was today. So far all of those decisions worked out perfectly.

"I think you know Korah's a good woman," Isaac said. "Maybe even the one you're supposed to be with, you know, *'til death do you part.*"

He chuckled when Brick rolled his eyes at that.

Isaac waved him off. "I know you ain't the marrying type, Brick. But if you ever decide you *might be* that kind of guy, I don't think you could do much better than Ms. Korah. But hell, what do I know?" he asked as he rose to his feet. "I'm just a guy who's been married and compromising with the same wonderful woman for almost thirty years. Tomorrow I'm taking my lovely wife on a road trip to Oklahoma – in the new car you bought me."

Brick continued to give him a dirty look.

"But you enjoy your weekend," Isaac said on his way out of the office. "Hope it's not too lonely... But then again, you're used to that. Ain't you, boss?"

It took Brick thirty seconds to come up with a snappy comeback for that, but it was too late. Isaac was long gone by then.

• • • • • •

On Saturday afternoon Devin met with his sister for lunch at Smokey's Barbecue on Lancaster. The restaurant was in a nice area, once upon a time. But over the past twenty years the region endured a steady economic decline. Smokey's was now in a part of town that Devin would generally have no cause to visit. But this was once his father's favorite barbecue joint.

Devin was thirteen when his dad died of prostate cancer in 2001. Stephanie was only six, so her memories of Devin Sr. were a bit foggy. She did know that her father was a hard worker who always put his family first. She knew that he loved Korah fiercely, and Devin Jr. was the spitting image of his father. The resemblance was so strong, she sometimes felt a tug in her heart when she stared into her brother's eyes.

Today was no different, but it wasn't nostalgia that brought a gloom cloud over their table for two. Devin picked at his food

203

like a bird, even though his ribs were so tender, you could literally shake the meat off the bone. Stephanie had a heartier appetite, but her brother's mood threatened to spoil her meal as well. She knew he wanted to talk, so she continued to stuff her face until he was ready.

"How's everything at work?" he finally asked.

Stephanie looked up at him, and he looked down at his plate sheepishly. She rarely saw him this depressed and unsure of himself.

"Okay, I guess," she replied.

"Everything's working out with Baron?" he asked, and he did meet her eyes then.

Stephanie was the one who had to look away this time. She knew he wanted the truth, but sometimes a lie will make people feel better.

"He's doing fine," she said.

"He took over at the school?"

She nodded. "Yeah. Last Monday."

"I guess Brick likes him better..."

She shrugged. "I don't know. I guess. He hasn't complained, or anything."

Devin nodded. "What about Mama?"

"What do you mean?"

"Did she say Baron was doing better than me?"

His little sister frowned. "No. Why would she say that?"

"I don't know. I was just wondering."

"Haven't you talked to her?"

"She called a couple of times this week," he said. "We didn't talk for that long."

"Are y'all still mad at each other?"

"I'm not mad at her. She didn't sound like she was mad at me."

"Did she ask you to come back?"

He thought for a second and then nodded. "Yeah. I guess so."

"What does that mean? She either did, or she didn't."

"She wants me to come back. But she also wants to know how things will be different. I don't have an answer, so I guess I'm not coming back yet."

"Different how?" Stephanie asked around her corn on the cob.

Devin shrugged. "I don't know. I mean, she wants me to get along with people better. I guess she thinks I have an anger problem."

"You are the angriest man I know."

He frowned. "What's that supposed to mean?"

"You're always yelling at people."

"What, you mean at work?"

"Yes, at work. You probably do it in your personal life, too. I don't know about all that."

Stephanie clearly didn't know how to pull a punch, but that was fine. It was actually the reason Devin sought her out for this conversation.

"At work, I just want to make sure the job gets done right," Devin said in his defense.

"Baron gets the job done right, too," his little sister countered. "But he doesn't have to yell at people."

Devin's stomach twisted with envy. Baron was his protégé. He definitely wanted production to continue without him, but, "So you are saying he's better than me..."

"It's not about him being better," Stephanie said. "He's just different. He gives people a warm, fuzzy feeling."

Devin's frown intensified.

"But he's only been a lead for a few months," Stephanie conceded. "I know he did a good job at the airport, but it's too soon to say how he's doing at the school. All I know is there haven't been any complaints."

"What, what about the other jobs? Who's in charge of those?"

"Baron picked a few people. I don't know their names, though. You have to ask him, or Mama."

Devin shook his head. He wasn't ready to talk to either of them about business.

"So are you gonna get fixed or what?" Stephanie asked.

"Fixed? How am I supposed to do that?"

"Stop being so mad all the time."

"It's not like a switch I can flip," he informed her.

"Well, if you want to get back to work, you'd better do something. You know how it goes: The longer you're gone, the more people will see that they can keep it moving without you."

Devin thought that was a horrible thing to say. A dark chill swept over his whole body. But he caught himself just as quickly. There may be qualified foremen who could do what he did, but there was one advantage Devin would always have over them: Texas Builders was a family business, and they weren't family. He was pretty sure his position as lead foreman would always be his, whenever he decided to reclaim it.

"What about Yolanda?" he asked. "Is she still training with ol' boy?"

Stephanie nodded. She dropped the mangled cob on her plate and used a napkin to remove the barbecue sauce that had accumulated on her fingers. "I think I need a wet wipe," she said.

Devin waited impatiently for her to respond to his question.

"They're almost done," she finally said. "I think she'll be on her own next month."

"Really? She's going to take over Priscilla's position all by herself?"

"That's the plan."

"Is she ready?"

"I don't know," Stephanie said. "Why don't you ask her?"

"We, um, we're not talking much."

"That's got to be awkward. Don't y'all live together?"

He sighed and shook his head. "She hasn't been home in a week, since me and Mama had our fight."

Stephanie was surprised to hear that. "Y'all broke up?"

"No. Not officially. I don't think so. She took a lot of stuff out of the house, but she left most of it."

"Wow. That's crazy. What happened?"

Devin continued to shake his head. He didn't know how to explain it. "I think it's been building up for a while. We been arguing, a lot."

For the first time since they sat down, Stephanie looked seriously concerned. "Arguing about what?"

"I don't know," her brother grunted. "Everything. She thinks I have some anger issues, too."

"*Damn.* I hope she doesn't let Tyson swoop in, while y'all are mad at each other."

That comment made Devin's heart freeze up. He tried not to show how rattled he was. "What, why do you say that?"

"Well," Stephanie said, "you know they been really close, since he started working with us..."

Devin knew they were working side by side, but he didn't think anything of it.

"They're good friends from high school," Stephanie went on. "Did she tell you that?"

He nodded. "Yeah, but they never dated or nothing, did they?"

"I don't know. What did she say?"

Devin searched his memory bank, but he didn't think he'd ever asked her.

"Me and Mama were talking about them a couple of weeks ago," Stephanie recalled. "We thought they were getting a little *too* close. You know? Always talking and laughing. They go out to lunch together, be in Priscilla's office all by themselves every day..."

Devin felt sick to his stomach. He knew about most of this, but he never considered anything was amiss. He and Yolanda had been in a relationship for over a year. She'd never cheated on him – or at least not that he knew of. He doubted that she'd get too cozy with Tyson right under Korah's nose, but he knew that it could happen, especially with the way he and Yolanda had been at each other's neck every day.

"I don't think they're doing anything," Stephanie offered. "I'm just saying, if you and Yolanda are arguing, you might wanna watch out for that man. Tyson is fine as hell. And he's successful, too."

Devin felt like he might vomit. He'd lost so much recently. Would he lose his woman too? He'd been so wrapped up in his own problems with his mom and Brick, he didn't realize how bad things were at home until it was too late.

"*And* you messed around and made Mama and Brick break up *again*," Stephanie said.

Devin sighed. His sister sure knew how to kick a fellow while he's down. The last time he interfered with his mother's relationship, he accused Brick of being a woman-beater. That turned out to be untrue, but Korah believed him initially and gave her boyfriend the boot. When they reconciled, she implored Devin to stay out of her relationship – especially with the bogus information he was feeding her.

"How did I break them up?" he asked.

"After you and Brick had your little argument, or whatever, he told Mama they needed to chill for a minute."

"How is that my fault?"

"No one wants to be with a woman who got some bad-ass kids," Stephanie informed him. "You don't even live with her, but he still had to put up with your shit."

Devin swallowed roughly. "He told her that? That's why he broke up with her?"

"I don't know," Stephanie admitted. "All I know is he came to the office after you and him got into it, and that's when he said they needed to chill."

Devin grimaced. He felt lower than dirt. Initially he would've preferred to see his mother alone, rather than with someone like Brick. But the contractors had been together since September, and Korah was genuinely happy with him in her life. Regardless of how Devin felt about her boyfriend, he would never intentionally take his mother's joy away.

"Maybe it wasn't about me," he mumbled.

"Maybe," Stephanie agreed. "Maybe Yolanda's not cheating with Tyson, either. And maybe Baron's not a better foreman than you. You got a lot of maybes in your life."

"Nice to see you're still the same annoying, little brat you were when we were kids."

Stephanie ignored him. "If you're not gonna eat that," she said in reference to his meal, "let me take it home."

Devin frowned and slid his plate across the table. Stephanie grinned as she moved her leftovers to the side to make room.

• • • • • •

The next day Korah attended Sunday services at Sunrise Baptist, her mother's old church. She wasn't the church-going type, generally. But the pastor at Sunrise was retiring, and this would be his last sermon. Korah knew the pastor well, from back when her mother attended the church. And she would never forget the beautiful eulogy he gave at her mother's funeral. She also spoke with Pastor Miles on a regular basis when she remodeled the building.

Korah took her friend Priscilla with her that morning. Priscilla was Jewish but said she didn't mind Christian services. She was nearly back to her old self by then, and she really wanted to return to work. Failing that, she was always eager to spend time with her "daughter," no matter where they went.

After church, the ladies had lunch at Julie's Café on McCart. Priscilla wanted to know about everything that was happening at Texas Builders, and Korah gladly filled her in. The questions from Yolanda and Tyson were coming so infrequently nowadays, Priscilla knew they were ready to fly without her. It was upsetting to hear that Devin's anger issues had finally led to his suspension.

"He'll be fine," Priscilla assured her. "He does need to mellow out. Maybe this will be the catalyst he's always needed."

"I hope so," Korah said. "It was hard to sit him down, but he didn't leave me a choice. There was no way Brick would take him back on his site."

"That's awful," Priscilla said. "I wish those two boys would find a way to get along. What about your relationship with Brick? Are any of these problems with Devin taking a toll?"

Korah knew the question was coming. "Yeah, they are," she said with a sigh. "Brick and I aren't talking right now."

Priscilla's eyes widened. "What? Why?"

"It was him," Korah said. "He said this was getting to be too much; working together and going together."

"That's silly."

Korah shrugged. "Not for him, it's not."

"Does he hate Devin that much?"

"I don't know. I've been thinking that's just the excuse he's using. You know? I don't think Brick has ever been in a relationship this long. I used to wonder what our expiration date was. I guess now I know."

Priscilla was surprised she could speak about it so calmly. "Are you going to be okay?"

"Me? Sure," Korah said. "You know what they say; everything's a learning experience."

"And what have you learned?"

"I'm getting a bigger shop for our construction team."

Priscilla looked confused. "I don't understand."

"Brick came to the office complaining because Devin told him we couldn't do a roof design," Korah explained. "I don't ever want to be put in that position again. So I'm getting a bigger shop. More workers, less outsourcing."

"Oh. That's, um, that's great, Korah. But I thought you meant you learned something about you and Brick."

"What's to learn?" Korah was surprised to find herself fighting back tears. She thought she was all done crying for that man. "I knew what I was getting into ahead of time. We had fun, and now it's over. Nothing to be upset about."

"Oh, I think there's more to it than that."

Priscilla's motherly wisdom made Korah feel safe and nurtured. A solitary tear spilled from her eye. She wiped it away without embarrassment. She wouldn't feel comfortable displaying this much weakness in front of anyone else.

"It's alright, dear."

The older woman reached across the table and took hold of Korah's hands.

"I don't think this is the end for you two," she said.

Of course Priscilla had no way of knowing that, but Korah clung to her words as if she had an inside scoop.

"Why do you think that?"

"Because you are so good together. He's never going to find another woman who completes him like you do."

Korah agreed with that, but, "I don't think he wants to be complete. He's been single for so long, that's all he knows. He's not willing to put up with anything that makes him uncomfortable. It's too easy to just get rid of it."

"He can get rid of Devin," Priscilla agreed. "But no one can get rid of you – not without it hurting a whole lot. He'll be back."

Korah didn't know why she was putting so much stock in her opinion, but Priscilla's words gave her hope. They also made her cry a little more. But these didn't feel like the same lonely tears.

"The only question is," Priscilla continued, "will you take his silly butt back when he comes crawling?"

That made Korah laugh. It felt good to laugh while thinking about Brick.

"Maybe if he comes bearing gifts," she joked.

"Hiram always does," Priscilla said. "This is from when he called my mother *fat* to her face," she said, showing off an old tennis bracelet that had never lost its beauty.

"Wow. I know Hiram's got a mouth on him, but I never thought he'd do something that crazy."

"My mother was very overweight," Priscilla acknowledged. "But she didn't need to hear it from him. But then again, I wouldn't have got these diamonds if she didn't." She smiled at the memory. "Can't wait to see what Brick gets you," she said with a wink of her eye.

Korah knew she might be waiting on a ghost, but her friend's confidence made her heart flutter. "Yeah," she said. "Me neither."

CHAPTER EIGHTEEN
HUMBLE

Devin spent the rest of the weekend battling stress, depression and jealousy. These were the type of inner conflicts that would usually result in his anger getting the best of him, but anger was the one emotion he would not give into. He dared not. He understood that his temper was on the verge of costing him everything he loved and held dear to him.

He was not yet sure how to combat his anger, but he did know that it was something that must happen – not just for his own sake, but for the sake of the company his father worked so hard to build.

He called Yolanda twice on Sunday. She didn't return his call until sunset.

"Hey," he said. "What took you so long to call me back?"

"You didn't leave a message. I didn't know what you wanted," she replied tersely.

"I thought you'd call me back, just because you saw that I was trying to get in touch with you."

"You didn't say what you wanted," she repeated.

Devin felt like she was trying to goad him into an argument, which was the exact opposite of what they needed right now.

"Okay," he said. "I just wanted to see how you've been doing."

"I'm fine."

"Where are you? Is it okay for me to ask that?"

"I'm at my mom's."

"Is that where you've been living?"

"No. I've been with my sister."

"Which one? Verna?"

"Mmm hmm."

Devin suspected as much. He also knew that Verna was talking shit about him on a regular basis. She was the one who warned Yolanda that a man who was so quick to anger would most likely take his fury out on her one day, be it verbally or physically. It appeared Verna was half right. Devin never hit any woman, but Yolanda was his emotional punching bag night after night.

"When are you gonna come home?" He regretted the question the moment he asked. Yolanda was too confident for him to boss around. And she left for a reason.

"When are you gonna get some help?" she countered.

"What kind of help? I feel bad enough already, after everything that happened. I'm not gonna be the same person I was."

"You said that before."

Devin didn't think he had, but he didn't want to contradict her. "What are you saying, I need to go to counseling or something?"

"Actually, I think that would help a lot. There are a lot of programs for people who need help with anger management."

Devin felt his temper rising. She was talking to him like he was a drug addict. He didn't think he needed counseling. All he had to do was calm down.

"So if I sign up for some classes, you'll come back?"

"I'll come back when you change."

"I feel like I've changed already."

"Really? Are you sure you're not getting mad right now?"

Bitch.

Devin's eyes widened, as if he had said the word aloud. He couldn't believe he just thought it. Grudgingly, he had to accept that Yolanda was right about him. As usual.

"Is something going on between you and ol' boy?"

That was another comment that got away from him. *Way to go*, he told himself. *Let her see that you're mad and jealous.*

"Who the hell is *ol' boy?*"

She was definitely trying to upset him now. Devin was sure of it.

"*Tyson*," he said. "How many guys you palling around with?"

"There is nothing going on with me and Tyson. He's just my friend."

"I heard y'all been getting pretty damned cozy."

"So you called me to argue?"

He caught himself. "No. That's not why I called."

"Good, 'cause I don't have time for that. Talk to you later."

Devin wanted to stop her, but he couldn't think of anything else to say that wouldn't lead to an argument. "Fine," he grunted. "Bye."

• • • • • •

On Monday morning Devin had to contend with another issue that had been tormenting him since he and his mother had their big fight. Even without an alarm clock, he woke up at seven a.m. and wanted to get ready for work. Trying to convince his brain that there was no need to be awake at that hour was futile.

Devin got up, took a shower and got dressed anyway. He didn't have anywhere to be, so he turned on his computer and tried to find a solution to his problems on the internet. He did find some useful information about coping with anger, but not the classes or counseling everyone thought he needed.

He gave up and called his little sister, who was much more skillful with the World Wide Web.

"Hey. What are you doing?"

"At school. Finna go to class."

"You really think I need some kind of anger management?"

"Yes," Stephanie said right away. "Hell, yes and Lawd, yes."

Devin rolled his eyes. "I been looking, but I don't know how to find nothing like that. Can you help me?"

"Yep. Do you want classes or counseling?"

"I don't want to be in a room with one person," he said. "They gon' make me think I'm crazy."

"You *are* crazy," Stephanie said. "But not that crazy. I'll call you back."

• • • • • •

Stephanie did call back later with good information. In the meantime Devin continued his own personal research. But even with this, the day seemed to drag along. Were Mondays always like this? Devin was used to hearing complaints from his men about how slow the time was ticking by, but he never experienced it himself.

Being on a construction site was a playground for him. There were never enough hours in the day. Being away from construction was his own personal hell, which is why he found himself on Baron's doorstep at six-thirty p.m.

He knocked hesitantly, not sure what he was doing there or what he wanted to say. Baron answered a few moments later. He still had on his work clothes, which broke Devin's heart. There was supposed to be dirt from the school site caked around *his* boots, not Baron's. But Devin wasn't even wearing boots that day. He had on a pair of sandals with no socks. He felt like such a loafer.

Before he opened the door fully, Baron said, "Hey, hold on a minute. Let me put Pearlie up."

Devin caught a glimpse of a pint-sized terrier lurking in the background a moment before the door closed. When Baron opened it again, Devin saw that the dog was now secured in a large kennel next to the television.

"Come on in," Baron told him.

Devin stepped inside with a curious expression. Not only did Pearlie look too small to pose a threat to anyone, but Devin didn't expect a big, strong guy like Baron to have such a cute, little doggie. He grinned at Pearlie as he made his way to the sofa, while Baron went to the kitchen to get them a couple of beers.

Devin had never been inside Baron's home. It was surprisingly neat, considering his friend was a bachelor. He also noted that Baron didn't have a flair for interior design. His entertainment center was impressive, but other than that, the construction worker was only concerned with the necessities.

He returned with the beers and handed one to Devin. Baron took a seat on his loveseat and immediately placed his bottle on the coffee table. He looked nervous and unsure of himself, which was odd, considering this was his home. Devin had to remind himself that up until a week ago, he was Baron's boss.

Depending on what Korah told him, Baron had to assume that was still the case.

"How's everything going at the school?"

"Good," he said. "We got no problems at the school. You coming back?"

Devin shook his head. "I'll come back to work soon, but not at the school. That's your gig, man. Congratulations."

The news didn't appear to make Baron happy. "Is everything okay, sir?"

"You can call me Devin."

"Okay, but is everything okay? Ms. Stewart says you're on a leave of absence..."

Devin chuckled. He knew that his mother would want to keep their personal grievances private. She was a great leader.

"Actually, I have a problem with my temper," he said, "but I'm sure you know that already..."

Devin told him the whole story, ending with his argument with Brick and his subsequent argument with Korah. Baron had been working alongside him for years, so he wasn't surprised by anything Devin said. What surprised him was why no one had called Brick out for his shenanigans.

"We're building that roof," Baron said. "But even if we weren't, why would he get on your case about it? That ain't right, man."

"I'm sure he gave me a hard time because I gave him a hard time first," Devin said. "That man never gave me a reason to hate him, but I hated him anyway. I didn't care that he was my boss while I was over there. I didn't give him the respect he deserved."

"But when are you coming back to work?" Baron asked. "You shouldn't have to stay gone this long, just because of that."

"I'll be back soon," Devin promised him. "I just have to get a few things squared away first."

"You should come back to the school."

"Why?"

"Because that's our biggest project," Baron said. "You're the head of construction. You're supposed to be there."

"Everything happens for a reason," Devin assured him. "You been chilling on the sideline for a long time. Now it's your time to shine. And you deserve it. I'm telling you; when I come back, nothing will change on that site. That's your baby now.

Take advantage of the opportunity, and learn as much as you can. We're gonna depend on you more and more in the years to come – if you decide to stay with us."

Baron frowned. "What do you mean? Why would I leave?"

"By the time the school is finished, you'll be a hot commodity. You'll get job offers from all over the place. Hell, Brick might try to steal you himself."

Baron shook his head. "No, sir. You and Ms. Stewart have been good to me. Got no reason to leave."

"Good," Devin said. "That's what I was hoping you'd say. Now are you gonna drink that beer with me or not? Coors is bad enough. But a *hot* Coors tastes like straight piss."

"Oh." Baron chuckled. "That's all I have to drink – unless you want a soda."

"I don't mind this," Devin said. "Just don't want to drink alone."

Baron hefted his bottle and took a manly swig.

"So how come you ain't married?" Devin asked.

Baron shrugged. "I don't know. I ain't smart enough for a girl who went to college, and I'm *too* smart for the girls I meet at the clubs. I guess I'm not looking in the right places."

"Probably not," Devin agreed. "We should hang out more."

Baron thought about that and said, "That'd be cool."

They watched TV for a while in silence while they drank, and then Baron spoke again: "If you don't mind me saying so, I think I caught your sister giving me the eye a couple of times."

That put a smile on Devin's face. Stephanie hadn't mentioned Baron to him, but she was always on the prowl.

"You like her?"

"She's pretty," Baron said. "And she's smart. She's definitely the kind of girl I'd go for. But with us working together, I don't think it would be a good idea."

"Proceed with caution," Devin advised him.

"Oh, because of your mom?"

"No, because of *Stephanie*. She hasn't met a man yet who can handle her."

Baron considered that as he emptied his bottle. He rose to his feet and took Devin's empty bottle from him.

"You want another one?" he asked as he returned to the kitchen.

"Nah, I'm trying to cut down. It is about time for dinner, though. What you cooking?"

Baron laughed. "Nothing. I was finna go get me some yard bird before you showed up."

"Churches or Kentucky?"

"Neither. Popeyes."

"I'm parked behind you," Devin said. "I'll drive."

● ● ● ● ● ●

On Tuesday morning Devin woke up at seven a.m. again. This time he showered and dressed in his work clothes. He didn't have any definite plans on where he would need the outfit, but he did plan on working today – somewhere.

Rather than head to one of Texas Builders' worksites that morning, Devin got in his work truck at eight o'clock and drove to Dallas. After fighting through multiple traffic jams, he eventually found himself at the Brick House headquarters. He entered the building and was greeted by a remarkably unattractive woman named Susie.

"Hi. May I help you?"

"I come to see Brick."

"Oh, um..." She looked him over, her eyes lingering on the Texas Builders logo imprinted on his tee shirt. "May I have your name, sir?"

"Devin."

Susie was clearly confused by his presence and the fact that he and Brick seemed to be on a first name basis. She told him, "One moment, sir. Would you mind taking a seat over there?"

She gestured to an area that was not close enough for him to hear her next phone call.

Brick started his day at the school that morning. He didn't mean to startle his secretary, but when she told him about the visitor, he had to ask, "Does he have a gun?"

"Uh, no, sir. I don't think so. Would you like for me to ask him?"

Brick laughed. Susie was extremely obedient. Almost to a fault.

"No," he said. "Tell him I'll be there in thirty minutes."

218

Brick called Isaac's office while Susie delivered the message.

"Hey," Isaac said.

"Hey. Just wanted to give you a heads up. Korah's son is in the lobby."

Isaac frowned. "What lobby?"

"*Our* lobby. He's talking to Susie right now."

"What does he want?"

"Hell if I know. Susie says he doesn't have a gun with him."

Isaac took the joke a little more seriously. "Should I sneak out the back?"

"No. You know it's not you he wants."

"Yeah. I guess."

"I'd ask him to meet me at the school," Brick said. "But if things get out of hand, I'd rather it happened at the office."

"I think I will sneak out the back," Isaac decided.

"You can't leave Susie alone with a deranged maniac," Brick kidded. "I'm afraid it's time for you to take one for the team."

"I've taken plenty for the team, Brick. But I'm not taking a bullet."

● ● ● ● ● ●

The Brick House CEO arrived at his office twenty-nine minutes later. His visitor was still waiting patiently in the lobby. Brick's chest tightened when he approached Devin and they locked eyes. But he wasn't too nervous. They were on Brick's home turf, which gave him a psychological advantage. Plus he was still in control of the school job. Devin wouldn't do anything foolish, if he had any hopes of returning to that site.

Korah's son stood and said, "Morning. Thanks for meeting with me."

Brick nodded. His eyes remained narrowed. He was clearly guarded.

"Step into my office," he said. "It's down the hall, on the right." Brick followed him rather than turn his back on the hot-headed foreman. Devin didn't look like he wanted to fight today, but Brick had been in enough scraps to know that you don't expose your vulnerable side to a potential enemy.

When they entered the office, Brick left the door open. "Have a seat," he said as he rounded his desk and took a seat himself.

Devin looked worried, which was something Brick had never seen in his eyes before. Even when he was wrong, the boy usually exuded confidence and power.

"I came to apologize," he said, which raised Brick's eyebrows. "I was wrong to argue with you on your site," Devin said. "You're the contractor, and I should've treated you with the same respect I treat all of our customers with. I know that I was upset about your relationship with my mother, and I brought that frustration to work with me."

Brick knew how hard it was for him to say that. He considered letting him off the hook right away, but he remained silent. The apology was necessary, and it was okay to take a little time to let it sink in.

After a few moments, Devin said, "I would also like to apologize for anything I did to come between you and my mother. I don't want to interfere with her personal life, and I don't want to be the cause of any trouble between the two of you. I love my mama, and I want her to be happy."

That was even more of a shocker. Brick felt his heart squeeze uncomfortably. He didn't realize that he hadn't responded to the boy until Devin looked around the office and sighed.

"That's, uh, that's all I wanted to say."

He started to stand, but Brick said, "Wait. Hold on a moment," and he sat down again.

"I owe you an apology as well," Brick said, which immediately caused a huge weight to lift from his shoulders. "My partner says I picked on you at the site. And, after thinking about it, I realize he was right. If you wanted to outsource the roof on the training center, there's nothing wrong with that. I shouldn't have given you a hard time about it."

"That's okay," Devin said. "It's your site. If you didn't want–"

"No." Brick shook his head. "That didn't have anything to do with what I wanted to happen at the site. It was all about me and you. When you came to work there, I knew we had our issues, but I was willing to start off with a clean slate. But when I came to talk to you about the surveyors, I felt like you were giving me an attitude."

"I was," Devin admitted. "And I was wrong for that, too. This is all my fault, sir."

Brick felt like this conversation was surreal. Isaac told him that if he simply sat down and talked to Devin, they could've worked out their differences. Brick never thought it would be that easy, but it appeared his partner was correct once again. Was Isaac ever wrong about anything? Brick wondered how much more smoothly his life would flow if he listened to him more often.

"Okay," he said. "It looks like both of us were wrong at some point. I'm sorry things went as far as they did. I respect you for being a bigger man than I am. I don't think I would've had it in me to initiate this conversation, if I was in your shoes."

Devin nodded. As far as he could remember, this was the most humbling thing he had ever done. When he decided to make the trip to Dallas, he thought Brick would make him feel like shit. But he didn't feel bad at all. In fact Devin felt stronger and more sure of himself. Maybe this was a sign that he could get his whole life back on track, if he continued to humble himself.

He stood and reached over the desk to shake Brick's hand.

"Well, thanks again for agreeing to see me. I hope there's no hard feelings."

Brick rose to his feet as they locked hands. "None at all. Are you gonna come back to the school today?"

"No," Devin said shaking his head.

"Why not? I think you should come back. That's your job. You deserve to be there."

"That's Baron's job now," Devin said. "He's the one who deserves that spot. He's a hard worker, and this is his time to shine."

Brick was even more impressed by that comment. This wasn't only about money. It was also about the notoriety and prestige all of the lead foremen on the school site would garnish. If Devin was willing to give that up, then maybe he wasn't just blowing smoke, and his change of heart was real.

"Okay," Brick said. "That's your decision, son."

He didn't mean to refer to him as *son* again, especially after the way Devin responded to it last time. But Devin was half his age, and that was the way Brick was used to speaking to young men.

Fortunately the comment didn't upset him. Devin smiled slightly and said, "Have a good day, sir," before he turned and left the office.

● ● ● ● ● ●

An hour later Devin showed up at one of his own sites. It was a convenience store under construction in a small neighborhood on the north side of Overbrook Meadows. This was one of the sites Baron was in charge of before he got promoted to lead foreman at Brick's school.

In Baron's absence, a less-experienced worker had been selected to lead the project. Larry Merchant had been with Texas Builders for four years. He was a hard worker, and Devin didn't object to Baron's decision to elevate him above the rank and file.

Devin parked his truck amidst the other workers' vehicles and stretched like a tom cat when he got out. The feel of the warm, morning sun on his dark skin was a blessing. The scent and sounds of construction vehicles and manual labor made his heart skip a beat. He scooped a hardhat from the bed of his truck and secured his tool belt around his waist as he stepped onto the property.

The building they were working on would be a 7-11 one day. But it was early in the project, and they were still working on the foundation. There were plumbers and electricians on the scene as well as half a dozen Texas Builders employees who were laying rebar in the unfinished parking lot. The men were surprised to see Devin on the site. They were even more perplexed when Devin pulled on a pair of thick gloves and began to work alongside them.

Larry watched him for a few minutes before he approached and asked, "Um, morning, sir. You, you taking over this site?"

Devin shook his head. He grabbed as much of the cut rebar as he could tote and carried it to the men who were building an elaborate foundation for the concrete. Larry followed him uneasily. Devin wiped the sweat from his brow before he set off to get more rebar. Larry didn't want to get fired for upsetting him, but this was a very peculiar scene.

"Sir, are... You, um... What's going on?"

Devin stopped long enough to respond to him. "Morning, Larry."

"Uh, morning, sir."

"Looked like you guys could use an extra hand out here," Devin said. "I'm just helping out."

"But, but you're the lead," Larry reminded him. "Want me to switch places with you?"

"Naw. This is your site, Larry. Today I work for you. If you need me to do something other than what I'm doing now, let me know. I can do whatever you want."

What Larry wanted was for him to offer a better explanation for what the hell was going on, but he didn't push it. He knew that there were some problems at the school site, and Baron was now in charge over there. If Devin got demoted, Larry sure wished someone had filled him in.

"No, sir. I guess what you're doing is fine," he said.

Devin nodded and returned to his task.

Larry hurried to his trailer to make a phone call. He was nervous about calling Ms. Stewart on her cellular. This wasn't an emergency, but it was definitely abnormal. Korah answered after a couple of rings.

"Hello?"

"Hi, um, Ms. Stewart?"

"Yes."

"Hi. This is Larry, from the 7-11 on Yucca Avenue."

"Hi, Larry. Is something wrong?"

"Uh, not really. But, um, your son is here."

"Devin?"

"Yes, ma'am. He just showed up and started working, right alongside the other men. I asked him if he wanted to be the lead, and he said no. He said he wanted to work with the guys, and I was supposed to tell him what to do today."

Korah didn't respond for a couple of seconds, which indicated she wasn't expecting this either.

"Is he being disruptive?" she finally asked.

"No, ma'am. He's working just fine. I'm just surprised, is all..."

223

Korah thought about it for a moment longer and then said, "If he's not doing anything wrong, I think you should let him work – unless he's making you uncomfortable."

"No ma'am. Not at all."

"Alright," Korah said. "Thanks for calling."

She sat at her desk with a perplexed expression for a few minutes before she called Devin on his cellphone. It took four long rings before he answered.

"Eh, hey, Mama."

"Morning. What's going on?"

"Nothing. Working."

"Yeah. I heard. Why are you at the Yucca site?"

"Why not? This is as good a place to work as any."

"Okay," Korah said. "And what exactly are you doing?"

"Moving rebar right now. Helping out with the parking lot. We should be ready for the concrete tomorrow."

Korah's eyebrows were bunched in confusion. "Larry says you don't want to be the lead on that site."

"This is *his* site," Devin confirmed. "I don't want to take anything away from him."

"So you're ready to come back to work, but you don't want to be the lead?"

"That's right. Is that okay?"

It was, but at the same time it wasn't. Korah didn't know how to respond to him, so she said, "You and I need to talk. When can you make it to the office?"

"After work," he said. "I guess that depends on what time Larry lets us go."

Korah couldn't believe he was going to do grunt work all day. But she thought it would be wrong to tell him he *couldn't* do it.

"Alright," she said. "But could you try to leave a little early? I want to get out of here by five."

"Okay," Devin said. "See you later."

"Alright. Bye."

Korah disconnected just as Malcolm entered her office.

He noticed her demeanor and asked, "Is everything alright, Ms. Stewart?"

"I don't know," she told him. "Devin just showed up at one of our sites. But he doesn't want to be in charge. He said he wanted to work alongside the other men."

"Well, you wanted him to come back to work, didn't you?"

Korah nodded. "Yeah. I guess so."

"Maybe he wants to punish himself," Malcolm offered.

Korah considered that. "Maybe. He said he'd stop by the office when he gets off. I guess I'll have to wait until then to find out..."

CHAPTER NINETEEN
BACK TO THE BASICS

Devin knew that his mother was eager to get home at the end of the day, but he purposely waited until after five before he went to the office. He knew Yolanda was still training with her old friend from high school, and he didn't want to risk an ugly confrontation with Tyson.

When he showed up at the Texas Builders' headquarters, there were only two vehicles in the parking lot. One was his mother's Pathfinder. The other was a Camry that he'd never seen before. Devin entered the building with his pants and shirt soiled. His hands were dry and dusty and a little sore, but his spirits were high. He hadn't felt this good about himself in a long time.

He encountered Malcolm at Yolanda's old desk.

"Good evening, Mr. Stewart. Your mother is waiting on you."

Devin continued down the hallway until he reached Korah's office. She looked up at him and then turned away from her computer. Her son's appearance was startling, but not in a bad way. He reminded her of the old days, before they had a team of sixty men spread out at their various sites.

Back then Devin was the company's workhorse. Korah knew that they ran him ragged when he graduated college and began working at the family business fulltime. She used to feel guilty about the amount of work they assigned him, but Devin never complained. Like his father, he believed a man should never be too proud to get his hands dirty.

Devin took a seat and relaxed his tired muscles. "Hi, Mama."

"Hey," she said. She looked over his shoulder and shouted down the hallway, "Malcolm, we're done for the day. You can take off anytime you're ready."

"Yes, ma'am," he said. "I'm leaving now."

"Is he doing a good job?" Devin asked when she returned her attention to him.

Korah nodded. "Better than I could've hoped for. Malcolm's a godsend."

They watched each other for a few seconds before she asked, "So what gives? Why'd you work on Larry's site today?"

"I was ready to come back to work," he said simply.

"I get that. And I'm glad to have you back. But why aren't you taking over one of the other sites? We're still working on the bank. Why didn't you go there?"

"I don't want to be the lead," Devin said. "I've been looking into my problems lately. I know I have a bad temper, and I get frustrated easily. I don't mean to. When I'm in charge, I yell at the guys a lot. I don't want to do that anymore."

Korah was startled to hear him acknowledge his faults. Devin had been behaving that way for so long, at some point she stopped considering it a problem. It was just the way he was.

"Stephanie helped me find some classes," he went on. "For anger management. I don't want to be mad all the time. I think I can change."

Korah continued to stare at him in disbelief. This was one of the best decisions Devin had ever made. She was so proud of him, her eyes began to well with tears.

"In the meantime," he continued, "I decided to get back to the basics, back to where it all started. I remember when I first started doing construction. It was fun to me. I loved being on worksites. I loved starting at the crack of dawn, eating lunch on the back of the truck with the fellas, packing up our tools at quitting time. That was all fun for me. I know this sounds weird, but it was pure. It was real.

"I don't know when it changed, but over time I started to get upset when things didn't go my way. Even if it was just a minor inconvenience, I would yell and curse at somebody. I thought it helped us get the job done, but it didn't have to be that way. *I* didn't have to be that way. I know Baron doesn't get mad all the time, and Larry didn't get mad today, either. That's why I decided to start over; to remember how much I love the work, before all the drama."

"That's fine," Korah said. "I'm very proud of you, Devin. It takes a strong man to admit when he's wrong and to do what it takes to fix it."

Devin nodded. It always made him happy to know that he pleased his mother.

"You can work under Larry for as long as you want," she said. "Whenever you're ready to take over again, the job will be waiting."

"Thanks, Mama."

"I hope it doesn't take *too* long," she added. "The company is growing by the day. We really miss your leadership."

Devin smiled. "I understand. I'll let you know when I'm ready."

Korah realized she wasn't going to get a definitive answer to how long his self-imposed therapy might last, so she let it go for now.

"Did Brick call you?" he said.

Korah frowned. She shook her head slowly. "No. Why? Is he supposed to?"

"I went to his office today," Devin reported. "We had a little talk."

Korah was both surprised and apprehensive about that. "You went to his office?"

"Yeah. This morning, before I went to Larry's site."

"Wh, why'd you do that?"

"I wanted to apologize to him. I apologized for what happened at the school, and I apologized for whatever I did to come between you two."

Korah brought a hand to her mouth. Her eyes were wide and unblinking.

"Is everything okay?" her son asked.

Korah couldn't answer until her heart started to beat again. "What, what'd he say?"

"He accepted my apology. He asked me if I wanted to return to the school as lead foreman."

Korah's mouth was completely dry. "What'd you tell him?" she managed.

"I told him that was Baron's site now, and I wouldn't take it away from him. But me and Brick are good now. He didn't call you?"

She shook her head stiffly.

"I thought everything would be better, with you and him," Devin said.

Korah swallowed and regained most of her composure. "Don't blame yourself for what happened with me and Brick."

"But I heard that you and him are on the outs because of me."

"No. We're on the outs because Brick can't decide if he really wants to be in a relationship. He may have used you as an excuse, but it has nothing to do with you. It's all about him. Don't blame yourself for that."

"Are you sure, Mama?"

"Yes. I'm positive."

"Okay," he said and allowed that guilt to dissipate as well.

"How are things with you and Yolanda?"

Devin's expression changed so quickly, it nearly broke Korah's heart. She regretted asking the question.

"I don't know," he said. "I guess we're on the outs, too."

"I'm sorry. When was the last time you talked to her?"

"A few days ago. She won't come home. I guess my anger issues affected her the most."

"Problems like that always hurt the people closest to you," Korah agreed. "Have you figured anything out yet, about why you get so angry? I think the problem is deeper than what you said..."

Devin sighed, and then he nodded. He took a deep breath before revealing something he had never shared with anyone. "I think it's because of Dad."

Korah was taken aback. Her late husband was not like Devin, when it came to the way he interacted with his employees. Devin Sr. was very even-tempered. And he always treated both of his children with compassion and fairness.

"What do you mean?" she asked.

She thought her son's eyes watered as he said, "I miss him so much, Mama. I think about him all the time, when I'm on construction sites. Sometimes it makes me happy, because I know how proud he'd be, if he saw some of the work I've done. But deep down I think it still depresses me, because I'm living his dream and he *can't* see it.

"He should be here to see how far we've taken his company. I'm so grateful, but when I'm depressed, I keep those feelings bottled up. Over time, I think it led to irritation and then flat out anger. I took it out on my crew, but I didn't mean to. I love those guys. All of them. They deserve better."

Korah had a lump in her throat. She wiped her own tears and said, "I'm proud of you, Devin. I'm glad you're willing to take a look at yourself and try to figure some of this out. I know Yolanda's going to be happy to know that you're getting help with your problem. Have you told her yet?"

Devin shook his head. "No. The last time I talked to her, we ended up arguing again. Do you think something's going on with her and that Tyson guy?"

Korah had her suspicions in the beginning, but she was surprised to hear it from Devin. "No. Who told you that?"

"Stephanie."

She frowned. "Figures."

"You see them together every day," Devin said. "What do you think?"

Korah didn't want to talk about one of her best employees behind her back, but family always comes first. "I won't lie to you, Devin. They are very close. And sometimes when I see them together, they'll be laughing and giggling, and I know they're not talking about work. I was worried about it too, so I asked her straight out. Yolanda assured me that they are just friends. They were really close in high school, and, you know how things can be when you reunite with an old friend."

Devin still looked doubtful.

"Yolanda told me that she would not bring a man into this office and have an affair with him right under my nose," Korah said, "and I totally believe that. This company means a lot to her. She wouldn't do anything to jeopardize her position – especially now that she's been promoted."

Devin thought that sounded reasonable. "She does love this company," he mused. "That was one thing that we argued about: I didn't understand why she would always take your side or Brick's side when I had a problem. I expected her to automatically side with me, because I'm her man. But if I did something that hurt the company, she always told me when I was wrong."

Korah's heart swelled with pride. She knew Texas Builders meant a lot to Yolanda. But she didn't know that Yolanda would risk losing a relationship over it. Loyalty like that was hard to come by.

"A good woman will support her man when he's right," she said. "And she will be strong enough to tell him when he's wrong."

"I see that now," Devin said. "Mama, what if I lost her?"

Korah could see the love and hurt in his eyes. She was currently going through something similar with Brick, so she knew how deep his pain was.

"I don't think it's over between the two of you," she said. "Sometimes, when the arguing gets to be too much, you have to take a step back and reevaluate your feelings for each other. You have to go back to what made you fall in love with her in the first place; kinda like you're doing with your job right now."

Devin mulled that over. It was easy to go back to the grunt work in construction, but how do you do that with a relationship?

"You ready to go?" Korah asked as she hefted her purse and stepped around the desk.

Devin nodded. He stood and wrapped her up in an unexpected bear hug. Korah was taken aback, but she could never get enough affection from her baby boy. Devin was taller than his father and as strong as Brick, but he would always be her baby. She closed her eyes and savored the awesomeness of his embrace.

● ● ● ● ● ●

Devin called his girlfriend when he left the office. He was surprised when she answered right away.

"Hello?"

"Hey."

"Hi," she said.

The sound of her sweet voice made Devin's heart sigh. She didn't sound like she was still upset with him, but Devin was apprehensive. He hadn't felt this way since they first started dating and they were trying to hide their relationship from his mother.

"Are you still at your sisters'?"

"Yeah."

"Can I come see you?" That was the first time he'd asked since she left. He was maneuvering through traffic, but it felt like his whole world stood still until she responded.

"Yeah."

Devin sighed with relief. He wasn't sure when or how it happened, but at some point his very existence became intertwined with hers. She had the power to break him down completely or fully nourish his soul with just a few words.

"Alright," he said. "I'm on my way."

• • • • • •

He pulled to a stop in front of her sister's house fifteen minutes later. Verna lived on the south side of town, not far from their mother's home. Devin saw Yolanda's car parked in the driveway, and he didn't like it. Verna's neighborhood was a certified ghetto, had been for the past twenty years. There was at least one vacant, ramshackle home on nearly every block. The only businesses that thrived in that part of town were corner stores, liquor stores, churches and pawn shops.

Devin mounted the front steps with his heart in his throat. He considered his grubby appearance after he knocked on the door, but by then it was too late to do anything about it. He had dirt under his fingernails. His shirt and jeans were also soiled. Yolanda answered the door in the exact opposite condition.

She wore a pair of short shorts that showed off her smooth legs and thick thighs. Her tee shirt wasn't too small, but her breasts stretched the fabric, slightly exposing the shape of her nipples. The house smelled like soul food, but Yolanda's scent was fresh and fragrant. She was barefoot. Her recently manicured toes had pink polish.

By the time Devin made eye contact, he felt weak in the knees. Yolanda was gorgeous. Perfect in every way. He couldn't believe he ever came home and yelled at this woman. Regardless of how bad his day at work was, coming home to this voluptuous goddess should've made him feel better in an instant. It was at that moment Devin realized how crazy he was, how he had come to take her for granted.

Yolanda noticed he had something in his hand. Devin followed her gaze and offered the gift he brought her.

"This is for you."

Yolanda had been given many gifts over the years, but she didn't think a suitor ever brought her a sour pickle in a plastic bag. But that didn't mean she wasn't appreciative, especially when Devin reached into his pocket and produced an accompanying pack of Now & Later candy. Cherry flavor.

"I remember when we first started dating," he said. "Every time we came to visit your mother, you wanted to stop at the corner store to get a pickle."

Yolanda smiled and blushed a little. Some days she felt far removed from her hood-chick upbringing. But it didn't take much to transport her back in time and make her remember the good old days.

She took the pickle and the candy.

"Thank you."

Devin looked around uneasily before asking, "So how's everything going?"

"Fine," she said.

"This, uh, this doesn't seem like a safe place for you," he said. "You're not scared to be over here?"

She shook her head. "Nope. This is where I grew up. I'm fine."

Devin knew he couldn't get her back that easily, but he figured it was worth a shot.

"It's not fine for me," he said. "I miss you."

Yolanda nodded and her smile slowly disappeared. "I miss you, too."

"How long are you gonna stay over here?"

Rather than answer his question, Yolanda looked him up and down and said, "You went back to work today...?"

He nodded. "Yeah."

"You went to Larry's site?"

"Yeah. I guess word gets around pretty quick."

"The office isn't that big."

Devin sighed. He wanted to reach out and touch and caress her. But he feared she might run away, like a startled fawn.

"You weren't the lead today?" she asked.

He shook his head. "Nope."

"What'd you do?"

"Just worked," he said. "Worked with the rest of the men."

"Why? You wanted it like that?"

"Today was one of my best days ever," Devin told her. "I felt good the whole time. When we shut down for the day, I was tired and sore. It was great. This is the way it used to be; how I used to feel about work."

"So, you don't want to be in charge anymore?"

"I do," Devin said. "But not now. I feel like I have to work on some things. I have to work on myself. I didn't have any stress today. I didn't get mad at anybody."

Yolanda wanted to believe him, but Devin had promised to mellow out before. Each time he went back to his old self within a matter of days.

"I went and saw Brick today," he said.

Yolanda couldn't hide her surprise then. "What happened?"

"I apologized," he said. "I know I didn't give him the respect he deserved on his site. I also apologized for anything I had to do with him and Mama not talking. I don't want to be the reason they don't work out. I would do anything to make Mama happy."

The sincerity in his eyes and voice touched Yolanda's heart. She wanted to keep her defenses up, but she did love him and miss him. Her goal in leaving was to help him, not hurt him.

"What did Brick say? Is he going to let you go back to the school?"

"He offered, but I turned him down. That job's already taken. I had dinner with Baron yesterday. He's a good dude. A hard worker. I want him to go as far as he can. He's a natural leader."

Devin's words made Yolanda melt, little by little. She knew he was career-driven. In all the time she had known him, Devin always wanted to be on top. He wasn't one to sit back and take orders from another man. The fact that he was willing to do so now didn't mean he changed, but it was a start. It sounded like he recognized his problem and was looking for ways to fix it – which was all Yolanda ever wanted.

"What are you going to do about your temper?" she asked.

"Stephanie found me some classes," he said. "They're at night, so I can go after work. It's not *counseling*, but I will get to talk to people who are like me. They'll give us strategies to control our anger. Baby, I want to change. Not just for you. I know I need to do it for myself. For the company. For everybody."

Yolanda's eyes watered. Devin gave in to his desires and reached for her. She didn't stiffen or pull away. He drew her closer, until her clean body pressed against his dirty one. The delightful scent of her skin filled his nostrils. Devin sighed pleasantly. She fit perfectly in his arms. Without her, he felt like he was missing a limb. Now he was whole again. He didn't think he could bear it, if she made him leave this house without her.

"Please come home," he pleaded. "I'm so sorry, baby. I never meant to hurt you. Please. Come home."

She nodded, or Devin thought she did. He backed away with a lump in his throat. His eyes were glossy as well.

"Did you say yes, baby? Are you coming home?"

She nodded again, and this time there was no mistaking it. Devin's heart kicked and then swelled with pure joy, flooding his bloodstream with perfect bliss. He suddenly felt excited and energized. He could work another eight hour shift at that moment, or throw Yolanda over his shoulder and tote her all the way back to their love nest. His smile was ear to ear, but it ebbed when he remembered the things he heard.

"Baby, tell me the truth," he said. "I've been hearing stuff about that guy, Tyson. Is something going on with y'all?"

Yolanda's smile faltered, which made Devin's heart squeeze uncomfortably.

Yolanda's thoughts returned to the night she visited her friend after the big argument with Devin. She told him she only needed a shoulder to cry on, and Tyson had told her, "That's fine. Tell me what happened."

But as the minutes rolled into an hour and the darkness outside deepened, her friend's remarks became more and more critical of Devin:

"*You don't deserve that shit.*"

"*You're a good woman. Doesn't he know how to treat a beautiful, black queen?*"

"*I would never make you feel like that, not if you were my girl.*"

235

"I don't think we should've broken up in high school. Do you ever think about what our lives would be like, if we had stayed together and got married?"

The final straw came when Yolanda asked for a cup of water, but Tyson went to the kitchen and brought back a glass of wine. Rather than return to his spot on the loveseat, he sat on the couch next to her.

Yolanda took the glass from him and placed it on the coffee table. She then shot to her feet when she realized Tyson was leaning in for a kiss.

"Wait. Stop," she had told him. "What are you doing?"

"I want you to be happy," he had said. "I want you to be with me, and I feel like you want the same thing."

Yolanda shook her head as she backed away from him, moving in the direction of the front door. "I shouldn't have come here," she told him. "I love Devin. I know we've had problems, and I do feel like we shouldn't be together sometimes. But I still love him. I wouldn't cheat on him."

"I'm not asking you to cheat on him," Tyson had said. He rose to his feet as well. "I'm asking you to leave him, Yolanda. You deserve better. I want you to be with me."

He moved closer, but he didn't attempt to stop her when Yolanda undid the deadbolt on the door. She opened it and took a shuddering breath as she stepped out into the night.

"I'm sorry," she had said. "I..." She shook her head. "I really appreciate your friendship. But I don't want this. I..."

Rather than finish her thought, she closed the door and hurried to her car. She drove straight to her sister's house and had been living there ever since.

The next morning Tyson texted her, simply stating, "I understand." Yolanda didn't respond, and she hadn't spoken to him since.

"Baby, I would never cheat on you," she told Devin. "Tyson is just my friend."

But Devin saw the worry in her eyes, and he knew that something had occurred between them.

"He never tried to push up on you at all?"

Yolanda nibbled on her bottom lip. "I did start to confide in him," she admitted. "I went to his house, after we had that fight. He, he did try to kiss me."

Embarrassed, she looked down at her shoes. When she met his eyes again, she saw that Devin was doing his best to remain calm.

"I swear nothing happened," Yolanda said. "When I saw what he was doing, I left. I left as fast as I could. I'm sorry I went over there in the first place. I would never disrespect you or your mom by bringing some man to the office and starting a relationship with him. I wouldn't do that, Devin. That would be crazy."

This was the second time he heard that. It made sense when Korah told him, and it also made sense now.

"Besides," Yolanda said. "I'm not into skinny, pretty boys. I like a man who works with his brain *and* his hands. Someone who ain't afraid to get down and dirty."

The way she was looking at him made Devin wish he had even more dirt under his nails. He let go of his anger and accepted the love she was offering him. It was a wonderful feeling; to know that Yolanda wanted to be with him because of who he was – not because she didn't have other options. It was one of the best feelings in the world.

"Are you coming home now?" he asked. "I don't want to be without you for another night."

"Yes," she said excitedly. "Let me go grab my things."

Devin waited anxiously on the porch until she came back. It didn't take long. She only had one bag, and it may have been packed already. Devin toted it to his truck and then rushed to her car to open the door for her.

"Were you really going to leave me?" he asked before she sat down.

She shook her head, still grinning. "No, Devin. I took some clothes but only a few pairs of shoes. If I was leaving, trust me, you'd know it because the closet would be empty."

If Devin wasn't grief-stricken at the time, he might have figured that out on his own. He shook his head as she got behind the wheel and pulled her seatbelt on. He didn't notice that she still had the pickle until she pushed the plastic back and took a cursory lick.

Devin's eyes widened. The pickle was short, but the girth was approximately the size of his manhood. Yolanda looked up at him and noticed his expression. She kept her eyes locked on his as

237

she took another slow lick. She kissed the tip and then pushed it slowly into her mouth – not too far, but it was enough to make Devin's dick start to swell in his boxers.

"Damn," he muttered.

"Did you miss me?" she asked when she removed the pickle.

"Yes. In a lot of ways."

"If you get home before me, you should take a shower," she suggested. "Make sure you get your pickle nice and clean. I promise I won't bite."

Devin closed her door and forced himself to walk rather than run back to his truck.

Not only did he make it home first, but he was halfway done with his shower by the time Yolanda entered the house; which truly was her home.

CHAPTER TWENTY
A VERY LATE RESPONSE

A week later, Devin woke up on Friday morning and found himself alone in bed. For a moment a sense of despair washed over him, a reminder of what life without his woman was like. But when he sat up, he saw a light shining under the bathroom door. And then he heard the shower.

A gratified smile softened his features as he rose to his feet. He shook off the last vestiges of sleep as he headed for the bathroom. He opened the door and was greeted by a thick plume of warm water vapor. He approached the sink, but the mirror was too foggy to see his reflection. Yolanda peeked around the shower curtain when he started brushing his teeth.

"Hey, baby."

"Morning," he told her.

Devin wore only a pair of boxer shorts. Yolanda marveled at the muscles stacked on his dark chocolate frame. Even in a state of relaxation, his body was powerfully built.

She closed the shower curtain and resumed her bath. "Where are you going today?" she asked.

"The bank," Devin muttered around his toothbrush.

Since returning to work, he was at liberty to lend his services to any Texas Builders' site he wanted. He still hadn't taken the lead at any of their constructions, but that was by choice. Devin said he enjoyed experiencing every aspect of construction; from roofing to flooring to forklift driving.

Korah didn't mind him operating behind the scenes, but she was eager for him to resume his position as the head of their construction empire. All of their foremen were eager for that, too.

Devin didn't realize how awkward it was for them to give him instruction. Telling their boss to go sweep up a mess was something they would never get used to.

Towards the end of Yolanda's shower, Devin pulled the curtain back and revealed his totally nude body. Yolanda looked him up and down longingly, but she was determined not to give in to his horniness this morning. Ever since she came home, Devin's appetite for love was insatiable. Even now, his dick grew steadily as he watched the water cascade over her body.

Yolanda shook her head. "*Oh, no you don't.* Baby, I can't be late today."

"Yes you can." Devin's eyes were dark with desire as he joined her in the tub.

"No, I can't," Yolanda insisted. "Today's my first day flying solo, and I have a meeting at nine. I need to make sure I have everything ready."

Devin was happy that Tyson's services were no longer needed at the office on a daily basis, and he was proud of Yolanda for excelling at such a difficult task. But none of that took away from his hunger. He placed both hands on her luscious hips and pulled her closer.

Yolanda, however, was quite serious about shutting him down that morning. She squirmed out of his grasp and exited the shower on the other side.

"Baby, I'm sorry. I'll make it up to you later."

"Later when? Don't you have school today?"

"Yes, but I should be home by the time you get here."

As planned, on the first of June, Yolanda began her studies in accounting at the junior college. Korah was worried that she'd have trouble juggling her education with her full-time job, but Yolanda was fiercely determined to make it all work. Devin was proud of her for that, too. But it didn't solve his current boner problem.

He stepped out of the tub in time to see Yolanda's fair-skinned booty exit the bathroom. He followed like a dog in heat. When she turned and saw him, she laughed nervously as she backed away.

"Devin, are you serious? You left the water running. Did you even close the shower curtain?"

"I'll get it in a minute," he promised.

His eyes continued to roll up and down her body. Yolanda had the best natural breasts he ever had the pleasure of fondling. They were big and perky with dark areolas and tender, suckable nipples. Her stomach was flat, with just a little pudge. Her hips were wide, her waist slim. She kept her pubic hair shaved low. Devin's eyes fixated between her legs, until she brought her hands together in front of her erogenous zone.

"It's not happening," she said. But her eyes weren't that convincing. Her smile didn't help at all.

She continued to back away until her butt encountered the bed. Devin didn't give her an opportunity to flee to the right or left. He reached and grabbed her hips with both hands. He pushed until she had no choice but to sit on the mattress. His hands then moved under her thighs. He lifted them, and Yolanda reclined even further, until she lay flat on her back.

"Oh, baby, you gotta hurry up," she murmured, now resigned to her fate.

Devin stared down at her until she made eye contact. His hands slid up her legs and settled on her knees. She was still dripping wet. He was too. He pulled her legs apart and grinned at the beauty he found at their intersection.

The look in his eyes made the muscles in Yolanda's stomach flex nervously. She tried to spy the alarm clock behind him, but his massive girth blocked her view. But then he moved, and she could see the clock clearly. It took her a moment to realize that he'd dropped to his knees in front of the bed.

She sat up on her elbows, and they made eye contact again. This time she could only see half of his face. The rest was obscured by her body. Devin's eyes slipped closed as he kissed and then gave her labia a delightful lick. The slight sensation of his lips and tongue caused an unexpected tremor to rack her whole body. Her stomach clenched again. This time the quiver rolled down her legs as well.

Devin lapped up all of the water on the outside of her kitty, and then his tongue sought the moisture within. Yolanda emitted a slow, sweet moan that excited Devin even more. His manhood continued to swell until it was rock hard, but he wasn't a greedy lover. Despite her protests, he wanted his woman to know that her needs would always supersede his. He would work his fingers to the bone to fulfill even the smallest of her heart's desires.

241

After a few minutes his licking and sucking drowned out the sound of the water still running in the bathroom. Yolanda laid her head back on the mattress and gripped the sheets as he zeroed in on her hardening clitoris. He kissed and titillated it with his lips and then began to stroke it with his hot tongue.

Between the blood rushing past her ears and her mingled moans and harried breaths, she barely heard Devin when he asked between licks, "How much time I got?"

But time no longer seemed like an issue. And for the life of her, Yolanda couldn't remember why it ever was. What did she have to do today? Did she even have a job? She felt like she might have, in a past life. But in this life, there was only pleasure, from start to finish. As her wet ass jumped and slid on the wet sheets and her wet god plunged his tongue in her wet center, there was only one thing that truly mattered:

"*Uhn. Don't. Stop.*"

Devin was attentive, and he was dutiful. He didn't stop when her legs began to tremble like the slopes of a volcano or when she reached between her legs and grabbed hold of his head, pulling him in so deep his whole nose felt submerged. He didn't stop when a mighty orgasm caused her to whip back and forth on the bed like she was possessed.

He did stop when her movements gradually winded down and her screams subsided to soft, breathy whimpers – but that was only long enough for him to rise to his feet and spread her legs again. From a standing position, he rubbed the tip of his dick around her opening until it was sufficiently lubricated with her essence. He slid in slowly and deeply. The expression on his woman's face as he filled her completely made his dick jump and squirt pre-cum inside her.

Yolanda was hot and wet all around him. Devin knew he wouldn't last long, but he desperately wanted this moment to last forever.

"*How, how much time I got?*" he asked again.

It took a bit of effort to focus on him. When she was able to meet his gaze, Yolanda smiled wistfully before her eyes fluttered closed again.

"*Don't stop,*" she whispered. "*We got, we got plenty of, uhn... Time.*"

• • • • • •

Yolanda rushed into the Texas Builders' headquarters at 8:25 wearing a stylish, new pants suit with two inch pumps.

She stopped by her boss' office and told her, "I'll be ready to go in five minutes."

Korah nodded. "That's fine. Did you finish the proposal?"

"Yes," Yolanda said. "I finished it yesterday before I left. I just need to make a couple of notes. I was looking it over last night, and I have a few questions I wanted to ask you before we leave."

"We'll have time," Korah said. "It only takes twenty minutes to get to the site."

Their meeting was with the owners of a new gated community on the west side. The architect added six more homes to the development, which changed the price on their original bid. Yolanda drew up the new proposal without help from Tyson or Priscilla, and she was understandably anxious.

"Where is Devin working today?" Korah asked her

"He said he's going to the bank."

"He's still not taking the lead?"

Yolanda shook her head. "No, Ms. Stewart. Not yet."

Korah sighed. "How's he doing?"

"He's a lot better," Yolanda said. "He's in a good mood every day when he gets off work."

"And the two of you are getting along better?"

Yolanda's fair skin reddened. She felt like the naughty deeds that transpired an hour ago were written all over her face.

"We're fine, ma'am."

"Alright, go ahead and get your notes together," Korah told her. "And try to calm down. Don't worry, you'll be fine. I'll be there with you the whole time."

"Thank you, Ms. Stewart."

Yolanda hurried down the hallway and Malcolm quickly took her place. He walked into his boss' office looking through a stack of envelopes. "Got the mail," he announced.

"Anything good?"

"Mostly bills," Malcolm said as he sorted through the correspondences. "I don't know what this is..." He placed one of the envelopes on Korah's desk.

She picked it up and was surprised to see Quincy's name in the return address.

Quincy McGee was her most recent boyfriend, before Brick. She dated him for several months before she decided he was a little too boring for her tastes. That should've been the end of it, but Korah made the mistake of accompanying Quincy to his birthday party after their break-up. Four hours and five drinks later, the night ended with a round of sloppy sex. The next morning Quincy was none too pleased when Korah told him the intimacy was a one-time thing, and it did not mean their relationship got a kick-start.

That should've been the end of it, but someone started vandalizing Korah's work sites less than a month later. It turned out to be another contractor, but Korah questioned Quincy about it before they found the true culprit. To say things ended on bad terms would be putting it mildly.

Korah tore the envelope open and was surprised to find a wedding invitation. It appeared she was cordially invited to celebrate Quincy's union with a woman named Desiree Mills. It had been eight months since she and Quincy last spoke. Korah figured that was enough time for him to meet and fall in love with another woman, but she didn't understand why he would invite her to the wedding. And why would he send the invitation to her place of business?

Clearly this was an attempt to get under her skin. And it couldn't have come at a worse time. Korah hadn't spoken to Brick in more than two weeks, so she had plenty of time to reevaluate their wild ride. She certainly had fun, but maybe it would've been better if she had stuck with a more stable suitor, like Quincy.

No. She shook her head and tossed the invitation into the waste basket. That's what Quincy wanted her to think. He knew the news of his wedding would probably irritate her. And he wasn't satisfied with irritating her at home. He wanted to piss her off while she was at work. That was a dickhead move.

"Is everything alright?" Malcolm asked, noticing her change in disposition.

"I'm great," Korah said and plastered a smile on her face. "Yolanda and I are leaving for a meeting in a few minutes. I need you to stay here and hold down the fort."

"Yes, ma'am," he said and returned to his desk.

• • • • • •

The meeting lasted a little over an hour, and it went off without a hitch. Yolanda was a little nervous at first, but she settled down midway through and had the property owners eating out of her hands towards the end. She was a beautiful woman, and she knew her stuff. Korah began to wonder if the men were prolonging the meeting, just so they could remain in her presence for a while longer.

Korah missed several calls while they were at the development. She listened to her messages while Yolanda drove them back to the office. One of the missed calls was from Brick. His message simply said, "Hey, can you call me back?"

Hearing his voice sent Korah through a wave of emotions, none of which she wanted to contend with at the moment. She wouldn't have returned his call, if not for the fact that she had a construction team working on his school at the moment. There was a chance his attempt to reach her was work-related.

She called Baron first. He answered after several rings.

"Hello? Ms. Stewart?"

"Hi," she said. "How's everything going?"

"Great. No problems here."

"How far along are you on the project?"

"Foundation's been laid for the training center and the bleachers. We're still smoothing out the football field. Should be able to dig holes for the goal posts on Monday."

"Have you talked to Brick?"

"No, ma'am. Haven't seen him since Monday. Is everything okay?"

"Yes," she said. "Just checking on your progress. I may stop by sometime today."

"That'd be fine, ma'am. We'll be here till five-thirty."

"What's wrong?" Yolanda asked when she disconnected.

Korah shook her head and then shrugged. "Nothing, I guess. Brick called while we were at the meeting."

"Really?" Yolanda struggled to keep her eyes on the road, rather than try to read Korah's expression. "What'd he say?"

"He just asked me to call him."

"Is it about work?"

245

"I don't know."

"Are you going to call him back?"

"Doesn't look like I have a choice."

"Maybe he wants to apologize and win you back..."

It seemed everyone was hoping for that, Devin included. But renewing her relationship with Brick wasn't a priority for Korah. She remained bitter about the things he said to her the last time they talked.

They drove in silence for a while. Yolanda kept stealing glances at her until Korah said, "Alright, I'm calling him now."

Yolanda returned her attention to the road and tried her best to suppress a giggle.

Brick didn't answer his cellphone, but he called back before Korah had a chance to leave him a message.

"Hello?"

"Hey," he said. "You just called."

"Yeah, I was about to leave you a voicemail."

"Oh, well, how's everything going?"

"Fine," she said tersely. "What can I do for you?"

"I would like to see you. Are you free tonight?"

Korah was, but, "What's this regarding?"

"Nothing," he said. "Dinner. Would you like to have dinner with me?"

Korah couldn't believe his audacity. He was a fool, if he thought they could simply pick up right where they left off. But she didn't want to have that conversation in front of Yolanda.

She told him, "I don't think that's a good idea."

"Are you mad at me? I know you are," he said before she could answer. "I'm sorry for what happened between us. I was wrong, and you didn't deserve that. I apologize for everything – especially the things I said about your company. It's not true. Texas Builders is amazing. Would you please let me take you out to dinner tonight?"

Korah missed him so much, her chest hurt. Her anger had the upper hand, but her heart quickly won the battle. "Fine," she muttered.

"Great. I'll pick you up at six-thirty. Dress formal."

Formal?

He disconnected before she could ask him why.

Yolanda waited thirty seconds after Korah returned the phone to her purse before she asked, "So, what did he say?"

"He apologized. He wants to have dinner."

"That's great," Yolanda said. Her smile was big and bright. Korah didn't share her enthusiasm.

"You're not happy?" she asked.

"I'm sure he has more bullshit up his sleeve."

"I don't think so," Yolanda said. "I think he finally sees the error of his ways."

"Does your crystal ball also come with lottery numbers?"

"Ha-ha. I guess you'll find out for yourself tonight."

"I suppose I will."

"What are you going to wear?"

Korah frowned. She had no idea.

●●●●●●

For dinner that evening, she selected a long, black chiffon gown that was strapless with a cinched waist and a sweetheart bodice. She chose diamonds as her accessories, including the diamond-encrusted panther pendant Brick gave her for Christmas.

When she checked herself in the mirror, Korah thought the amount of cleavage she had on display was sinful, which was perfect. Brick had made a bone-headed decision when he pressed the pause button on their love affair, and he deserved to suffer. His apology over the phone was terribly insufficient. Until he made things right, he could look all he wanted, but touching was out of the question.

He rang her doorbell at exactly six-thirty. His eyes became instantly wolfish when Korah opened it. He wore a full tuxedo, complete with a black cummerbund that matched his bowtie. Korah couldn't imagine where he planned to take her that required such attire.

"Good evening," he said. "You look ravishing."

He reached to take her hand, but Korah pulled away from him.

"Where are you taking me?" she asked.

He grinned and stuffed his hand in his pocket instead. Brick looked unbelievably handsome beneath the fading sunlight. He was clean-shaven. His haircut was fresh. His hazel eyes

247

twinkled as he smiled at her. A slight breeze brought Korah a whiff of his cologne, which smelled like Tom Ford.

"Reunion Tower," he said.

His voice was deep and confident. He returned to his vehicle to open the door for her, while Korah turned to secure her home.

"You don't have to wear a tuxedo to Reunion Tower," she said when she stepped his way again.

"You do if it's a formal occasion."

His smile made Korah want to slap him – or kiss him. She wasn't sure which.

"And what's the formal occasion?" she asked as she took a seat in his Navigator.

"It's a surprise," Brick said before he closed her door.

Korah had to wait until he went around and got in on his side before she could ask, "What surprise?"

"Wouldn't be much of a surprise if I told you, now would it?" Brick replied. "Hey," he said when she rolled her eyes. "You don't look like you accept my apology."

She folded her arms over her stomach. "Brick, you hurt me. You can't just slap a Band-Aid on it and make it better."

He half-turned in his seat and faced her. His smile was completely gone now.

"I didn't mean to hurt you. And for the record, I never said I didn't want to be with you anymore."

"No. You said you *needed time to think*," Korah said with a condescending tone. "I don't know how it is where you're from, but in the real world, that's not what decent people do. They don't back out of a relationship like that. But then again, I don't know if we ever even had a *relationship*. So maybe I'm the stupid one."

"We've been together since September," Brick said. "Of course we have a relationship."

Korah noted how he referenced their relationship status in the present tense, but she didn't let it go to her head. Brick had already proven how shifty he could be.

"I'm sorry," he said. "I know I was wrong." He looked into her eyes. The lingering pain he saw there made his heart ache. "I'm embarrassed," he revealed. "There's no excuse for the way I treated you. Please forgive me."

Korah saw that he was sincere, but she couldn't forget how he abandoned her.

Before she could respond, he said, "And to answer your question, *yes*, I do love you."

Korah was so stunned, her first thought was when had she asked him that, rather than the belated response he just gave.

"I haven't told a woman that in a long time," he said, still staring deeply into her eyes. "I'm sure it's been over ten years, maybe longer..."

Korah's brain raced. Her heart did, too. When Brick decided he needed time to think, she did ask him if he ever loved her. But she never said those three words to him. For him to make such a significant declaration without being prompted was **HUGE**. It was the biggest thing that had ever happened during their courtship.

Korah thought she might cry. Priscilla told her Brick would come bearing gifts when he apologized. This announcement wasn't what Korah was expecting, but as far as gifts go, she didn't think he could've done any better.

"So, do you forgive me?" he asked.

She nodded. She sniffled and wiped the mist from her eyes.

"We're going to have a great evening," Brick promised her. He put his car in gear and rolled slowly out of the driveway. "You don't even have to tell me you love me back, or anything..."

Korah chuckled. She couldn't stop smiling. "I didn't think men cared about stuff like that."

"I may be a dick, but I've got a heart of gold," he assured her.

Korah reached and took hold of his hand. She squeezed it tightly. Brick stopped before his Navigator made it to the street. He turned to face her.

"I do love you, Brick."

He grinned. "I know you do. I mean, how could you not?" He laughed when she rolled her eyes again.

CHAPTER TWENTY-ONE
THE FINAL CHAPTER
REUNION

I wait
For you to create in me a wave
Of ecstasy previously unknown
Anticipation makes my love grow stronger
Until you return, and I long no longer
To hold you
And want you
And feel you
You are
My sunlight
A diamond
To me
A star

Reunion Tower was one of Dallas' most recognizable landmarks. No picture of the city's skyline was complete without the tall, cylinder shaped building which was topped with a dazzlingly bright sphere that rotated slowly, giving diners and sightseers a 360 degree view of the impressive city.

In addition to a five-star hotel and the "GeO-Deck," the tower was home to the Five Sixty restaurant, which offered extraordinary culinary delights from the world-renowned chef Wolfgang Puck.

Korah and Brick dined on steamed Scottish Salmon and crispy Maine lobster while they watched the sun set over the bustling city. Korah hadn't been to the tower since her college days, but of course everything was bigger and better with Brick.

He was more charming than their waiter. Korah didn't realize how much she missed being pampered by her hunky cowboy.

Towards the end of the meal he asked, "When is Devin coming back to the school?"

"Why?" Korah asked. "Did Baron do something wrong?"

"No. Not at all. He's a very good foreman. Very respectful."

"Then why do you want Devin back?"

"I still feel bad about running him off," Brick confessed. "When he came to my office last week, I realized what a fool I was. I'm glad he was man enough to take the high road, because I wasn't ready to do that yet."

"That surprised me, too," Korah said. "I had no idea he was going to visit you."

"What site do you have him on?"

"I don't have him anywhere. Devin wanted to take a step back to deal with a few personal issues. He works every day, but he doesn't want to be in charge. He's been doing grunt work; sweeping, taking out the trash, you name it."

Brick found that very peculiar. "He demoted himself?"

Korah shook her head but said, "I guess that's a way to describe it. He said he wanted to get back to the basics, to remember what he loved about construction in the beginning. Yolanda said he's never been happier."

"Yolanda, your assistant?"

"Well, now she's my bookkeeper. You know she and Devin have been dating for a while now."

"You're keeping the business in the family *for real*."

Korah hadn't thought about it like that before, but if Devin and Yolanda got married, that would be the case.

"So what's the big surprise?" she asked with a smile. "Since you already told me we were coming here, I'm guessing this isn't it."

"You guessed right," Brick said. He winked at her as he waved a hand in the air and summoned their waiter. When the youngster approached their table, Brick told him, "The lady is ready for her special dish."

The waiter nodded and said, "Right away, sir," before hurrying to the kitchen.

Korah wore a look of confusion when Brick's gaze returned to her.

"You still hungry?" he asked.

She shook her head. "Actually *no*. I'm stuffed. Why didn't you tell me to save room for your *special dish*? I'd hate for you to go out of your way for nothing."

"Really? You're not hungry at all? You can't eat one bite?"

"Is it a desert?"

He shook his head. "No. It's a full meal. A delicacy."

Her eyes widened. "Brick, you know I can't eat another *full meal*. What were you thinking? I hope I can take it to-go. Are you serious?"

"Yes. And, yes, you can take it to go."

That was a relief. But Korah continued to frown at him until their waiter returned. When he did, Korah saw that he toted a humungous platter. It was big enough for a whole turkey, but the contents were concealed beneath a decorative silver lid.

Their waiter was not alone. A second waiter stepped forward and removed all of the dishes from the table. When the space before Korah was clean, the first waiter deposited the platter, lid included, and said, "Enjoy," before they left them alone.

Korah reached immediately for the lid, but Brick reached to stop her.

"Wait. You can't have it until you agree to something first."

Korah never heard of a meal that came with a prerequisite, but she found it amusing. She sat back in her seat and gave him her full attention.

"You know," Brick said, "I'm a very successful man..."

His date shook her head, but her smile remained. "Yes, Brick. I know that."

"No, I mean *really* successful," he said.

"And boastful."

"Yeah, that too," he agreed. "But lately I've come to realize something: Success can only bring a man a certain amount of happiness. I didn't recognize how much was missing from my life until I met you. Actually I didn't know there *was* something missing until I met you."

Korah's smile faltered slightly. She looked from the platter to Brick. His eyes were beautiful and serious.

"A man can spend his whole life chasing dreams," he continued. "Or in my case, he can spend his whole life chasing a fantasy. But sometimes dreams and fantasies come true, and that's what I've found in you. And now I don't have to keep looking for anything else."

Korah continued to stare at him; her lips parted, her eyes unblinking. She looked from the platter to his eyes and then back again.

"What's in here?" she asked, her voice barely above a whisper.

"What do you think is in there?"

Her breaths quickened. "Brick, I'm about to faint. Tell me what's in here."

He stood and slowly strode to her side of the table. He removed the lid and carefully placed it on his side. Korah began to hyperventilate when she saw that there was no special meal. There was only a ring box in the center of the platter. Brick picked it up and dropped to one knee as he opened it.

Korah really did think she would faint. Her hands trembled, and her eyes filled with tears, so thick she couldn't tell if he had a ring or a pair of earrings. She wiped her eyes and gasped when she saw that it was definitely a ring – with a diamond so big all of the stars in the sky would be envious.

"I want to spend the rest of my life with you, Korah," Brick said. "With you and *only* you. Will you marry me?"

She brought a hand to her mouth as fresh tears squirted from her eyes. Her heart was beating so fast, she couldn't articulate a response. But she could nod. She nodded fiercely, like she invented the gesture and was giving lessons.

Yes! Her heart sang. *Yes! Yes! Yes!*

Brick turned to the waiters, who hadn't left them after all, and gave them a thumbs up. The room then erupted in music and applause. Korah looked around with a bewildered expression. She had no idea so many people were watching them, or for how long.

But of course none of that mattered when Brick reached for her hand and slipped the ring on her trembling finger.

No one else mattered at all.

● ● ● ● ● ●

Brick took her on a leisurely stroll down Main Street when they left the tower. The dark sky was filled with stars. The city was alive with night life. Korah and her fiancé walked arm in arm. Brick was breathtakingly handsome and debonair. Korah couldn't stop smiling and looking down at the rock on her finger.

When a vendor approached with a dozen roses in hand, Brick purchased them without hesitation. He presented them to his queen, and she cradled them like she won a beauty pageant.

The clapping sound of horse hooves on the street pulled their attention in another direction. Brick saw a team of two horses pulling an elegant white carriage, and he knew that God had aligned everything perfectly for them on this blessed night. He flagged down the driver and was grateful to find the cushy seats in the back of the carriage empty and ready for new passengers.

The glowing couple boarded and cuddled and smooched as the driver piloted them past popular attractions on the thoroughfare. Each time he mentioned that their ride was coming to an end, Brick told him, "We'll take another," and the carriage kept rolling.

Korah was still in shock, not fully believing this evening was real. Brick had always been faithful to her, but throughout their relationship she worried that his playboy lifestyle would one day make a resurrection. Apparently that was not the case. Korah would be the one to take him off the market for good. She felt like the luckiest girl in the world. But the look in Brick's eyes, as he held her under the moonlight, made it clear that he considered himself the luckiest guy.

● ● ● ● ● ●

It was after eleven when they left the downtown area. Rather than head straight to his place or hers, Brick took his woman on a drive along beautiful Dallas streets that were still filled with party-goers and club hoppers. Korah held her man's hand as she took in the scenery, the people around them. She wondered if any of them were as happy as she was.

The drive eventually took them to the freeway and then to an unexpected exit in an industrial district. Korah was curious about their destination, but she kept quiet until they came upon a huge construction site with an unambiguous **BRICK HOUSE** sign planted out front. Her smile was quaint as Brick pulled onto the property. They didn't get far before their progress was impeded by a locked chain-link fence.

"Isn't this something," Korah said when he put the car in park and turned to grin at her.

"Yes it is. Thanks for noticing."

She giggled. "You're so silly."

"What do you think this is?" Brick asked, looking out at a mostly complete factory of some sort. The main building was a hulking structure; three hundred yards in width and two stories high. Two impressive smokestacks added to the building's height.

"I don't know. A rendering plant?"

He frowned. "No. And *gross*. Why I would bring my fiancé to a rendering plant?"

Korah's smile was whimsical. "Say it again."

"What, my fiancé?"

She nodded. "Yes. I like the way that sounds."

"My *soon-to-be wife*," he said.

"Mmmm. *That's even better!*"

He leaned over and kissed her slowly. When he backed away, Korah's eyes were dazzling, despite the dark setting.

"Why me?" she asked. "What made you decide to finally get married?"

"I don't ever want to live without you," he said earnestly. "You're the perfect woman. You're strong. Smart. *Gorgeous*." He smiled. "You compliment me in every way. If I met you ten years ago, I would've asked you then. It's not about me changing. It's about me finally meeting you."

Korah's heart quivered and then swelled to the point of bursting. She reached to wipe the new batch of tears from her eyes.

Brick kissed her again, on the lips and then on her nose and forehead. His sweet breath on her face made Korah numb.

"So, what are you building?" she asked, looking back at his latest masterpiece.

"A glass factory."

"That's some glass factory."

"Yes, we do it big at my company," he agreed.

Korah giggled. "Alright. I know you want to show off your building, but it's a bit dark, don't you think?"

"We have lights on the inside."

She didn't think he was serious, but Brick reached and opened the glove compartment. He had four sets of keys in there. Korah watched as he fished through them. The ring he selected had over a dozen keys on it. He found the one for the lock on the gate in front of them and said, "Are you down?"

Korah nodded. He wore a tuxedo. She wore an evening dress with her best jewelry. But they were there, and he was eager to boast, so why not?

"Great," he said.

Brick got out of the car and unlocked the gate. He then rolled it open to make room for his vehicle.

●●●●●●

He gave her a tour of the factory, which was impressive by any standard. It was even more amazing for Korah because this was her future husband's work. The inside was surprisingly clean. The clicks of Korah's heels echoed throughout the main floor as Brick led her past work areas that were designed for efficiency but were still aesthetically pleasing.

The night felt like an elaborate cocktail of her hopes and dreams masquerading as real life. She had never been with anyone as spontaneous as Brick. He was a fireball of energy and excitement. He didn't live like a man in his mid-forties, and Korah was learning to experience life in the same manner.

She tried her best to pay attention as Brick walked and rattled on about his unquestionable feats, but Korah was so giddy, her thoughts kept returning to the ring on her finger. Brick held her hand and strutted in his tuxedo.

Korah was most impressed with the enormous furnaces, which were complete and ready for use. Brick told her his favorite part of the factory was a courtyard near the west entrance. He led her there, and Korah had to say she was surprised by his selection. The factory was so solid and manly. The courtyard was serene and beautiful – almost out of place with the rest of the building.

"This area is designed for smoke breaks," Brick said as he led her down a cobblestone sidewalk that was lined with dense shrubbery, Japanese maples and bonsais. "It will also be used for parties and company picnics."

Korah thought it was a nice touch for the designer to add a human feel to such an industrious structure. The courtyard had plenty of seating in the form of concrete benches that stood on Romanesque legs.

They stopped when they reached an open area where the vegetation had been cleared. It appeared the cobblestone sidewalk once extended into this space, but most of it had been broken down and carted away. A couple of nearby wheelbarrows contained remnants of the demolished sidewalk.

"What's going on here?" Korah asked, careful not to step into the work area.

"Minor problem," Brick said. "They're going to lay grass here. The concrete landscapers got a little over zealous."

"How far did the sidewalk go?"

"About twenty more feet before I caught them."

"So you had to tear it down?"

"A minor inconvenience," he said.

Korah lifted her dress and stepped onto the soil beyond the remaining sidewalk. She thought she saw... Yes, there it was, lying inconspicuously in the grass less than ten feet away.

"Is that a jackhammer?"

Brick's eyes narrowed as he focused on the muscle machine. "Why, yes, Ms. Stewart. That is a jackhammer."

Korah noticed the tone of his voice had changed slightly. She looked back and saw him standing stiffly, watching her. He had his hands stuffed into the pockets of his slacks. He looked totally scrumptious.

He grinned. "You wanna, um..."

Korah laughed, though the look in his eyes made her nipples harden.

It had been nine months since the last time the two of them came across a jackhammer. She could tell by the look in his eyes that Brick had fond memories of the incident as well.

"We're so far from the nearest neighborhood," he said, "I'm sure no one would hear you. If you wanted to..."

Korah looked around as her blood gradually heated. The area they were in was not visible from the street. And most of the neighbors were other factories that appeared to have shut down for the day. There were security cameras mounted above the doorway leading back inside the building. But before she could inquire about them, Brick said, "They're not on yet. The technician's setting them up on Monday."

Korah's nostrils flared. Her muscles tensed as she looked from the jackhammer to Brick. The sound of the powerful machine would be enormous at that time of night, but there was no one around to complain. Even if there was, Korah was sure that he wouldn't let her play with it for very long.

"You want me to use that jackhammer?" she breathed.

"You can. If you want to."

She bit her bottom lip. "I never get to play with tools that big anymore."

He nodded. "I know."

Unlike the last time Brick let her fool around with this much horsepower, Korah knew exactly what his reaction would be. Their tool play had become a powerful aphrodisiac. It was silly in a way. But it was also appropriate, given their professions. And it was only for the two of them. The rock he put on her finger tonight was a precursor to a lifetime commitment, so Korah knew that she would not deny him tonight. Plus she really did want to use that jackhammer!

"Can I break off some more of that sidewalk," she asked as she stepped further into the unpaved area. Her pulse quickened as her heels sank into the soft ground.

"Yes," Brick drawled. "That would be marvelous."

He moved swiftly to the side of the building where the jackhammer's cord was coiled. He bent to plug it in and then found a pair of work gloves on one of the benches. He handed them to her and said, "Wait. I gotta find some goggles."

Korah giggled nervously as he began his search. In the meantime she pulled the oversized gloves over her dainty fingers and bent at the knees to lift the weighty jackhammer. The feel of the hard metal in her hands made her sigh pleasantly.

Every year she erected buildings that were smooth and polished. They were so finessed, a layman might not consider the powerful equipment involved in the building process. The drilling and the pounding. The sweat and muscle of a hundred men who may never visit the site after the grand opening. That was the stuff that made Korah's pulse race, and she knew Brick felt the same way.

He returned with a pair of safety goggles and was surprised to see that she had already brought the jackhammer to a standing position.

"Whoa. I thought you were gonna wait for me."

"Just getting a feel for it," she said with a smile.

"Here, let me move it over here for you..."

He handed her the goggles and then took the jackhammer from her. He lifted the nearly hundred pound machine from the ground effortlessly and toted it ten feet, to where the remains of the cobblestone sidewalk still needed to be destroyed. He didn't care any more about his Stacy Adams getting soiled than Korah did about her heels.

When he had everything set up, Korah approached with her safety goggles in place. A floodlight near the building's entrance offered enough illumination for her to see her workspace fairly well. She wasn't nervous about damaging any more of the sidewalk than he wanted her to, but she was a little apprehensive about controlling the jackhammer when it sprang to life. When she used the one at Brick's house, it jumped a full foot to the left before she got it under control. Tonight she wanted to show her man – her *fiancé* that is – that her skills had improved.

She took hold of the jackhammer, and Brick backed away a few feet. He watched as she gripped the handles firmly and located the ON switch. She hunkered over the tool, knowing she'd need her body weight to control the mechanical beast.

Brick told her, "You look real sexy right about now."

She looked up at him and smiled. She would've imagined she looked quite foolish in her formal dress with work gloves and goggles on. "Really?"

He nodded. His eyes were dark, his smile slightly threatening.

Korah returned her attention to the task at hand. She took a few deep breaths and held the last one as she turned the machine on. As expected, the first kick was the hardest. The jackhammer's strong piston jerked forward with enough power to punch a hole in a tree. The blade encountered unyielding concrete and sent an explosive tremor back up to the user.

Korah's grip on the machine tightened, and she managed not to lose hold of it as the piston jerked again and again with blinding speed. The noise was immediate and deafening. Korah began to second guess Brick's assurance that no one would hear them. But more important than the noise was the steady drum of energy the jackhammer fed her with each thrust. Korah felt her whole body jerking and jiggling. She kept her eyes on the machine's blade, which was making quick work of the remaining sidewalk.

TAT-TAT-TAT-TAT-TAT-TAT-TAT!

After twenty seconds she was in the groove. She hefted the massive tool, pushing it further onto the sidewalk, breaking the concrete down by the inch and then by the foot. A maniacal smile spread her lips as her arms and shoulders absorbed wave after wave of tension. She was surprised to feel her clit awaken with bright, eager eyes. The quivering of her thighs floated upwards, until she felt it between her labia.

TAT-TAT-TAT-TAT-TAT-TAT-TAT!

She thought Brick would stop her when she moved within a foot of the good sidewalk, but he didn't. Korah grudgingly released the trigger on the machine's handle, and everything came to a complete stop. Her deep, harried breaths filled the vacuum of silence, but Korah couldn't hear much besides the ringing in her ears. Her arms felt tense, but her legs were like jelly. The goggles hung askew on her face. She was exhausted and completely energized at the same time.

Her pants were laced with laughter, but Brick displayed his amusement in a different manner. He shook his head slowly as he approached her.

"That's the hottest thing I have ever seen," he muttered.

Korah's throat caught when she noticed the new bulge in his slacks. She continued to stare at it as he made his way to her. Brick took the jackhammer from her limp fingers, and let it fall onto the soft dirt. Korah still hadn't caught her breath before he kissed her. Intensely. He reached and gripped her body with both hands. She moaned when he grabbed hold of her ass and drew her hips so close to his she could feel every inch of his erection. His tongue slipped inside her mouth, and he swallowed down her startled sighs. He sucked her lips and squeezed her ass with urgency.

Having made love to him outside before, Korah knew he had a voyeuristic streak. But she honestly thought they would make it home before they consummated their engagement. She realized she was wrong about that when she felt her skirt rise high, all the way up. She felt the cool, evening air on her bare butt cheeks that were separated by a mere thong. And then her man grabbed hold of her panties and began pulling them down.

"*Brick. Wait.*"

He removed his mouth from hers and stared at her startled expression. Korah thought his eyes were wild and sexually deranged.

"I'm sorry," he said. He jerked his jacket off roughly and tossed it to the ground behind them. "Is that better?"

Korah looked back in confusion. She had no idea what he meant by that, but then he began to lower her, until her bare ass was on the ground with only his jacket as a barrier. She couldn't help but laugh then. Out of all of the inappropriate things they were doing, he thought she was complaining about their lack of linens.

All traces of amusement left her when he dropped to his knees between her legs and ripped his cummerbund off like it was on fire. He unbuttoned his pants and pushed them and his underwear down his thighs. His dick jumped up to greet her. Korah's clit trembled in anticipation. She moistened her lips and bit down on the bottom one as she lay back on the ground. The soil was soft and processed, ready for the layer of grass they were rolling out next week.

Korah barely had time to wrap her mind around all that had transpired today and the massive dirty deed they were about to partake in before Brick lowered himself and she felt his fat head spreading her slick opening.

"*Oh! Oh, Brick!*"

She cried out as he pushed in hard and deep, sliding in so smoothly there was no doubt that he was the missing part of her, and her body would always belong to him.

She reached and dug her nails into his sides as he pumped his hips, slowly at first. Her clitoris devoured every pleasing sensation his friction provided, and her walls stretched and sucked him down deeper, until their bodies meshed and she felt him in her lungs.

261

She stared at the stars over his shoulder, her fingers gripping him tighter and tighter. *"Oh God! Damn, baby..."*

"You feel so good," he growled next to her ear. *"This is mine,"* he grunted, the speed of his hips increasing. *"All mine."*

His declaration made Korah's heart and clit shudder simultaneously. The scent of the fresh soil and Brick's cologne and the exhaust fumes from the jackhammer filled her nostrils, solidifying everything that he was and everything they were together. He propped himself up on his forearms and made eye contact as her legs wrapped around him, encouraging him to go deeper and harder.

Brick readily complied. The speed of his hips soon felt faster than the piston in the jackhammer, and Korah felt as if he was pounding her box with the same intensity.

"Oh! Yes, baby! Yes! All yours!"

Her orgasm tap-danced down her spine and collided with her clitoris with so much force Korah could not stop herself from throwing her head back and howling at the moon like a horny alley cat. Brick felt her legs trembling around him. He watched her luscious breasts heave as her climax enveloped her, and he could hold his excitement no longer.

As he came, he savored the feel and the sounds and the smell of her. He loved how her walls squeezed him even tighter as his manhood jumped and pulsated inside her. He loved the look on his woman's face; her lips, her tongue, the ecstasy in her eyes.

He whispered, *"I love you,"* which was something he said so infrequently, it was like a foreign language. Declaring it during sex was even more taboo.

But this wasn't sex. This was the woman he was willing to change his life for. He did love her, with all his being, and their lovemaking was pure, no matter how wild and unconventional.

He knew that he would never want another because of the overwhelming *fullness* that enveloped him when Korah's eyes fluttered open and she mustered the energy to tell him, *"I love you too..."*

EPILOGUE

Korah and Brick were married four months later on Saturday, September 26th.

Either of their estates was lavish enough for the event, but the wedding was held at the picturesque Avery Ranch. Korah's dress was elegant, with a sweetheart neckline and glimmering bodice. The train flowed several feet behind her.

In addition to her immediate family and friends, many of her relatives from Chicago came to celebrate her special day. Her cousins Tina and Patrice were gorgeous bridesmaids. Korah's father Franklin stood tall and proud as he marched her down the aisle and placed her hand in Brick's, who looked obscenely handsome standing next to his best man Isaac.

When he was allowed to lift her veil, Brick stared at Korah as if it was the first time he realized how beautiful she was. A dozen doves were released into the air when they kissed for the first time as husband and wife.

The reception at the ranch was one for the ages. The Avery clan showed up in droves. They danced and dined and drank with merriment. After dinner a handful of Brick's nephews changed into cowboy wear. They bridled and saddled the horses in their best gear. All of the guests were welcome to partake in leisurely horseback rides around the corral. Others followed the trail to Brick's lake to see if the legend about his famous fishing hole was true. Brick's ranch hand made sure there were enough rods and reels for everyone.

As night fell, the Avery men became more loud and boisterous with every sip of alcohol. The carriage rides through the wooded area on the west side of the ranch seemed to never end. The bride and groom were long gone by then. Their flight to Bora Bora would take nine and a half hours. But even that was a wonderful experience. Brick chartered a private jet, so they did not have to contend with other passengers or a pushy flight crew.

The champagne continued to flow as their plane broke through the cloud cover. And the newlyweds stumbled upon another first. Brick said he was not a member of the mile-high club. Korah giggled and told him she wasn't either. She thought it would be a shame for them to have such a great opportunity and not partake. Brick wholeheartedly agreed.

Bora Bora was the most beautiful place Korah had ever visited. For seven days and six nights she and her husband were seduced by sandy beaches, emerald lagoons and golden sunsets that took her breath away every single time. She didn't want to leave. But when they returned to Texas, they would embark on a new era of their lives together, and that prospect was just as thrilling.

• • • • • •

Yolanda didn't catch the bouquet at the wedding, but Korah knew that it was only a matter of time before she impressed upon Devin the importance of solidifying their union before God and all of their family. Or maybe it was the bun in her oven that spurred their wedding.

Whatever the case, Yolanda wasn't showing when she and Devin met at the altar three months after Korah and Brick tied the knot. The bride looked unequivocally gorgeous. And for Korah, she was already family, so her tears of joy were for Devin as well as Yolanda.

Seven months later the young couple welcomed Korah's first grandchild into the world. They named her Deborah Lynn Stewart, after Korah's mother Debbie. The joy Korah felt when she held her granddaughter for the first time could only compare to the happiness she felt when she gave birth to Devin and Stephanie. Even Brick had a gleam in his eye when she handed him the little bundle of joy.

He told Devin, "This is the most beautiful baby I've ever seen! Whenever you and Yolanda need help babysitting, you gotta bring her to us."

Devin gave him a celebratory cigar and a pat on the back. Grinning broadly, he said, "Don't worry. You know we already got y'all penciled in."

• • • • • •

Over the next two years Brick House and Texas Builders continued to experience gains that moved them closer to the top of the go-to list for construction. The work at Brick's school continued without a hitch and was completed on February 1st, 2017. The school district, as well as the rest of the city, was extremely impressed with the finished product. Brick House got a nod for more construction work and renovations for Overbrook Meadows ISD. And Baron, who led Texas Builders' portion of the construction after Devin's departure, received praise and recognition from everyone involved with the project.

Devin predicted other contractors would try to lure Baron away after the school was completed, and he was right about that. Korah was, however, surprised by where some of the offers came from. She called her husband one day after Baron gave her a bit of unsettling news.

"Hey, baby." A racket of construction sounds in the background told Korah that he was at one of his sites.

"Did you offer Baron a job?" she asked directly.

"Oh, um. Heh-heh."

"*Heh-heh* my ass."

"If he told you, I guess that means he's not going to accept my offer – or did he give you two-weeks' notice?"

"He did not give me two-weeks' notice, you snake. Why would you try to take one of my best foremen?"

"If you agreed to the merger, we wouldn't be having this problem," Brick stated. "But as it stands, you're still my competition. So, you know, it's business, baby. Nothing personal."

"No, I am taking this personal," Korah decided. "I'ma kick your ass when I get home."

"Don't make promises you can't keep."

"I should've known you'd like that, you freak."

"So did Baron say he's at least thinking about it?"

"Kiss my ass, Brock."

"I will, baby. Soon as I get home. Sorry for being underhanded. I'll make it up to you."

"Oh, well I look forward to it."

Korah's smile remained for a couple of minutes after she disconnected.

● ● ● ● ● ●

On Thursday, February 2nd Korah held a meeting with her core team, which now included Malcolm and Baron, in addition to Yolanda, Stephanie and Devin. Thanks to an incredible influx of new contracts, Devin had to resume his role as the head of construction less than a month after his self-imposed demotion. Korah was very proud of his accomplishments.

He'd completed a six-week course for anger management, and everyone agreed that he was a different kind of leader now. He was as productive as before, but his crew joked that he didn't have a stick up his ass anymore. Devin's new approach to work translated to a better home life as well. Plus the baby kept a smile on his face every time he thought about her. Even Yolanda was surprised by what a nurturing father he turned out to be.

The meeting that morning focused on two Walmart supercenters Texas Builders was in the process of erecting as well as more kudos for Yolanda, who was just named Employee of the Month for the third time in a row. But more importantly, Korah wanted to address rumors that had been circulating throughout her company since her wedding a year and a half ago – despite repeated attempts to dispel them.

"Listen folks…" She stood at the head of the conference table wearing a tweed skirt suit that was both stylish and form fitting. Her shoulder-length hair was straightened and tied up in a professional bun. She was the perfect blend of elegance, style and power.

"I sent another email this morning, but I need everyone – especially Devin and Baron – to follow up with our crew members. Everyone's waiting for us to merge with Brick House. I've even heard that Brick House is going to *absorb us*, and Texas Builders won't exist anymore. But for the umpteenth time, that is *absolutely not going to happen*."

Korah watched as everyone in the room blew out a collective sigh of relief.

"I understand why the rumors were started," she continued. "And I won't tell you this is not something Brick and I have discussed. But I told him the same thing I'm telling you now: Texas Builders is an independent enterprise. This company was founded by my late husband, and it will *always* belong to my family. If Devin and Stephanie choose to sell-out once I've retired, that will be their choice. But it certainly will not happen on my watch."

Both Devin and Stephanie shook their heads, indicating they wouldn't sell the company either.

"Honestly," Korah said, "it's a little disheartening to know that some of our employees think merging with Brick House would be a good move for us. Some even believe we would be a more successful company under the Brick House umbrella."

She paused for a moment to let that sink in.

"But the fact of the matter is," she continued, "Texas Builders is a force to be reckoned with *on our own*. Our crew is just as big as Brick House, and our leadership is just as solid. As far as our earnings, we're nearly neck and neck.

"I know a lot of this thinking is the result of us working under Brick House on the school. But that was an isolated event. And we're certainly not *under* them now. In fact, every month I see reports that put us *on top* of Brick House – which is right where we want to be.

"So I need everyone here to do their part in shooting down these rumors. Devin, you and Baron need to make it known that working for Brick would be a *step down* and not something our crew members should ever look forward to. We're the McDonald's of Texas construction. Brick House is like Burger King. And we all know McDonald's beats Burger King every single quarter."

"Those Whoppers do taste better, though," Stephanie said and everyone laughed.

Korah smiled too, and she took note of how Baron's amusement to the joke seemed a little *extra*. Devin warned her that Stephanie and Baron might be seeing each other outside of work, but Korah was reluctant to believe it until she heard it directly from her daughter.

As far as boyfriends went, Korah would have to say Baron was an excellent candidate. But she wasn't eager to give them her seal of approval. They were lucky that Yolanda and Devin's interoffice romance worked out as well as it did. Baron and Stephanie giving it a try might be pushing it.

"Alright, that's it for now," she told her beloved employees. "Everyone's doing a great job. I couldn't be more proud of you. Oh, and before we go, let's give a big hand to Yolanda, who completed her associates degree in December."

Everyone, including Korah, gave their bookkeeper well-deserved kudos.

"I meant to make the announcement last month," Korah said. "With Christmas and the last bit of work on the school, her success got lost in the mix. But I want to officially acknowledge the work Yolanda has done for our company since Priscilla retired.

"This young lady took over a very difficult task at a time when we needed her the most. And she never stopped giving it her all. Even through a marriage and a new baby, Yolanda never missed a day of school. She's a shining example of the spirit and work ethics that makes this company so great."

Yolanda blushed as the round of applause turned into a standing ovation.

"Thank you Ms. Stewart," Yolanda said. "I mean *Mrs. Avery*." She giggled. "I swear I'm gonna get that right one day..."

• • • • • •

After the meeting, Korah worked alone in her office for half an hour before Malcolm appeared in her doorway with a huge smile on his face. Korah looked up at him and she smiled as well. The young man's cheerfulness was always infectious.

"What's up?" she asked.

"We got it," Malcolm announced. "Got a call from Powers and Bingham."

Korah's eyes lit up. "Really? When?"

"Just now," he said. "We won."

Korah's mouth fell open. She felt tingles all over her body.

"Wow. I really didn't think we would win that one."

"I can't tell," Malcolm said. "After that speech you just gave, I thought we were number one."

"Well, hell, maybe we are!" Korah said. She was so ecstatic, she wanted to leap from her chair and do cartwheels down the hallway. "Did you tell Yolanda yet?"

"No. Not yet."

"When you go in there, tell her not to make any plans for lunch today," Korah told him. "It's on me."

"Awesome!" Malcolm said. "Congratulations, Mrs. Avery!"

"Thank you, Malcolm."

Korah was too excited to continue her work when he left the office. Powers and Bingham was a big-time corporate group. They owned more than a dozen high-rise office buildings in the south and were looking to build a new one in Louisiana. The price tag on the job Korah just won was four times the cost of Brick's school, easily making it the biggest project either of their companies had ever won a bid on.

When she told her team that Brick House was not as good as Texas Builders, Korah's goal was to build morale. But this new contract gave her declaration credence and power. She sat grinning wildly for a few minutes before her cellphone rang, snapping her out of her trance. She was not surprised to see her husband's number on the caller ID.

"*Good morning,*" she sang.

Brick cut straight to the chase. "How the hell did you beat me out of that office building?"

Korah laughed. "Aw, what's wrong, baby? Did you get some bad news?"

"Yes. You know I did. What'd you do, bribe them?"

"Sorry to disappoint you, but Texas Builders operates with honesty and integrity. Is it so hard for you to believe that we beat you fair and square?"

"Bullshit," Brick grumbled. "Not after the work we did on that school."

"From what I've been hearing, the football field and training center are the best parts of your school..."

"Really?" Brick said. "You wanna egg me on?"

Korah laughed. "Honey, I know you're not really upset."

"Actually, I am very disappointed," Brick said. "I thought Industrial Works might take it from us, but I never suspected you guys would."

"Well thanks a lot," his wife said. "I guess that's what you get for underestimating the competition."

"So, are you gonna tell me how you did it or not?"

"I will if you admit that we're better than you."

"Fat chance."

"Well, can I at least get a celebratory bottle of wine?" Korah asked with a giggle.

"Yes. I can do that."

"And a massage?"

"Sure," Brick said. "Now spill it."

"Okay. I don't know if this is definitely the reason," Korah said, "but from what I understand, you may have a problem with your head of construction."

That caught Brick off guard. "What are you talking about? You mean Hector?"

"Yeah, him," Korah said. "Rumor is he's a bit of a drinker. And I hear he got a DUI in December."

Brick was floored. "How'd you know about that?"

Korah shrugged. "I forget where I heard it. But I think the same little birdie who told me may have passed the word to Powers and Bingham as well. *And* I'm thinking they don't want an alcoholic to lead construction on their new building..."

It took Brick a few moments to recover from that news. "But, but Hector is good now. He completed inpatient rehab and everything."

"Oh. Well maybe that's something that would've helped your chances. Hmmm. Too bad."

He chuckled. "So what you're saying is you had dirt on me. And rather than tell me, *your husband*, you allowed it to interfere with a contract we were both bidding on?"

"As *your wife*, I really wanted to tell you," Korah said. "But as your competition, I could do no such thing. You know that. No hard feelings?"

He laughed. "No, baby. I guess not. But I never figured you'd be such a ruthless competitor. I think it's time for us to take you seriously."

"My new contract is four times bigger than your *biggest* job," Korah quipped. "If you're not taking us seriously, that's probably why you're losing. But hey, you'll get 'em next time, champ."

"Oh, no you didn't."

She giggled. "I love you."

"Love you, too, babe. But, hey, you're gonna bring us in to do some of the work, right?"

"Mmmm... I don't know. I think we may be big enough to handle it all by ourselves. Plus you've been talking all kinds of noise. I should let you sit this one out."

"You know you ain't right."

"Maybe you can persuade me," Korah offered.

"You take bribes?"

"You already offered me wine and a massage. I don't think you have anything else to offer."

"Not true," he said. "I got a big brick in my boxers."

Korah laughed. "That's not – you know what, I can't even lie. Your brick is very impressive."

"Good. I'll draw up a subcontracting agreement, and you can sign it when you get home."

"Yeah, okay."

"Hey, all jokes aside, congratulations," Brick said before he disconnected. "I didn't think you'd beat me, but you deserve that job. You impress me, woman."

"Why thank you, sir."

"I love you, Korah."

Even after being married for over a year, it always warmed her heart when Brick told her that.

"I love you too, baby. Talk to you later."

THE END

ABOUT THE AUTHOR

Keith Thomas Walker, known as the Master of Romantic Suspense and Urban Fiction, is the author of nearly two dozen novels, including *Life After, Dripping Chocolate, The Realest Ever* and *Brick House.* Keith's books transcend all genres. He has published romance, urban fiction, mystery/thriller, gay/lesbian, poetry and erotica. Originally from Fort Worth, he is a graduate of Texas Wesleyan University. Keith has won or been nominated for numerous awards in the categories of "Best Male Author," "Best Romance," and "Author of the Year," from several book clubs and organizations. Visit him at www.keithwalkerbooks.com.

www.ingramcontent.com/pod-product-compliance
Lightning Source LLC
Chambersburg PA
CBHW020609110726
47899CB00002B/437